Trust No Bitch

Lock Down Publications
Presents
Trust No Bitch 2
A Novel by *Ca$h & NeNe Capri*

Lock Down Publications
P.O. Box 1482
Pine Lake, Ga 30072-1482

Lock Down Publications
Ca$h
Email: ldp.cash@gmail.com
Facebook: Cassius Alexander
Like our page on Facebook: Lock Down Publications @
www.facebook.com/lockdownpublications.ldp
Amazon: http://www.amazon.com/Ca$h
NeNeCapri
Facebook: NeNeCapri
Twitter: @NeNeCapri
Instagram: @NeneCapri
Cover design and layout by: **Marion Designs**
Book interior design by: **Shawn Walker**
Edited by: **Shawn Walker**

Acknowledgements

We would first like to acknowledge our fans nationwide. Thank you for supporting our individual careers and this collaboration Trust No Bitch. To our loyal supporters on the social websites, in the book groups, and the distributors, you fuel our drive. To the readers, you make us what we are authors. Thank you Shawn Walker for your boss editing. Keith, we thank you for the cover and look forward to more of your work. Friends, family, associates, and fellow authors we thank you all.

Dedications

CA$H: To the one who prefers to remain anonymous, they can't destroy what they can't see.

Nene Capri: To My beloved daughter Princess Khairah everything I do is for you. Mommy loves you.

Prologue

Kiam sat in silence on the burgundy Italian leather sofa in his living room. His ratchet sat on the marble and glass cocktail table in front of him fully loaded with one already in the chamber. Next to the Nine sat a half empty bottle of Jack Daniels and a bottle of pain pills.

Kiam's dark eyes seemed more frightening with the two week old beard that framed his normally clean shaven face. His left arm hung down by his side in a sling but there would be no doubt after this evening that he was still deadly.

With his free hand, he stroked the hair on his face as he looked around the living room at the upper echelon of his team. Lissha sat across from him on the loveseat studying his expression. She knew that something real serious was about to go down, but even her wildest imagination couldn't have prepared her for what she would soon witness.

Lissha could see Treebie in the dining room loading a plate with food that Kiam had laid out. That bitch would have an appetite at her own execution, Lissha thought.

Donella and Bayonna sat across from each other in twin recliners with plates of untouched food on their laps. JuJu, however, chose to stand close to the door. He had already decided that if one of them were flawed, the only way they would be leaving was twisted, wrapped in sheets and black plastic.

Lissha's eyes rotated from Kiam to the Nine on the table, and the half bottle of Jack Daniels. Donella fidgeted with her hands and Bayonna shook her foot as the silence became thick with anticipation.

Treebie entered the living room and sat down on the other end of the loveseat. She was cool as a breeze with her legs crossed and a heaping plate of food balanced on her lap. She bit into the drumstick then filled her mouth with a fork full of spaghetti. "What kind of meat is in this? Ground turkey?" she asked, looking at Kiam.

"Humph," he grunted.

"Whatever that's supposed to mean. Anyway, it tastes like damn jerky."

Kiam didn't comment, he was steady staring her down.

Treebie felt his gaze hot on her face but she kept on eating. She didn't know why Kiam had called them all together; she suspected that it had something to do with the angry phone call that he'd received from Riz the other day, but she wasn't sure. She knew she was strapped and if he was planning on acting a fool she would surely aid in his venture.

Kiam cleared his throat then spoke with words that were carefully chosen. "I sat and thought long and hard before I called y'all here to-night," he stated a little over a whisper. All eyes were focused on him and there was no other sound in the room aside from his voice.

He looked from one face to the other. "The last thing a general ever wants to do is wonder about the loyalty of his men," he continued as he picked up the medication bottle, popped it open and threw two pills in his mouth.

He poured himself a shot of Jack and locked eyes with Lissha. "I'm going to start with you. My product made it back here, but the money never made it to Riz, his people got jacked leaving the exchange spot. Now unless I'm stupid that tells me that it was set up on this end. You told me that you'd put your life on your crew."

"And unless you have proof that I can't, don't even bring that shit to me," Lissha defended her girls.

Kiam chuckled. "Besides you and me, they were the only ones that knew when and where the pickup went down."

Treebie stopped chewing and sat to the edge of her seat. "What the fuck is that supposed to mean?"

Lissha held her hand up gesturing for Treebie to be quiet. She sat up and looked him square in the face, the way Big Zo had taught her to face opposition. "Are you accusing me of something?"

"Until I find out exactly what happened, I'm accusing all of you muthafuckas," he said point blank.

"If Riz's people got jacked, why the fuck couldn't the cross come from his end?" Lissha contested.

"That's what I'm saying," Treebie angrily agreed. "And ain't nobody seen Gator's slick ass in two days, how we know he didn't have something to do with it? You need to find out where that nigga at."

"I already know where he's at," Kiam replied matter of factly.

"Well, enlighten the rest of us please," shot Treebie impatiently.

Kiam smirked. "You're chewing him."

Treebie gasped and spat out the spaghetti. She cocked her head to the side and looked at him crazily. "What the fuck, man!"

"I skinned that bitch nigga alive then I ground him up real good," said Kiam.

Treebie slung the plate off her lap and bolted to the bathroom. Lissha, Donella, and Bay stared at Kiam with their mouths open.

JuJu was still covering the door. He was not surprised by Kiam's revelation, he had helped him dice Gator up.

Treebie returned to her seat still gagging and waiting for Kiam to tell her he was only kidding, but the look in his eyes confirmed that he was dead ass. This nigga craze. Treebie shook her head in utter disbelief. The others were thinking the same thing.

Kiam looked at them as if to say they hadn't seen shit yet. "Gator was stupid," he said. "He should have known that he would be the first person I suspected. I thought he had something to do with the attempt on my life, but I was wrong. He jacked Riz's people. I couldn't get him to admit it before I ended his suffering but it don't matter, I know that he was skimming money for years. Riz told me that."

"You put a whole lot of faith in what Riz say. That nigga could be wrong about all this shit," Lissha voiced.

"You got a problem wit' it? 'Cause if I'm right about Gator having something to do with the jack then one of you had to help set it up." He paused and looked in the faces of the women one by one. He had to admit that they were tight lipped and unified. But in a minute Gator's accomplice would fold.

"I'm gonna give the guilty one a chance to own up to what she done. If you do that I'll show some mercy but if you sit here and play innocent, I'ma do to you the same thing I did to your boy," Kiam promised ominously.

Neither of the girls expressions changed a tad, noted Kiam. "Y'all gon' play this shit all the way out, huh?" Still he got nothing but four blank stares. The silence in the room was profound.

Switching tactics Kiam said. "I give that soft nigga, Gator, credit; he wouldn't tell me nothing. Nah, he took that to the grave with him. But I'ma still find out which one of you crossed me."

On cue, Daphne came sweeping into the living room. Four sets of eyes focused on her.

Kiam chuckled and picked his gun up off of the table. He looked at Daphne and said, "Point out the bitch that you saw with Gator when he met with Wolfman."

Daphne locked eyes with the guilty one and did not bat an eyelash as she raised her finger and pointed directly at the traitor. "That's her right there," she said.

Chapter 1
Blood In, Blood Out

A wicked, foreboding silence hovered over the entire room as Daphne's accusatory finger landed on the alleged culprit. Everyone's head snapped in the direction that she pointed, knowing that an irreversible death sentence had just been issued.

Kiam's eyes instantly faded to a blackness that mirrored the inevitable punishment that he was about to hand down. His chest filled with murderous energy that surged down through fingers that were already gripping steel, ready to obliterate a bitch's whole mind.

Lissha's mouth fell open. Treebie gasped. Bayonna's heart raced with nervous trepidation for her girl. JuJu moved into position awaiting the slightest signal from Kiam. A simple head nod was gonna get a ho sent to the afterlife.

Daphne's voice reverberated off of the walls as her index finger jabbed the air. "Yeah, that's her," she repeated with certainty.

"Bitch, you a got damn lie!" cried Donella, springing up out of her chair, ready to attack her accuser.

"Sit the fuck down!" commanded Kiam in a leveled tone that was much more threatening than a raised voice.

Rising to his feet, he leveled his Nine dead between her eyes. The click-clack of him housing a slug in the chamber echoed as loudly as a cannon being fired inside a closet.

Donella froze and looked around at her girls as if she didn't know what the fuck was going on. In that brief moment of doom each of them refused to meet her questioning stare. Her eyes turned into slits as the implication became crystal clear in her mind, the cross was in effect—one of them had put some fuckery in the game.

JuJu walked up behind her and snatched her Celine bag off of the chair just in case she was thinking about reaching for the banger inside. "Sit bitch or get put on your ass," he spat, itching to display his gangsta.

"Nah, fuck that," Donella vehemently protested.

Whap! JuJu slapped her across the face with his tool, drawing blood from her mouth. Donella crumpled down in the chair and looked up at Kiam pleadingly.

"What the fuck is you doing?" Lissha yelled at JuJu.

"You want what the fuck she got?" he barked back, pointing his gun in Lissha's direction.

"Nigga, you must be fucking crazy," Lissha shouted, refusing to back down.

JuJu glanced at Kiam who gave him the eye to chill.

"I fucking thought so," Lissha stated before turning her attention back to Kiam. "Kiam, what the fuck is going on?" She announced each word as if it stood alone and carried with it the same threat as a hollow point bullet.

"Ya bitch ain't right and I'm about to give y'all bitches some new memories together," declared Kiam.

"Why? 'Cause this dick sucking ho say so?" she pointed at Daphne.

Kiam chuckled then he looked down at Donella. "Tell them what you and Gator been plotting. Tell 'em how you ate at the same table with us then consorted with the enemy." All eyes went in her direction.

"I ain't got shit to tell," she maintained.

Kiam shook his head. "Get ya life right with God and do it fast 'cause you're about to dwell in His house."

"Kiam, we don't know this trick." Lissha stated angrily, pointing at Daphne. "She coming up in here accusing people of treachery and you're fixin' to body Donella on this nobody ass bitch's words? Hell no," she objected.

"Lissha got a point Kiam. We all have gone places with Gator at one time or another. That don't make her guilty of betrayal. Gator was our brother," Bayonna tried to reason with him.

"Was all y'all fucking ya brother?" he asked accusingly. "Going with him to meet with the enemy behind my back? Is that the way all of y'all get down?" His tool moved from woman to woman.

Treebie looked at Lissha and Bay then at Donella.

"This bitch ain't got shit on me," Donella said in her defense.

"Only this," disputed Daphne. She pulled her phone out and played a recording of Wolfman confirming with Gator that Donella would be meeting with him about the business they discussed earlier. Further proving the conspiracy, Daphne pulled a picture up on her screen of Donella, Gator, and Wolfman.

She held her phone up and walked around showing the picture to each girl, presenting proof that could not be refuted. Kiam had already reviewed the evidence and had reached a tacit decision.

"That don't prove shit! I ain't never been around that nigga. Bitch, that picture is fabricated," cried Donella through her busted mouth. But even to her own ears her denial sounded weak.

Treebie's eyes lowered as they bounced from face to face. Lissha wanted to talk but the lump in her throat stopped her words from leaving her mouth. Bayonna knew in her heart that Donella was not capable of betrayal but the evidence that stacked against her was overflowing.

Kiam walked over and looked down in Donella's face with contempt that was thicker than ghetto stress. He flat out despised a Judas ass mutha-fucka as much as he hated a snitch. Donella's gender warranted no pity from him at all—pussy or balls, this was the life she had chosen and he was about to make her honor the code. *One hunnid or your ass will sit with Jesus.*

Showing no emotion, Kiam pressed the nose of the Nine against Donella's forehead. "You got some shit you need to say?" he asked, peering down at her.

"Fuck you, nigga. I'm an official ass bitch. I haven't did a got damn thing. If somebody crossed the family it damn sure wasn't me. Now do what you do," Donella muttered with angry tears rolling down her cheeks.

Kiam heard that hot shit but it didn't alter her fate. In a cold remorse-less tone, he uttered, "Look in my eyes and tell me what you see."

"I don't see shit."

"Exactly," he confirmed. "Because I don't feel shit. Take that picture to the grave wit' you." He re-tightened his grip on the Nine and caressed the trigger.

"Kiam!" Lissha shouted.

He eased off of the trigger and cut his eyes towards her. "Save that shit. Straight up! This bitch ain't gettin' no reprieve and you can get it next." His tone was merciless.

"What the fuck is you talking about?"

"You vouched for this bitch so her death is on your hands."

"Nah, it's on mine," Treebie interrupted, stepping in and putting her cold steel to Donella's head.

"Treebie, noooo." Lissha yelled out as she lunged toward her.

Boc! Boc! Treebie's Glock .40 clapped like thunder.

"What the fuck?" Bayonna belted, jumping from her seat as blood and brain sprayed onto her neck and face.

"Noooooo!" Lissha cried, falling to her knees, lifting Donella's head onto her lap and tenderly running her hand over her face and lifting her arm. "Aw, Momma," she sniffled.

Donella twitched for a few seconds before her arm went limp and her head fell slack. Blood trickled from her wounds and pooled beneath her head.

"Treebie, why?" cried Lissha.

"You know what the fuck this is." Treebie pointed the Glock at her. "If this bitch had conspiracy in her blood then you should thank me. Because what I can't live with is a traitor in my house." She held her gun firm, silently daring Lissha to test it.

Bayonna felt like she had walked into a bad nightmare. With her hands covering her mouth, she thought about the countless times the enemy had been at the other end of their unforgiving triggers but never would she have imagined that their ruthlessness would turn on one another.

Lissha stood up breathing heavily with Donella's blood all over her clothes. She locked eyes with Treebie and held her stare; two lionesses destined to lock ass. Treebie held her position, itching to be challenged.

Slowly, Treebie bent over Donella's dead body and ran her hand in the puddle of blood beneath her. It coated her palm in a ghastly wet thickness.

Bay looked on in shock as Lissha moved back towards Treebie.

"We shed blood to get in this muthafucka, and we'll bleed to get out," Treebie stated. She put her hand out towards Lissha then looked over at Bayonna.

Cautiously, Bayonna approached and placed her hand on top of theirs. Treebie slowly lowered her gun to her side. Tightly they gripped hands sealing their bond with blood.

Lissha turned to JuJu. "Tonight Kiam set the standard. Make sure from this moment forward you don't slip. Because as you see, the only penalty is death." Her voice cracked as the last word crossed her lips and her eyes settled on her sistah's bloody corpse.

14

Kiam nodded his affirmation. "The rest of y'all burn that shit in your memory because this shit is just the beginning." He eyed each of them trying to detect even the faintest sign of disloyalty.

Treebie was unfazed. Bay was stoic. Lissha was beyond reproach. Each, however, wore a poker face.

Kiam continued to study them as he went on. "We know who set up the robbery of Riz's people and they've been dealt with swiftly and without clemency. But somebody put those Blood Money niggas on JuJu and muthafuckas tried to come for me. Whether or not all of that was connected, I don't know. Until I find out who was behind those moves, none of you bitches are safe. Get the fuck outta my house." He sat on the couch with his gun rested on his lap.

The three women took one last look at Donella's dead body, grabbed their shit and headed to the door. As they filed out the house they made sure to throw JuJu some shade on the way out.

Treebie was the last to leave. She stopped at the door, slowly turned around, glared at Kiam and left some parting words that were coated in acid. "I hope you find a good ass hole to hide your rat in." She gave Daphne the look of death as she closed the door.

Daphne's heart sank to her feet. She knew she was living on borrowed time. Her false accusation had been well planned and rehearsed but if and when the truth came out she planned to be nowhere around. Kiam was not playing with a bitch. It was time for her to collect the money and get in the wind.

Ca$h & NeNe Capri

Chapter 2
A Tangled Web

Daphne could barely hold the steering wheel steady as she drove home. Her nerves were frayed and her mind was racing out of control. Visions of Donella's wig getting puffed out and her brains being sprayed all over the living room was already haunting her and the girl's body wasn't even cold yet.

Before the meeting Daphne had held her composure under Kiam's intense questioning, making her studied lies sound authentic. She didn't have to lie when he asked what her connection was to Wolfman and why she was willing to sell him out.

"Because I hate that black bastard," she replied.

That was indeed the truth. She lived for the day she could help somebody knock him to his muthafuckin' knees.

She had used the revulsion that she felt for Wolfman to help her convincingly lie on Donella. The clincher had been the picture; that shit had withstood Kiam's closest scrutiny. The marvel of *photo shop* had sealed poor Donella's fate.

Daphne wondered if she had figured out which one of her so-called sistahs had set her up before Treebie's gun put her thoughts on the floor. She shook her head over the part that she had played in the complicity and reminded herself to *Trust No Bitch.*

Her cell phone rung just as she pulled into her driveway. She parked next to DeMarcus' truck and reached into her purse. Her hand shook as she held the phone and stared at the screen. The call was from a restricted number which meant that it was *her* calling.

Daphne nervously cleared her throat. "Hello?" she answered.

"You did good. I'll have the rest of the money for you tomorrow. Remember, this stays between you, me and God. If you get loose lips on me I'll do to you what the Lord can't reverse."

The screen went blank.

Once Treebie dropped off Bayonna, she drove out to Lake Erie. Pulling up to the side of the bank, she deaded her headlights then parked under

17

the nearest tree. Reaching into her bag she pulled out a blunt and lit up. Taking pull after pull, she tried to rationalize her actions. *It had to be done.*

Tears weren't an option and neither was regret. Each of them had chosen their path. Prison or death would be the only way out. Treebie didn't give a fuck about Gator other than the sickening thought that she had swallowed a piece of that weak ass nigga. Just knowing a bit of him was in her digestive system made her want to stick a finger down her throat and force herself to throw up. She still couldn't believe Kiam had done that shit! But what stood out more was Donella's demise at her hands.

Treebie puffed until the last bit of smoke left her fingertips then she grabbed her gun and got out. Walking over to the edge of the bank, she looked down at the tool that had ended life and love. She choked back her tears then tossed the gun as far out into the dirty lake as her strength allowed her.

"Rest in peace, ma," she said as she stepped back and just looked out over the water.

Bayonna sat in the middle of her living room floor crying and laughing at the same time. She caressed the pages of a photo album full of vacation pictures that she and the girls had taken over the years. Each picture was filled with irreplaceable memories.

Donella had always been the adventurous one which made their little trips so much fun. And in a blink of an eye that was all gone.

Gator too.

Donella had tried to warn her that fucking with him was gonna get her killed, but she hadn't been able to leave him alone. He had his flaws but away from the others he had been so sweet.

I told you not to get at Riz's people. Damn baby, why didn't you listen? She reflected solemnly as the thought raised serious questions in her mind. She had refused to help him set up the robbery but obviously someone had.

Treebie? Lissha? Bayonna tried to decide. Neither made much sense, but one of those bitches were guilty because she knew for sure Donella wouldn't have rocked like that. Donella was her thorough bitch and she would not have betrayed her with Gator. It didn't matter how high the evidence was stacked, Bayonna didn't buy that shit.

That bitch came in there and lied on you Nella. But why? I was the one fucking with Gator.

Guilt and anger grabbed ahold of her soul as the evening's chain of events clouded her mind. Hugging the open album to her chest, she began devising a plan.

Bayonna dismissed all thoughts of going to Kiam and coming clean. She also decided against walking away from Blood Money; they had done too many things to turn back now. She was going to stick around and pretend to be as loyal as always until she found out which one of them had set Donella up. Then she was gonna murder that ass.

"Nella, I owe you that," she said affectionately as her tears dripped down on a photo of her and Donella on ski jets in Aruba.

"You're my bitch for life," she vowed. "Sleep in peace. I *will* avenge you."

Lissha rushed into her house and quickly closed the door. She looked down at her blood soaked clothing and immediately took off for the bathroom, stripping herself of each soiled article along the way.

Slamming the bathroom door, she rushed to the sink and turned on the water. With the night's episode drumming in her head, she scrubbed her hands almost violently, desperately trying to rid herself of the blood from her sistah that stained her hands.

Reaching in the medicine cabinet she grabbed her toothbrush and ran it back and forth across her nails as tears began to cascade down her cheeks. "Why, Nella?" She repeated to herself as she damn near scrubbed the skin from her hands.

Heavy emotion took over her heart as she sat on the edge of the tub and cried. It seemed as if the pain was punishment for all the lives they had taken and all the misery they had caused.

It's your fault. Kiam's words bounced through her mind. Lissha wrapped her arms around herself and rocked back and forth as the permanent picture of Donella laid stretched out with a hole in her head flashed through her memory every time she closed her eyes.

Once Lissha was finally able to stand on steady legs, she turned on the shower, stepped inside and attempted to wash away the last traces of

Donella's blood. She watched it rinse down the drain, carrying with it a part of her that was lost forever.

Her body felt laden as she reached to turn off the water and all of a sudden the burden of her secrets began to crack her hard shell. Her shoulders rocked as a loud sob escaped her lips and she fell back against the wall. For a moment she couldn't move. The pain in her heart seemed physical. She took a few deep breaths then willed her legs to move.

Walking into her bedroom she felt even worse as her eyes scanned the many photos of her and the girls. Rushing to her dresser, she snatched each frame and threw them in a drawer—she could not face those happy memories at the moment. A breath of air came out her mouth in a whoosh as she fought back a sob and collapsed onto her bed.

Caressing her pillow, Lissha silently cried and prayed for God to have mercy on Donella's soul.

When she felt she could talk, she picked up the phone from her nightstand and called Big Zo.

"Hey baby girl," he answered.

"Daddy," she managed to get out a little over a whisper.

"Lissha, what's the matter?" He sat up in his bunk with his ear pressed to the phone.

"Daddy, everything is fucked up," she blurted as tears began to flow down her face.

"Lissha, calm down and tell me what's wrong," he pressed.

"Donella is dead. Gator too."

Big Zo paused to allow her words to sink in. "I need you down here immediately," he ordered in a stern voice then disconnected the call.

Lissha rose to her feet and headed to her closet to get dressed and pack a bag. She needed to get out of the city right away.

Big Zo dropped his cell phone on the bunk and ran a hand down his face as concern began to overtake his thoughts. *Donella and Gator—dead? What the fuck happened? Is shit unraveling already?* he fretted.

Instinctively he knew that their deaths couldn't have been from an enemy's bullets or else Lissha would have also reported that Kiam had slayed a whole community in retaliation. And Treebie would be going slap off killing everything moving.

No, this had to be some in-house shit, he correctly concluded.

Big Zo dropped his head and reflected back to when he had recruited Donella out of the strip clubs and onto his team. He had promised to change her life and he had definitely done that. Under his tutelage she had elevated from tricking for a little bit of a nigga's bank to balling with her own money. But now she was dead.

Big Zo didn't exactly know how he felt about that and whose ass would suffer for it until he found out what the fuck had happened. If Donella's death turned out to be unwarranted some heads were going to roll.

He reached for his Newports and fired one up, inhaling the smoke deep into his lungs then blowing it out slowly as he tried to wrap his mind around the news.

Gator too, Lissha had said.

This made Big Zo reflect a couple years back.

Big Zo awakened to the vibration of his cell phone. Trepidation leapt up in his chest because calls in the middle of the night were never good news. He was already stressing trying to keep his operation afloat from prison. "Hello?" he answered, sitting up and swinging his feet over the side of his bunk.

"Old man, I got your daughter. If you want the bitch back alive you better have five bricks and $200,000.00 on deck the next time I call or I'm going to send you her obituary in the mail."

"Who in the fuck is this?"

"I'm the one that you saw so much potential in before you went down."

The words resonated in Big Zo's mind with clarity, he had uttered them to a young boy named Trill. The kid had begun making a name for himself in the streets with his murder game and Big Zo had tagged him to become one of his enforcers. That union had never occurred because the Feds snatched Big Zo up, and now this little reckless clown was trying to extort him.

"Muthafucka if you lay one hand on her I'll..."

"You can't do shit from where you're at old man. Your reign is over and you're about to sponsor mine," Trill cut him off with a chuckle in his tone.

Big Zo remained calm, he was not the type to let another man force his hand. "What I'ma sponsor is your funeral if you harm Lissha," he threatened.

"You're at my mercy. You know not to fuck with me. Have that shit ready or prepare yourself to receive some condolences." The phone went dead.

Big Zo sprung up off his bunk and began pacing the cell as he tried to think of a way to turn the tables. He made a few frantic calls to the streets and found out that Trill was disliked by many. He also found out that Trill had a friend who could be flipped for the right price.

A few phone calls later Big Zo talked to Gator for the very first time. After a long conversation he was convinced that Gator wasn't in on the kidnapping so he made him an offer that he couldn't turn down.

As Big Zo awaited the next call from Trill, he had already devised the youngster's demise.

The call never came because the cross was applied swiftly and ruthlessly. What Trill found out a second before Gator stamped his one-way ticket to hell was that in the game it's always the one closest to you that will take you out.

Big Zo smiled at the memory; nothing beat the cross but the double-cross. There was no greater feeling than to be able to move niggas around like pawns on a chess board. He was still a boss even from behind the walls.

Gator had been rewarded for selling his soul but he proved to be the wrong piece to the puzzle. Big Zo had no tears to shed over his death because in all honesty he had known that Gator's life expectancy was short from the moment Kiam stepped out of prison. Still he needed details to put his mind at ease.

Lissha needed to get her ass down there ASAP. He wanted to look in her eyes and see into her soul while she delivered her report. Her eyes could not lie to him like her mouth could.

He stood up and paced back and forth in the small cell while trying to keep his mind from racing. *Don't fuck up Lissha.*

He needed to re-strengthen his influence over her and keep her focused on the mission.

Chapter 3
Love or Loyalty

Kiam pulled up in front of his condo, popped the trunk and jumped out. His left arm was still in a sling due to the gunshot wounds, but he managed to carry his bags inside. As he closed the door behind him his cell phone vibrated in his pocket.

Kiam dropped the bags beside the couch and hurriedly answered. He was hoping that it was Eyez. When he finally dug the phone out of his pocket and saw a Pennsylvania number he knew exactly who it was. He had been expecting the call for days.

"Hello," he answered as respectfully as he could.

"What's going on soldier? How are you?" Big Zo asked as he looked out his cell window at a huge expanse of nothing.

"I'm good Pops. Had a few problems that had to be permanently erased but that happens from time to time. I'm sure you know how it goes."

"I do," Big Zo confirmed. "And I just saw my little princess, she explained what happened. Are you sure that they were in violation?"

"I did my homework," Kiam assured him.

"I trust that you did. It's just that I would've never expected the girl to violate," said Big Zo purposely omitting names. "As for the other individual, I wouldn't put it past him. He always felt he was owed more than I could ever give him for saving Lissha's life."

Kiam chuckled, he still didn't know that story but whatever it was it meant nothing now. Gator could not be resurrected. "Yeah?" he replied. "Well, that wasn't my debt. I didn't owe him nothin' but what he ended up gettin'." His callousness was for Gator, it wasn't aimed at Big Zo.

"Indeed," Big Zo understood. He paused to gauge Kiam's mood. "Is there anything else I need to know or do you feel I am well informed?"

Kiam also paused for a minute to make sure he wasn't in violation. "I trust that she would tell you everything,"

"Don't ever leave anything to chance. Real men always make sure."

Kiam nodded his head then put together a sequence of coded statements that detailed the treachery, murder and losses that had taken place. When he was done he sat down on the couch awaiting his mentor's verdict.

"Is that all?"

"Yes," Kiam quickly responded.

"Son, I know that I've placed a huge responsibility on your shoulders, but I have no doubt that you're capable of handling it. I don't have to question your officialness or your commitment to this thing of ours. Whatever problems arise, I am confident that you will do what is needed. Always act on knowledge and certainty. Emotion is a bitch's game. If you need me, reach out. Don't do what you think I would do, do what you *know* I would do."

"I got you, Pops," Kiam affirmed.

"Lastly, my daughter is hurting right now but she will get past it. Don't coddle her. The last thing I want is a weak ass team. Make that trip and get us back on point." He made his orders clear.

"Already on it," said Kiam.

"I'm proud of you son. There is no other man whom I would've entrusted with this. Regroup and take over the city. No one is built to stop you."

"No one," Kiam echoed confidently.

Zo ended the call and stood staring out the window and thinking back to a time when the world was his and muthafuckas bowed at his feet. Now he was living life vicariously through Kiam. It wasn't much but it was all that he had.

Kiam placed the phone on the coffee table as his heart filled up with pride and relief. Pops' approval meant as much to him as Faydrah's love. The last thing he wanted was to let Pops down or fuck up what had been entrusted to him.

Always act on knowledge and certainty. Emotion is a bitch's game. That sage advice alone reminded him that he needed to make sure he was carefully calculating each move.

Reaching over and grabbing the phone, he called Riz to set up a meeting. From the sound of his connect's voice Kiam detected that the nigga was still salty but fuck it, he had to make shit right so they could get back to business.

After ending the conversation with Riz, Kiam went up to his bedroom and threw some clothes into an overnight bag. He went to his closet and retrieved a bag of money and hit the door.

As he drove through the streets he hit JuJu up, letting him know he would be there shortly. Then he placed a long-overdue call to Faydrah.

The first call went unanswered, causing Kiam mild agitation. Was she purposely ignoring him? he wondered. "Call Eyez," he repeated to his voice command.

This time she answered and Kiam's thuggish heart jumped like a teen hearing the sweet purr of his crush's voice for the first time.

"Hey you," he said, regaining his swag but uncertain of where he stood in her world now.

"Hey you," she returned their affectionate greeting.

A brief silence claimed the moment but Kiam refused to acquiesce to it. What they had transcended his stubbornness.

"How you doing baby?" he asked softly.

"Doing what I do. You know, working and trying to keep busy. How are you?"

"Missing my woman," he replied honestly. With her he was never averse to putting his heart on the line.

"I miss you too," she admitted with reservation in her tone.

Kiam immediately picked up on it and even though he understood what it was about, it still hurt him a little. "Where are you?" he asked.

"I'm at Mommy's."

"Can I see you?"

She didn't respond right away and that fucked with his heart too. *Was it really like that?* he asked himself. *Nah, shorty can't just walk away.*

After a brief pause, she proved him right. "You can come over to Mommy's if you want to talk," she invited.

"A'ight. I'm on my way."

Faydrah stared at the table as she turned her phone in her hands. She had not seen Kiam since she left the hospital and was trying to come to grips with the idea that she was going to leave him alone.

"Faydrah? Where is your mind at child?" her mother asked as she slowly stirred her chili.

"That was Kiam."

Her mom turned to face the picture window over the stove as she sprinkled fresh basil into her mix. "So what are you going to do?" she asked continuing to face forward.

"I don't know, Mama," she replied truthfully, hearing the pain in her own voice. "I know I love him and that I've forced every man I've met away from me so that I could save my love for him but he let me down."

Ms. Combs smiled then turned the fire down on her chili and put a lid over it. Grabbing a towel, she wiped her hands as she walked over to her precious child who now had tears filling her eyes.

She pulled a chair out from the table, sat down and reached for Faydrah's hand, holding it in hers. "Listen honey. He didn't let you down. You let yourself down. Kiam has always been honest with you. And you did him a disservice by fabricating parts of your love for him."

Faydrah lowered her eyes because the truth hit hard.

Ms. Combs lifted her daughter's head up and looked her in the eyes. "You have to love him for who he is, not for who you want to change him into. You know Kiam loves you. He would do anything in his power to make sure you never see a day of hurt or sadness. But you have to decide if you're willing to wait until he is done growing," she advised.

Faydrah took her mom's wisdom to heart but she was still undecided about what to do. Giving up Kiam would be so hard on her, but remaining with him and having to endure everything that came along with his lifestyle was a whole different type of pain.

Her mind went back and forth as they continued to talk about other things. Faydrah could barely pay attention to anything else her mother said; her thoughts were consumed by the choice she'd have to make.

The doorbell chimed breaking her thoughts.

"I'll get it," Ms. Combs quickly volunteered.

Faydrah stood up and drifted over to the sink and ran water over her face in an attempt to get it together. When she walked into the living room her mom had Kiam in a warm embrace. That was the type of history that they shared that could not be replaced.

Kiam slowly pulled back and out of her hold and locked gazes with the one that turned his gangsta into a love song.

"Let me let y'all talk." Ms. Combs squeezed Kiam's arm and walked back to the kitchen.

Kiam kept his eyes on Faydrah as she stood on the other side of the room looking at him apprehensively.

"Come here," he requested.

28

Reluctantly, she moved in his direction still battling with her thoughts. The little girl in her wanted to run into his arms and say fuck the world. But the woman in her spoke truth and logic. *Make him give you what you deserve.*

"Can I have a hug?" he asked, opening his arms.

Faydrah stepped into his embrace, careful not to hurt his arm. She melted under his touch instantly as her eyes closed and she took a deep breath, enjoying his scent.

A voice in her head whispered that she had to let go. But her heart blocked out the message and her body screamed for what only he could make her feel. She pressed against him tighter to quell the tingling between her thighs.

Kiam answered the call her body was giving; he gripped her back, sliding his hand down to her butt and planting soft kisses on her neck. Heat rose up from between her legs sending signals to Kiam's dick that she needed him.

Faydrah was on her way down *Memory Lane* emotionally naked and with rose colored shades on when she replayed her interpretation of her mother's speech. *You can't change him.*

Abruptly she pulled back, putting a little space between them so that her desire wouldn't take control of her tongue.

"What's wrong?" he asked, looking in her face for some of the passion she felt for him.

Faydrah sighed heavily. Then she straightened her shoulders and forced the words out of her mouth. "Kiam, I'm not ready for this. We have a lot of things we need to talk about. And if we push them aside because our asses are on fire then we will be living a lie."

"I don't have anything to talk about except when are you going to put my ring back on your finger."

"Exactly. It's all about what *Kiam* wants. But what about what Faydrah needs?" She walked to the other side of the couch putting more distance between them. She looked at him with embers of anger in her eyes. Anger that stemmed from her loving him so fucking much.

He felt the heat from across the room and saw the intensity in those beautiful eyes of hers.

"You know what?" She went on. "I have to accept that this is my fault. I have been loving you under an illusion."

"What are you talking about?" he was getting frustrated with her little tantrums.

"I knew what it was when I started on this journey, but I pushed that shit to the side because my life ain't right without you. Then I almost got killed and that shit forced me to accept that my life ain't right with you either."

Her words hit his chest hard as the weight of them pulled at his heart. "I already told you I'm not doing this without you."

"Then walk away from the streets Kiam," she challenged.

"Eyez, don't ask me to do that shit. Hold me down and let a man be a man."

She shook her head with profound regret. "You know what Kiam? Pride comes before the destruction of men."

"I'm not doing this without you," he repeated.

"Kiam, let me go," she said as tears began to run down her face.

"That ain't happening. I have to go outta town for a few days then I'll be back for you." He walked over to where she stood. "You belong to me. I'm not taking no for an answer." He opened her hand and placed the ring in her palm. "I know you need time and I'ma give that to you. Regardless to what you decide just know you are the only woman I will ever love." Kiam closed her hand then planted a single kiss on her lips. "I love you."

"I know," she responded as she watched him turn and move to the door.

"Bye, ma," he called out to Ms. Combs.

"Bye, baby," she yelled back from the kitchen.

She came back into the living room to see him off, but when she got there Kiam had already left out of the door.

Faydrah was staring out the window watching him back out of the driveway. When his taillights faded out of sight she ran into her mother's arms and broke down.

Kiam was weighted by emotion that he quickly checked. He had already been warned about that and was not going to let it cloud his mission. He put Faydrah to the back of his mind and business in the front. He knew that his life depended on how he played out his next move and he wasn't going to lose over being caught up in his feelings. At this level of the game one slip and a nigga's whole cranium got blown the fuck out. He was not letting that shit happen to him.

He flipped into beast mode and prepared to go handle his business—by whatever means necessary.

Chapter 4
A Stunning Revelation

Kiam looked at his young boy and spoke decisively. "We're going up in here to make shit right, but we're not bowing down to this nigga. If he don't have no understanding let your banger do the talking. If shit get hot we either come outta there together or we die side by side. There is no compromise to that," he instructed.

JuJu nodded his head and clicked one in the chamber of his Desert Eagle. From this point on, it was do or die. If Riz was on some gorilla shit he was gonna make that nigga the top story on the ten o'clock news. "I'm ready fam. Let's go see what it do," he said as they got out of the car at the same time.

Kiam had his heat on his waist and a small duffle bag slung across his good shoulder. JuJu followed him inside the building with his jaw set and his mind on creating chalk lines. He took in everything as they climbed the stairs to the sixth floor.

Bones opened the door and let them in. He had a mug on his face like something stupid was on his mental. Kiam looked him in the eye communicating that death was right around the corner if he was intent on having it pay him a visit. JuJu's grimace punctuated that message, but Bones wasn't shook. He had more than a dozen bodies on his street resume and the thought of adding two more made his nuts swell.

None of the men spoke to each other. JuJu kept his eyes on Bones as he closed the door behind them. Kiam's gaze immediately honed in on Riz who was seated on the couch with his two Rottweilers at his feet. His short dreads were neatly trimmed and the army fatigues that he wore were starched and creased. Nothing about his appearance was cruddy but his eyes; they were two black orbs that resembled the darkness that came before death.

With four killahs in one small room and a breadth of animosity between them, the tension immediately thickened.

Both canines rose and bared their teeth, letting out low growls. Kiam didn't flinch, he was gonna turn them into black and brown throw rugs the minute they pounced.

"Sit," ordered Riz without breaking the eye lock that he held on Kiam.

The well-trained dogs obeyed their master's command while continuing to watch Kiam. The dog's keen sense of smell picked up the heavy scent of danger that emitted from his pores.

Riz sized Kiam up. The reports that he'd gotten back from Cleveland confirmed what his first impressions had been. The man that stood before him personified realness but that didn't excuse what had happened.

Kiam dropped the duffel bag at Riz's feet. It landed with a thud. "I'm a man of honor," he said. "I would never betray the people that vouched for me nor would I dirty my name. A man's word is worth much more than money. That's every dollar that you lost in our last transaction. I hope that brings peace between us but if not, it's your move."

Riz duly noted Kiam's audacity; he had no choice but to respect the nigga's gangsta. Here he was with one arm in a sling, up in BK, in the crib of one of the most ruthless men in the city, letting his nuts hang to the floor.

Riz cleared his throat. Seconds later four cold-hearted assassins came out of the back wearing menacing frowns and holding assault rifles. They posted up around the room covering all sides and stood prepared to let their weapons bark at Riz's command.

Kiam's eyes scanned the room, the odds were seriously against him but that was the story of his life. He had never been one to fold against a stacked deck and that wasn't about to change now. Behind him JuJu wasn't sweating, he had resigned himself to kill or be killed. But he was going to take a muthafucka to the grave wit' him. Bones was going to be the first to get his top blown off, JuJu had already decided.

Quickly his eyes located the light switch on the wall. It was right there within arm's reach. With the lights out, the darkness would minimize their advantage.

JuJu took a mental picture of where each man stood, he could put them on their asses without accidentally shooting Kiam. *Yeah muhfuckaz, I'm 'bout to turn this lil' spot into Beirut.*

Kiam was thinking the same damn thing. He showed no fear. His persona remained all dick and balls. Wasn't no pussy inside his jeans so there was no chance of him bitching up. Fuck he care about a six against two disadvantage? For most of his life it had been him against the whole got

34

damn world. He looked at Riz's setup. There wasn't enough of those mu-hfuckaz to get at him and his vicious ass young boy. And what purpose did dogs serve in a gunfight? The thought brought a chuckle from his gut and his hand eased toward the strap inside his jacket. In that frozen moment of time, Eyez flashed in his mind. He hadn't told her goodbye so there was no way he was dying today. Fuck no! These niggas were about to get introduced to mass mu-hfuckin' murder.

The sound of the click clacks around the living room echoed in harmony as Riz's team peeped the move and clapped one in their chambers. Riz's hand shot up. "Everybody hold the fuck up!" he shouted. "There's no need for bloodshed. Let me talk to this man."

Kiam's whistle was halfway out of his waistband and JuJu's was already aimed at Bones' head, a fraction of a second away from decorating the wall.

Kiam studied Riz's face and saw what he needed to see in order to quiet that beast within. His hand came off the rubber grip around the handle of his banger, and he let it settle back down in its place. "We good Ju," he said without turning around.

JuJu removed his tool from Bones head but kept it out and ready to reverse the bodyguard's fate if the wind changed directions up in there.

Riz reached out, pulled the duffel bag to him and peered inside. He looked up at Kiam and nodded his acceptance. "Have a seat my friend," he offered.

Kiam sat beside Riz on the couch.

Riz leaned over and grabbed a blunt off the cocktail table. One of his goons walked up and put some flame to it for him. Riz hit the blunt and slowly blew the smoke out. "What happened? Who on your team betrayed us?" he asked pointedly.

"Donella and Gator," replied Kiam. "They both have been dealt with and can't possibly violate again."

Riz considered what he had just been told. "I didn't see that in Donella," he admitted. "I read her to be a down ass bitch. Maybe even loyal to a fault."

Kiam just listened, he didn't see where true loyalty had a limit.

35

"It doesn't surprise me about Gator because he crossed people he was down with to join up with Big Zo, though what he was really loyal to was Lissha's pussy. I guess you're coming in and taking over and probably taking Lissha from him too, pushed him to flip," Riz continued.

Kiam left him to think whatever he wanted, but something Riz had said caught his attention. "How did Gator cross someone to hook up with Big Zo?" he delved.

"Ask Lissha, she'll tell you. But you better watch that bitch, behind that pretty ass smile is a loaded gun. Her loyalty to Big Zo is impenetrable, never think otherwise."

"Mine is also," stated Kiam. "Never think otherwise."

Riz smiled appreciatively, loyalty was the attribute that separated real men from fakes. With a nigga like Kiam on his squad there would be no stopping him. He sat the blunt down in an ashtray and placed a friendly hand on Kiam's shoulder. "I like what you stand for. You're the type of man that can be trusted. Unfortunately, I don't feel the same way about the man you work for." Riz moved his hands back and forth animatedly.

"You can feel what you wanna feel Bleed, but I didn't come here for that. I came to straighten things up with you. Now that that's done where can we go from here?"

"Kiam, things aren't always as simple as that and not many people are who they appear to be. I used to have the same respect for Big Zo as you have for him now, but things started happening that has me wondering." He leaned back and gathered his thoughts before sharing them.

Kiam looked over at JuJu who was still posted up by the door surveying everything and everyone. Riz's voice brought Kiam's attention back to him.

"Kiam, let me tell you a story. When the feds hit Big Zo and snatched up everything he had, I was the one that fronted Lissha and Treebie blocks to help them rebuild his empire. Not long after I began doing that one of my stash houses here in New York got jacked and three of my men lost their lives trying to defend it. A fourth one was left alive by the robbers to deliver a message." Riz gestured one of his goons over to the couch.

The dreadlocked boy came across the room and stood awaiting Riz's order. "This is my son Jamaal. He is the one Blood Money left alive to deliver their message," he said to Kiam.

Blood Money! Kiam was shocked, but his expression did not change. JuJu had heard the name too but he did not allow his emotions to betray his calm.

"Jamaal, show him what Blood Money did to you," Riz prompted.

Jamaal let the stock of his chopper rest on the floor as he removed one of the gloves he was wearing and showed Kiam the scar left from the bullet hole that Blood Money had blown through his hand.

All kinds of thoughts ran through Kiam's mind but he revealed nothing to Riz. "What does any of this shit have to do with us?" Kiam questioned him.

Riz looked him in the eye and replied, "I had several of my men executed after that robbery. But as time moved on I have reason to suspect that Big Zo was behind it. I've tracked Blood Money to Cleveland, Ohio, Big Zo's stomping grounds. I don't believe in coincidence. I haven't been able to find out any of their identities but I will sooner or later, and if my suspicions prove correct I'm murdering everyone associated with Big Zo. You might wanna consider breaking ties with his organization."

"Loyalty or death," proclaimed Kiam, rising to his feet. "So I guess this ends our business."

"Only if you want it to. Like I said, I have suspicions but no proof. We can carry on with our dealings, it is very profitable to both sides. But I can't trust delivering to your people outside of New York. I'll lower the price five hundred a shoe but you'll have to come up here to get them."

"I can do that," Kiam agreed and they shook hands.

As Riz walked him to the door he told him that he hoped his suspicions turned out to be wrong. "I do too," Kiam replied. "Because when two giants clash a lot of little people get crushed."

As Kiam and JuJu descended down the stairs they both were wondering who in the fuck Blood Money was. Kiam's forehead was creased, he needed answers and this time he was not letting Lissha blow him off.

Inside of his apartment, Riz picked up his phone and dialed a number. "Yeah?" answered his man.

"What have you found out about Blood Money?" asked Riz.

"Nothing yet but I'm on it. And when I smoke 'em out, I'ma torture and kill 'em one by one," said Wa'leek.

Chapter 5
Shattered Trust

Lissha slowly moved around her kitchen trying to prepare a meal for the girls. This would be the first time since Donella's death that they were all together.

As she gathered all of the items she needed to make an eggplant parmesan dish, the recollection of the last meal the four of them had shared along with the laughter and the love, flashed through her mind and caused tears to form in her eyes. Up until now cooking for her girls had been therapy to her dark soul but now with the image of an empty seat at the table, her hands became heavy and her taste buds seized on her tongue.

Lissha wiped away the tears with the sleeve of her blouse then she placed the dish in the oven and prepared her house for Treebie and Bayonna's arrival. Taking a seat on the couch she ran the new plans through her head that she and Big Zo had carefully plotted.

When the doorbell rang she jumped and a surge of heat moved from her feet to the tips of her fingers. Walking towards the door her heartbeat increased two-fold. Lissha took a deep breath, calming the tidal wave of emotions that threatened to crash upon her mental shore and wipe out years of friendship.

What is already done can't be reversed. Now comes the ultimate test of your mettle. The blinders have been removed and you can now see the many different shades of black. If you're the Queen feline that I've schooled you to be you will show the face that they need to see. Tears are for weak bitches. A boss chic sheds blood— the blood of others. Zo's lecture from a few weeks ago drummed in her head verbatim.

Lissha stiffened her back, smoothed out her clothes, straightened up her shoulders, and opened the door with a look of purpose on her face.

"Hey momma," Bayonna said as she leaned in and gave Lissha a hug.

"Hey, girl. How are you?" Lissha responded then looked over Bayonna's shoulder at Treebie.

"You know me, taking it as it comes," Bayonna said, moving towards the living room.

"What you want, a special invitation?" Lissha said to Treebie giving her a little smile.

"Bitch, if you miss me just say it," Treebie shot back as she stepped through the doorway dressed like the CEO of a black-owned Fortune Five Hundred company. She wore a smart, pinstriped pantsuit with low heels and sharp toes, and her hair had been cut in a short bob.

"Whatever," Lissha said as they embraced.

Treebie walked over to the couch feeling slightly empty as her eyes rested on the chair that Donella would always sit in. She took a seat on the couch and reached in her bag and pulled out something to smoke.

Once the door was shut, Lissha went to the kitchen to retrieve a bottle of Amsterdam and three glasses. Treebie and Bayonna sat in the living room feeling very uneasy. Haunted thoughts of Donella filled the room as each of them tried to find comfort.

Lissha sat the glasses down then turned on some music to break the melancholy silence. As she poured the drinks she looked over at Bayonna who appeared to be slightly depressed.

"What's wrong, Bay?"

Bayonna took a deep breath. "I miss Nella," she said, gripping her hands and choking back her tears. Her bestie was gone and she was holding on to a secret that she didn't trust sharing with either one of them. *Both of them look like they have fangs.*

"I miss Donella, too," Lissha said, passing her a glass.

Treebie said nothing as she reached over and took her glass. Bringing their glasses together, she toasted, "To Nella."

Bayonna thought she could hear the insincerity drip from Treebie's forked tongue. Inside, Bayonna was bristling. *How she gonna toast to Nella and she's the one who killed her?*

Lissha looked at Treebie to see if there was any genuineness in her eyes. What she saw was a glimpse into the pits of Hell. Treebie had changed. But just how much only time would reveal.

Lissha effected a poker face. "To Blood Money," she said as she locked pupils with Treebie, silently conveying that she wasn't afraid off the devil because she wielded a pitchfork herself.

When the glasses clinked it was decided. They were moving forward with three because regardless of what the past had stolen, there was money to be made and greed drove them after it.

Each one of them had acquired a love for the kill that sent hot blood surging through their veins. Treachery had claimed one and no one wanted to be next. Though they smiled at each other, there wasn't one of them that wouldn't put something hot in the other's back to keep something hotter out of their own.

"Let's get this shit poppin'," Lissha said, slamming her glass on the table.

Bayonna got up and went to the kitchen to start making plates as Treebie began rolling up. After they puffed and passed, Lissha and Bay dug into their food. After the wicked stunt Kiam had pulled— feeding her Gator chopped up in spaghetti— Treebie was now much more cautious about what she put in her mouth. She lifted a fork full to her nose and smelled it. The parmesan smelled kosher, but she still waited to see Lissha chew and swallow before she dared to.

"Bitch, I'm not Kiam," said Lissha, observing Treebie's hesitancy. "I don't ground niggas up, I plant them *in* the ground."

"I apologize, LiLi, but that muthafucka has forever changed how I eat."

"I understand that but you know you can trust me."

Treebie knew no such thing. Not anymore. A lot had been said but not as much as what wasn't being spoken. Treebie considered herself a real bitch so she had to put it on the table what she knew was on their minds.

Removing a strand of hair out of her eye, she sat her glass down and looked at her sistahs. "Is either of you feeling some kind of way about what happened?" she asked outright. Then she went on without waiting for a response. "Because if you are, let's put that shit out in the open. I don't want to be running up in niggas' spots watching them with one eye and having to watch my own girls with the other. What I did had to be done. When one finger becomes rotten you have to cut it off to save the hand. If that's not understood and respected then I've been fucking with the wrong bitches."

"Street justice is a heartless bitch sometimes but it's the code we must live and die by. We all loved Donella, she was our sistah, but she chose her own fate," Lissha added.

Bayonna nodded in agreement because she didn't trust her mouth to move or her hand might've moved right along with it. One of those bitches was foul and she was going to find out which one it was then avenge her girl. Then she would make a real toast to Nella and blow some weed in the sky. "I'm down," she said, sounding oh so sincere.

They toasted again then Lissha laid out the ground work for the next moves with Blood Money. She explained to them how Big Zo wanted them to deal with Kiam. "Nothing has changed in that regard. Kiam is like a son to Daddy and he trusts whatever decisions Kiam makes. Our orders are to do as he says and follow his lead."

No one disagreed because Kiam had left the type of impression that visited a bitch in her sleep.

"What about JuJu? That nigga acted real disrespectful that day. And if it ever comes out that we're Blood Money, he's going to need more than an explanation about that hole I blew in his hand," said Treebie.

"Let me rock that ass to sleep," Bayonna volunteered.

"No," Lissha rejected. "Respect JuJu's get down and his loyalty to Kiam. With the numbers they're doing, they're making enemies and attracting haters. Sooner or later that will lead to war. And don't forget Kiam is going after Wolfman, Dontae, Money Bags Carter, the entire upper echelon. JuJu is a young killah and he's very valuable to all of us as Kiam's right hand. When he's no longer needed, trust me, I'm going to make that young boy regret the day he put a gun in my face."

Treebie accepted that.

"What about Gator's duties? What new nigga is Kiam going to have handle those? Another JuJu stepping in with his chest puffed out. I'm not feeling giving these young boys positions they haven't earned," she said, extending the blunt to Lissha.

Lissha re-lit the blunt, pulled on it a couple of times then passed it to Bay. "Replacing Gator is no real stumbling block since Kiam had him on minimal duties anyway," she explained to them both.

However, it tugged at Lissha's heart that after all he did for her she wasn't able to buy him more time.

Across from her Bayonna felt a pang of heartache in her chest as she reminisced on being in Gator's arms and getting to know him in ways he hadn't allowed the others to see. She wished Gator had listened to her.

"So is everybody still on deck?" Lissha's question brought Bayonna back to the present.

"You know I'm down," Treebie confirmed.

"I'm with you LiLi." Bayonna made it unanimous.

"Cool. It's only three of us now, we damn sure can't let any other bitches in the fold so we will have to tighten our shit up and make sure we are well prepared when we run down on niggas," Lissha stated firmly.

"You know my bitch stay ready," Treebie said as she pulled out her gun and placed it in her lap.

Chills shot up Bayonna's back as she recalled how malicious Treebie had been when she pulled out on Donella and ended her life like she was no more to her than a bitch in the streets.

"Y'all my bitches and I'll protect Blood Money with my life. Straight like dat!" Treebie reinforced.

"I hope so. Because we can't show any mercy," Lissha said, holding eye contact.

"They won't get any from me." Treebie's expression backed up her words.

Bayonna's head ping ponged between the two women as they hurled slick statements back and forth on calm breath, like each word was a reminder and a warning.

When their lips stopped moving, Bayonna's began. "So other than all the nonsense you had to tell Big Zo, how was he doing?" she asked, reaching in and grabbing another blunt from the ashtray and lighting it up.

"He was good," Lissha reported. "His main concern is our safety and our ability to bounce back from this situation and keep it moving." She reached out and accepted the fresh blunt from Bay.

Treebie was silent as she watched Lissha *puff puff.* Then she dropped the bomb. "Wa'leek was out here?" She calmly revealed, sitting back on the couch crossing her legs and placing the gun on her side.

The hair on Lissha's neck stood straight up. "What do you mean he was out here?" Her eyes got low as the crease in her forehead deepened.

"Just what I said."

"What did he want?" Lissha's mind began to wonder.

"Just some pussy. Is that a problem?" Treebie showed her a sinister smile.

"I don't know. Is it?" Lissha questioned her.

Treebie folded her hands in her lap and matched Lissha's penetrating gaze with one just as cautioning. She knew what her main concern was and she quickly addressed it. "Don't worry, all the cats are still in the bag."

Bayonna again looked back and forth but this time it was with confusion. "Who the fuck is Wa'leek?" she asked.

"Treebie's husband," Lissha answered with a worried look on her face.

"Damn, Tree, you married?" Bayonna asked with her head to the side.

"Something like that," she replied, waiting to see if Lissha would cut in.

"What does that mean? Either you are or you're not," Bayonna said, rising to her feet. She looked at Lissha, then back at Treebie. "Let me go to the bathroom since obviously this is none of my business." She walked out of the living room wondering what other fucking secrets they had.

As soon as Bay's footsteps could no longer be heard, Lissha hurriedly poured herself another drink and tossed it back. She looked at Treebie with fierce reprimand. "Keep that nigga calm," Lissha warned.

Treebie smirked. She kind of enjoyed seeing Lissha uncomfortable for a change. "You know how Wah do. It's only one part of him I can keep calm. The rest of him is going to be you and Kiam's problem." She sat up and poured herself a drink.

Lissha just shook her head. She could not wait for the girls to leave so she could call Big Zo and let him know that Wa'leek had removed the rock and crawled from up under it.

She replayed the recent events through her mind, searching for any sign that Wa'leek's hand prints were on any of it. With that nigga back in Treebie's ear, her loyalty was about to be severely tested.

Shit was bad enough, and with Wa'leek lurking around it was only going to get worse.

Chapter 6
On A Bitch's Trail

Wa'leek wasn't the only danger lurking in the shadows. Bayonna was prowling the streets too. She was looking for Daphne whom she felt held the answers that would seal either Lissha's or Treebie's fate. She didn't know the bitch but she figured that a couple of racks in the right thirsty person's hand would get her the information that she was in search of.

As soon as she left Lissha's house Bayonna made a beeline over to one of Wolfman's main drug houses on Superior Ave. There she poked out her titties and batted her eyes a few times and like presto, the dude that was over the spot made a call then put her on the phone with someone who could holla at her about the questions she had.

Bayonna took the phone, stated her business, and then was given an address to come to. She handed the man his phone back along with a G-note. "Thanks baby boy," she said.

"Let a nigga get your number so we can hook up," he tried but Bayonna's mind was on her mission. She flashed him a little smile and answered him by saying nothing.

She moved out the door with purpose, climbed in her car and headed to the location that she'd been told to come to. When she pulled up in front of the house she took a few deep breaths, grabbed her gun from her purse and tucked it in the back of her pants and prepared for the worse. She knew she was taking a chance going to the enemy's house; she damn sure had heard all the rumors about how greasy Wolfman's crew was, but she needed answers and she wasn't leaving without them.

As Bayonna stepped out the car she took inventory of the block. There were a few dudes standing against a Maxima and a few females trying to occupy their time. When she got close to the porch all eyes were on her. She walked fast and with confidence like she belonged there. Once on the porch she rang the bell and listened for anything strange.

"What you need little mama?" A big black dude stepped from the side of the house with a gun tight in his hand.

"I got business with Wolfman." She stood firm locking eyes with the man sending him the signal that he ain't run up on no dumb bitch.

"He expecting you?"

"Nah, I make it a habit to roam around in the middle of the night knocking on random doors looking for niggas," she spat, positioning herself where she would have easy access to pull out and get out the way.

"Damn, shorty, you got more heart than most niggas."

"I'm a'ight, just need to handle my business and swerve."

Dude rested the gun on his thigh then reached for his phone. "Yeah, she here," he informed the person on the other end then the door came open and a black husky man mean mugged her.

"You Bayonna?" he asked in a gruff and unfriendly tone.

Bayonna looked at his bandaged hand and chuckled inside. "You must be Nitti," she said with a straight face.

Nitti opened the door and allowed her enough space to come in. "He's in the next room," he informed her as he looked up and down the block. He gave the dudes on the car the nod and they dismissed the females and got on point. Nitti wasn't taking any chances. Kiam was not a nigga to fuck with and sending a pretty face could be the quiet before the storm.

Bayonna moved cautiously towards the living room taking note of everything in sight in case she had to visit this nigga again.

"You real brave coming here alone knowing there's beef simmering between our crews," Wolfman announced as she entered the room.

"No, not brave but I'm not scared either," she corrected.

"You ain't afraid of Wolfman?" He gave her a sinister smile from his reclined position on the couch.

"Look, we could go back and forth all night about my motivation. But on the real, I need answers." She put her hands on her hips getting them closer to her heat.

"Man, fuck this bitch, she coming up in here like we won't put her on her back," Nitti spat as he entered the living room with major attitude.

Bayonna turned in his direction. "You better watch who you call bitch before I finish what Kiam started," she replied boldly.

"What the fuck you say?" Nitti moved towards her.

"I think you heard every word." She eased her hand closer to her spine.

"Chill the fuck out!" Wolfman yelled at Nitti. "This is a guest in our house."

Nitti stood inches away from Bayonna breathing heavy and staring in her eyes like he wanted to choke her out.

46

"I don't give my orders twice," Wolfman stated calmly as he waited to see if Nitti was crazy enough to defy him.

Nitti gritted his teeth as he began to back up. "I'll see you again," he warned as he headed to the chair behind the couch.

Wolfman checked him with a cold stare then softened his expression when he turned back to Bayonna. "So, pretty lady, what can I do for you?" he asked politely.

"I need that dick sucking bitch that accommodates you."

"I got so many bitches sucking my dick you will have to be a little more specific."

She didn't know her name but she described her from head to toe. Wolfman didn't have to search his mind for a name, he knew exactly who she was looking for.

"Daphne," he said, lighting a cigarette and taking a deep pull.

Bayonna watched the thick smoke leave his lips and settle in the air as she reorganized her thoughts. "I need to speak to the bitch," she said flat out.

"It seems a lot of people need to see her these days." He smirked.

"I can't concern myself with a lot of people. *I* need to see her. Can you please point me in the right direction?"

Wolfman took another deep pull then blew it in the air. "You know what? I started to tell you. But you smell like that nigga that is gunning for me. So I can't give you shit but enough time to turn around and get in your car before these niggas try to find out how wet they can get their dicks." He gave her an evil grin.

"Fair enough. But remember I came to you in peace." She turned to leave.

Nitti jumped up and met her at the door with a victory smile plastered on his face. "Get yo ass outta here." He taunted as she walked onto the porch. The same dude who announced her presence was standing at the bottom of the stairs.

Bayonna started to keep on going but she had to let that bitch nigga Nitti know exactly how she felt. "Nigga you a puppet. Go on back inside so he can finish pulling your strings. Or maybe you one of the bitches sucking his dick."

"Nah ho, I'm that nigga that will cut your slick ass tongue out your mouth and wrap it around your muthafuckin' neck," Nitti threw back.

Bayonna stuck up her middle finger as she moved to her car. When she got in and started it up she let out a huge sigh of relief. She had taken a big chance going up in the enemies' camp. The fact that she had walked out of there alive prove to her that up under those niggas' gangsta lived nothing but some bitch ass imposters.

As she passed a McDonalds a few blocks away from the house she'd just left, she saw the same Maxima that had been parked outside. She pulled into the parking lot and watched the traffic going in and out. Just as she thought, the two females who were talking to Wolfman's goons were coming out with bags in their hands.

Bayonna grabbed two stacks and jumped out. Her heels clacked on the black top as she approached the two women. "Can I holla at you for a minute ma?" she asked.

"Didn't we just see you at Wolfman's?" the chic asked Bayonna.

"Yeah we cool. He put me on a little mission but I think I need a little help."

They lowered their brows and looked at her curiously but that didn't deter Bayonna from spitting her game. When she was done she looked at them expectantly.

"I don't know. Wolfman don't be liking us all up in his business," One of the chics said as they approached the vehicle.

"Look, you got what I need and I am sure I have what you need." Bayonna pulled the two bands from her pocket.

When the women eyed those green laces, Bayonna was sure she saw a little spit form at the corners of their mouths.

"What I gotta do for that?" she asked as she began planning her trip to the mall to cop those Red Bottom shoes she had been lusting for *for* two months.

"I need to holla at Daphne and I know you know where I can find her," said Bayonna.

"I hate that bitch." The woman turned up her face as if the name alone made her tongue itch.

"Good then tell me where I can find her."

48

The woman shifted her weight to the side and smacked her tongue. She toiled with the idea of crossing Wolfman and the repercussions but on the real he had giving her a dozen reasons to do so. Not to mention those green laces was screaming *handle your business*.

"Look I don't fuck with the bitch like that, but I know somebody who do. Let me get your digits." She pulled out her cell phone and locked in Bayonna's number as she read it off to her.

"What's your name?"

"Karma," Bayonna spat with one eyebrow raised high.

"I hear that," the woman said with an understanding smile.

"Keep this between us. I don't want you to get in trouble with Wolfman." Bayonna handed the woman the cash. "If I find her I will throw another two stacks your way. Oh, and you better share with your homegirl. She looks like the thirsty type," she said then moved back to her car and pulled out.

Now she was one step closer to the truth.

Ca$h & NeNe Capri

Chapter 7
A Boss Statement

As soon as Kiam got back from New York he dropped JuJu off and went home to shower and change clothes. Standing in the mirror, stepping into his pants, he realized that he needed a fresh cut. His circular brush waves we're still spinning but he needed the temple fades tightened up and a razor sharp line-up to set it off just right. Conceit wasn't part of his make-up but he liked to look good even when he was on that murder shit, so he made a mental note to stop by his boy Scooter's barbershop soon. Kiam needed to chop it up with him anyway and that would kill two birds with one stone.

He flexed his pecs in the mirror and was glad to see that his physique hadn't fallen off any since he came home from the joint; he still maintained a washboard stomach and a slim waist. He slipped his tool down in his waistband to complement those well-defined abs and peeped his profile. Yeah, he was that muhfucka, straight up.

Kiam dabbed on some Black Orchard cologne, put on a button down shirt, and reached for his phone to hit Lissha up. He had called her earlier and invited her over for dinner.

"I don't think so," she had turned him down.

"Why not? We need to talk," he'd insisted.

"Oh, we can talk but a bitch ain't eating nothing you cook," she protested.

Kiam had chuckled. "A'ight, I'll take you out to dinner. You choose the spot," he'd compromised.

Lissha had suggested a restaurant on the Westside which was all good with Kiam, but what she didn't realize was that this wasn't about food or pleasure. Kiam needed answers and if she uttered the wrong shit, her head could still end up on a dinner plate, fuckin' around with his intelligence.

The phone rung three times before she picked up. "Aren't you supposed to be on your way?" she said upon answering.

"Why you always trying to run something? Just be ready, I'm on my way." Kiam hung up the phone, put on his jacket and headed out the door. Tonight Lissha was coming clean or that ass was gonna rest at the bottom of Lake Erie, Zo's daughter or not.

51

Across town, Lissha looked at her reflection in the full length mirror in her bedroom as she glossed her pouty lips. Her face was framed by Chinese bangs that came down to her chin. Her hair was cut shorter on the sides and in the back, and new red highlights added something sassy to her look.

Her eyebrows were freshly arched and her naturally long lashes always gave her a bedroom type of sex appeal. A little eyeliner helped effect a sort of dreaminess to her look. Her titties stood up on their own and her small waistline flared out into hips that niggas referred to as gunslingers. She pirouetted in the mirror and looked over her shoulder at her ass. That muhfucka was swole up and poking out; if she was on pussy like that she would've been sprung on her got damn self.

The absurdity of that made Lissha giggle. She was a bad bitch and she knew it. What she couldn't understand was why Kiam wasn't all crazy in the head over her. She knew that Big Zo's warning was the main reason but they had come so close to violating that. Had she not reminded Kiam of it that time, they definitely would've crossed that line and Lissha couldn't say that she would've regretted it.

The smile that danced at the corners of her mouth disappeared when she considered the only other thing that stood between her and Kiam. The one thing that could interfere with Kiam's rise and change everything that was planned.

That bitch is getting put on her ass. Lissha recorded that thought on her mental list of things to do as she fastened on a necklace and anxiously waited for Kiam to arrive.

"I should have known you weren't inviting me out just to be nice," said Lissha, not hiding her disappointment. She twisted up her mouth and looked up from her fillet mignon.

Kiam hadn't ordered shit, the only appetite he had was for the truth. He rested is forearms on the table and stared across at Lissha with a face of stone. "I don't have time to be nice. Now, this is my last time asking you, who the fuck is Blood Money?"

Lissha dropped her fork down with a clink. "And this is my last time telling you I don't know." Her voice was low but unwavering. "Are you accusing Daddy of being on some shiesty shit because that's what Riz said? Because if you are, maybe you're down with the wrong team," she deflected the guilt away from herself.

"I'm gonna ignore that, otherwise you would be chewing with more teeth on the table than in your mouth."

"I keep telling you I'm not scared of you, you got some teeth too nigga."

Kiam reached across the table and grabbed her wrist, squeezing it hard. "Say one more word! Just one! Go ahead so I can slap it back down your throat," he threatened in a low guttural tone.

"Why you always putting your hands on me? Is that the only way you think that you can control me?" she said, giving him a low gaze.

"Act like you think I'm fuckin' playin'," he said with clenched teeth.

Lissha saw his eyes turn cold and decided not to test him this time. They stared at each other as Kiam continued to grip her wrist and send heat her way.

Lissha raised her hand like a student asking for permission to speak. "What?" gritted Kiam.

"You're hurting my wrist," she mumbled in a little bitty voice.

"Don't play with me shorty. I'm not fuckin' around." Kiam released his grip. "I want some answers."

"Okay, but not here." She pushed back from the table rubbing her wrist as she slowly rose to her feet. "I'm going to the ladies room, I'll be ready to go when I return. And thanks for ruining my appetite," she said before stalking off.

"You'll get over it," he called out.

Lissha looked over her shoulder and stuck her tongue out before continuing past the bar.

Kiam watched her walk away. He couldn't help but follow the sway of her hips. He briefly allowed his mind to wonder how it would feel to hold on to them and give her a shot of act right. But even quicker he erased it from his visual. Shit was too serious for that.

Kiam paid the bill and waited for Lissha in the car. She slid into the passenger seat and they rode back to her place in complete silence. Kiam was wondering what type of treachery the truth would reveal. Lissha was mentally molding her lies in a cast of concrete.

By the time they arrived back at her house Lissha had her game face on. Kiam sat down across from her in the living room. His silence was only broken when she lit a blunt.

"Put it out," he commanded.

"You know what, you're rude for no reason," she complained, putting the blunt out.

"Thank you," he said.

"What—ever." She looked up and wrinkled her nose at him.

"It's not going to work ma. Start talking."

Lissha feigned a deep sigh then she sat up on the couch. "I don't know what you're expecting to hear but this is not that. You have to understand that anything Riz tells you has to be taken with a grain of salt. Riz deals with us because it's profitable to him but he has never liked Daddy."

"That's personal so I don't give a fuck. Big Zo will always have enemies because he's his own man. Even from on lock his presence is still felt out here on the streets. I know how niggas move; they fear what they can't understand and they hate what they can't control."

Lissha nodded her head. What Kiam had just said was real spit.

"Trust me, Riz can't turn me against Big Zo. Your father has proven that he's legit, but I wanna know if Blood Money has any ties to our organization. I find it very hard to accept that it's just a coincidence that a local robbing crew struck way up in New York. Somebody would have had to put them on Riz." Kiam sat back and gauged her reaction.

Lissha was a skilled liar under pressure. She was the type of calm, cool and collected female that could stare down the barrel of a loaded gun and stand firm on her denial. "Kiam, have you ever considered that Blood Money might be out of New York? Riz has more enemies than a dog has fleas. Somebody up top probably put Blood Money on that nigga," she tossed out.

"If so, who put them on my gambling spot?" Something told him that Lissha could connect the dots, but the shit didn't add up.

Lissha saw his mind scanning over the possibilities. She could allow him to uncover the truth on his own then face his wrath once he had done so. Or she could put everything out on the table and ask him to understand.

She decided to play a pat hand because to do otherwise would put everything and everybody at risk. It was time to tie up the loose ends that

54

could expose her complicity. Spank, who had set up licks for Blood Money and knew other things that could blow up her spot, would have to go if things got hot. And he wasn't the only one.

In the meantime Lissha wanted to get closer to Kiam. She missed what was developing between them before things began to come apart at the seams. She understood why Big Zo didn't want her to become intimate with Kiam, but she couldn't fight her feelings any longer. Besides the thump Kiam caused in her chest every time he came around, a bitch needed some good dick in her life and she needed it attached to a boss.

Kiam was sitting there looking mean, sexy, and dangerous all at once. Lissha thought back to the manner in which he had murked Gator. That was so wicked it gave her pussy a fever every time she thought about it.

She unconsciously licked her lips.

"Why you staring at me? You got something to tell me?" asked Kiam, looking at her curiously.

Lissha got up and walked over to where he was seated. She sat down on his lap and placed her arms around his neck. "Why don't you trust me?" she whispered in his ear, then slowly ran her tongue over the lobe.

"Because too many people got bad shit to say about you and the serpent always wears a skirt," he said.

"You think I would bite you?" Her voice was husky with desire and her hand traveled down his chest. "This is what I want to bite but not hard," she said, grabbing that steel that shot out babies not bullets.

Kiam couldn't help it, he rocked up at her touch.

"You want to control me? Make me do what you say?" She breathed heavily in his ear. "Give me what I want. Make me submit to you."

Kiam closed his eyes as she maneuvered her hand inside his pants and released that Dominator that she needed to feel spread her wide open tonight.

Lissha went down to her knees and stroked him. Kiam grew large in her hand and hot to her touch. He stood up and placed his hand on the back of her head. "This what you want?" he asked

"It is," she panted. Her panties were soaking wet and he hadn't even touched her. Just looking at all that dick was about to make her cum.

"Close your eyes and let me put it in your mouth." Kiam's voice sounded thick with lust.

Lissha closed her eyes, licked her luscious lips, and opened her mouth to accommodate his girth. Seconds seemed like hours as she waited for that long, thick hardness to slide between her lips. When that steel pushed into her mouth Lissha's eyes shot open.

Kiam held his Nine steady as he looked down at her and gritted, "Try me like a trick again and I'ma puff that new, pretty hairstyle of yours out." He slowly removed the gun from inside her mouth and placed it in the center of her forehead.

Fear flashed in Lissha's eyes. "Who the fuck is Blood Money?" Kiam gritted.

Panic rose up in Lissha's chest and her life flashed before her as she saw Kiam's trigger finger poised to twitch. "I told you I don't mutha-fuckin' know!" she yelled, forcing tears from her eyes for added effect.

Kiam grabbed her by the face with his free hand and snarled, "If I find out you're hiding something from me your daddy won't be able to save you."

He slung her to the floor on her ass, fixed his clothes, and walked out the door.

Chapter 8
Back on Track

Lissha stared angrily at the door. If Kiam had been any other nigga, she would have run outside and emptied a whole clip in his ass for that fuckery he had just pulled. *He must have me confused with the average bitch!* She fumed. But the way he handled her made her want him even more. She was just going to have to play her hand better in the future.

She pulled herself up off the floor, went upstairs, undressed and climbed into bed. Settling into her favorite spot she let her fingers do what she wished Kiam had done.

She began by pinching her nipples, imagining that Kiam was biting them gently. "Ssss," she moaned still hot from what had almost occurred.

Her hand slid down her body and stroked her plump pussy as her ass rose off of the bed and her hips rotated in a slow circular motion. She closed her eyes and could almost feel Kiam's weight press down on her. "Ummm." Lissha spread her petals open and found her pearl.

She drew tiny circles around it until the heat inside her oven became intense and hot. Then she increased the pace and her legs began to tremble. Her mouth opened and she could taste him going inside, all the way to the back of her throat. Damn, he was rocked up and thick. She made slurping sounds as if she was Einsteining him for real. Her clit jumped and her pussy screamed out to be fucked, pounded into submission.

"Make me act right, nigga," she mumbled to herself as the fire became a blaze.

She was on the edge and needed to release.

Lissha opened her legs as wide as possible and plunged three fingers inside her purring kitty. The climax came instantly and with the power of a tidal wave. "Ahhhhhh—sheeiitttttt," she cried out as an image of Kiam popped up in her mind and intensified her orgasm. He was banging that ass like it belonged to him.

Take this pussy you mean ass muthafucka.

Lissha panted heavily as her juices flowed down and coated her whole hand. When the nectar stopped flowing she lied still for a minute and tried to recuperate. Within seconds her eyes were closed and she was in La La Land.

Early the next morning, Lissha was torn out of her sleep by the loud ringtone on her cell that boomed from across the room. "Shit," she cursed as she stumbled to the dresser to retrieve it.

"What you doin'?"

"Huh?" she responded with a froggy voice.

"Answer the question," Kiam ordered as he came to a red light.

"What do it sound like I'm doing?" she said as she moved to the bathroom.

"Get yo ass up and stop getting slick with your tongue. I need you to take care of something for me."

"Get somebody else. I'm not fucking with you today. I got shit to do."

"This shit ain't up for debate. Get dressed I'll be there in an hour." Lissha flushed the toilet and headed to the sink to wash her hands. "Damn ma, you in the bathroom?"

"Yeah, I had to flush this bullshit you talking."

Kiam had to chuckle. "Have your spoiled ass ready when I get there," he ordered.

"Get off my phone." Lissha disconnected the call, threw her phone on the counter and grabbed her tooth brush. "That nigga get on my nerves," she spat, shaking her head and applying toothpaste to her brush.

Kiam was thinking the same thing about her. It baffled his mind at times about the love/hate thing between them. Sometimes it was cute and entertaining and other times he wanted to knock her the fuck out. He shook his head at the way she had tried him up last night.

Pushing the whole incident out of his mind, Kiam focused on the trap spots as he made his early morning rounds to see what the streets were doing. He made a few stops and dropped a few orders before heading to pick up Lissha.

Lissha hopped out the shower and slipped into her skinny jeans and a Burberry top. She went through a few shoe boxes and found her Burberry loafers. Once she was completely dressed she grabbed her gun and purse and headed to the door. When she got into the living room her mind wondered over the things that were at hand. Donella was gone, Gator was gone and there were secrets out there that if exposed could threaten Big Zo's whole operation.

For the first time fear rose in her gut. Lissha and Daddy had worked so hard to maintain the organization and in a blink of an eye everything could come crumbling down. One thing she knew for sure is she needed to make certain that Kiam's head stayed in the game and his focus didn't waver from the blueprint that Daddy had drawn up.

Just as her mind had begun to roam down the road of "what if's" she heard Kiam's annoying horn waking up the whole neighborhood. "Why the fuck can't he just blow once?" she huffed, grabbing her keys and heading to the door.

Kiam looked up and saw Lissha coming down the walkway swaying her hips to their own little sexy beat. She had a heat that turned him on; it was a struggle to not say fuck it and rearrange her organs. Had she come at him a different way last night he wasn't certain that he could have resisted.

"Where to, Chief?" Lissha asked as she got in and closed the door. Her scent rose up in his nostrils enhancing his fantasy and causing a slight stiffness to his dick.

"I need to move some money around," Kiam said with his eyes fixed on her breast.

"Well is it in my bra?" Lissha joked and smiled as she caught him staring at her chest.

"They pretty but they can't pay no bills."

"Sheeit—you riding around and living in what my pussy paid for." She looked over at him with her lips twisted to the side.

"I made this happen shorty. The only thing pussy can do for me is make me nut," he clarified as he turned the corners headed towards Wade Park.

"That's what they all say," Lissha countered.

"Your mouth slippery today. I guess you still mad at me for putting my ratchet in it?" he remarked snidely.

"It's not the first time I had a gun put in my face. But I understand. You put that gun there because you know if you had put your dick in my mouth you would have to change your last name and address," Lissha spat slyly as she pulled down the sun visor and applied her lip gloss.

"Get your mind off my dick and put it on business."

"Whatever, with yo' scary ass." She flipped up the visor crossed her legs and smiled. "I still love you tho," she replied

"Shorty, you just talking 'cause you got a pair of lips. Anyway this is not the time to be fucking around. Pay attention because I'm about to take you by the new spots and introduce you in case anything was to happen to me."

Lissha didn't even want to conjure up that thought; she swallowed the lump that had formed in her throat and held a firm face.

As they rode through the different spots Kiam had set up on the east side, Lissha noted that he had really expanded the business. By the time he dropped her back off at home two duffel bags full of money were in the trunk.

"You need anything?" he asked as they pulled up in front of her house.

"What you giving up?" She looked down at his dick print and ran her tongue over her lips.

"Is that why Gator had to be replaced? Was his mind on your pussy too much to handle these streets?"

The question was aimed to cut but Lissha didn't wince. "Oh no baby boy, I didn't break Gator I *made* that muthafucka. Don't get it twisted. What, are you jelly?"

"Not at all," Kiam smirked. "How's he doing now?"

Lissha couldn't do nothing but respect that comeback because Kiam had shown his ass in handling Gator. "Point well taken," she conceded. Then she leaned over and planted a kiss on his cheek before he could turn away.

Kiam admonished her with a wrinkled brow that did nothing to stem her aggression. She slid her hand between his legs and grabbed a handful of his power. "This gonna belong to me. Fuck that bitch you're claiming, she better fall back or get stretched out."

Before he could formulate a comeback Lissha was out of the car and sauntering up the walkway with her hair blowing in the wind. Kiam shook his head and put the car in gear, more determined than ever not to give her what she wanted.

Nah, bitch, I'm the muhfuckin' puppeteer.

"Call Bayonna," he commanded as he drove off.

Chapter 9
Fearful Exchange

As Bayonna drove nervously to Kiam's house, her palms became a bit sweaty around the steering wheel and her gut filled with fear. She wondered why he had summoned her, of all people, to his house. Knowing her own secrets made her worry that he had something fatal planned for her soul.

Each corner that she bent brought her closer to the answer. Anxiety gushed up in her face like a sudden blast of putrid air, causing her to shudder and the car to serve. Had Kiam found out any new information? Would she be the next cuisine that he maniacally served?

She steadied the wheel and retrieved her gangsta from deep down in her gut. Quiet as it was kept, she was as do or die as any muthafucka on the team. And if this was Judgment Day she was gonna make the verdict a double death sentence.

When she pulled in front of Kiam's condo the first thing she noticed was JuJu's Rover. Now it was gonna be a triple homicide, Bayonna resigned herself to that fact. She parked her car, reached into her glove compartment for her gun and tucked it comfortably in the back of her tight fitting pants.

Exiting the vehicle she put together a plan of where she needed to sit and where she needed to hit a nigga to make sure she laid him out before they put her on her ass. Adrenaline pumped through her veins at the speed of light as she raised her hand to ring the bell.

"Why you look like a nervous girl scout trying to earn a badge?" Kiam asked as he opened the door to let her in.

"Just trying to see what this whole meeting is about, that's all," she said, moving her eyes around the room then resting them on JuJu who was comfortably seated on an arm chair next to the couch. She observed the deadly look on his face.

Taking an imperceptible breath to steel her nerves, Bayonna hoped for the best but feared the worse.

"Have a seat," directed Kiam. His deep voice on the back of her neck startled her.

Bayonna jumped. *Play this shit cool bitch,* she reminded herself.

She quickly took a seat on the other recliner closest to the door in case she had to shoot her way up out of there. Kiam took a seat on the couch and propped his feet up on the coffee table like he was about to uncover some shit. How in the fuck did he find out about her and Gator? She wondered.

"I thought long and hard about this decision I'm about to make," began Kiam, looking at her with those coal black eyes. "And in doing so I believe I have come up with the best solution to our little problem."

Bayonna's heart pounded as Kiam looked over at JuJu then back at her. She took in a little air as a knot formed in her throat.

JuJu sat up and moved to the edge of his seat. Bayonna did the same, she wanted to be able to easily get to her heat if he reached for his.

"We took a huge loss caused by inside deceit. That is intolerable," Kiam continued. Now Bayonna was certain she was about to go down.

She eased a hand towards her back.

"The one thing I don't wanna have to ever deal with again is my bands getting fucked up—a muhfucka play with my green laces they play with their life," stated Kiam as JuJu and Bayonna sized each other up.

"Usually I would never put my right hand man in danger, but with the stench of distrust that lingers in this organization I have no choice." Kiam spoke clearly.

Bayonna's heart raced a mile a minute; she played with the thought of just pulling out and ending the whole conversation. Fuck allowing them to pull out first and gain an advantage over her.

"Bayonna, I have studied you since I met you and I believe that you are the missing link," Kiam continued.

Bayonna stopped her hand inches from her strap. "What is that supposed to mean?" If his response was accusatory it was about to go down!

Kiam's voice remained non-threatening. "It's not supposed to mean anything but what I said. My words are clear."

"I can't tell. You have something on your mind and I feel you should just say it," she spoke directly, turning in his direction.

Kiam smiled at her courage. "I told you we had the right one." He directed his statement at JuJu.

JuJu nodded in agreement and Kiam returned his attention to Bayonna. "Look little mama. I know that you're very uncomfortable in my presence with all that has taken place over the last couple weeks. I understand your apprehension. However, I don't have to bring you all the way to my house to kill you. If I had a reason to push your forehead back, I would already be comforting your girls while they lay your ass to rest." He removed his feet from the table and sat forward.

Bayonna relaxed a little but she watched his muthafuckin' hands.

Kiam smiled at her observance, it reinforced in his mind that she was indeed the right one for the job. "This is a restructuring meeting," he clarified. "Riz will no longer meet us in Pennsylvania with the work. From now on I want you to make the runs with JuJu to New York to pick up the product."

Bayonna squinted her eyes. "Why me? Why not Treebie or Lissha?"

"Shorty, bosses don't give explanations. We give orders."

"I believe Big Zo is the boss," she countered bravely.

Kiam chuckled but left his banger on his waist. "You disrespecting me? Is that what you're doing?" he asked.

"Never that," she clarified. "I'm just saying."

"No, little mama, you ain't saying nothin'. You're making the trips with JuJu from now on. *I'm just saying.*"

"Whatever."

"Ol' girl got heart," JuJu said with a semi smile.

"More than you know," she shot back, causing him to drop the smile from his face. She turned back to Kiam, "I'm on board, *Boss.*"

"Good, now stop fucking around. The first pick up is in a couple of days. Things are back square with us and Riz, but once a man has been crossed the trust can never be the same so ya'll have to watch them as hard as you've been watching me since I arrived."

Bayonna's mouth turned up at the corners in acknowledgement of his keen observance.

Kiam smiled back.

"Y'all conduct on this pickup will determine whether the peace stands or if there will be cause for more bloodshed."

"You already know I'm official," JuJu said, looking over at Bayonna as if he was in doubt of her get-down

"I'm sitting across from you youngin so it's obvious my gangsta must match yours or some other bitch would be taking the trip with you," she responded, putting his ego in check.

Kiam smiled at the little tension that was building between them. He knew that JuJu was a beast and all he needed was a beauty by his side to level him out.

"Relax, youngin," Kiam joked seeing JuJu getting ready to go in.

"I'll be ready Kiam just let me know when." Bayonna stood up ready to be out of the tense situation.

"I'll keep you posted," he assured her.

"Alright," She said. Then she turned to JuJu and gave him a penetrating stare. "Have a nice day," she spat sarcastically as she turned to the door.

JuJu sat back and watched, allowing his eyes to wonder over her frame as she walked to the door. She walked like she had just dismounted a horse.

"Why you staring youngin?" asked Kiam with a hint of laughter.

JuJu shrugged his shoulders. "Nothing much," he replied.

"Yeah, I hear you nigga." Kiam rose to his feet. "If you're free I need you to take a run with me?"

JuJu sat thinking about Bayonna, tossing all that ass and thin waist around in his mind. The thing that stood out the most was her humble yet commanding personality. He was slick hypnotized.

Kiam made a few stops before he pulled up in front of Faydrah's house. He had JuJu put a package on her porch, ring the bell and hurry back to the truck.

Faydrah opened the door a minute or two after they drove off. She bent down to lift the box and heard a small whimper coming from inside. Reluctantly she pulled back the flap and saw the cutest little white Maltese puppy with a tiny red ribbon around his neck.

"Awww, who left you here?" she cooed as she lifted the puppy into her arms.

The box contained a silver bowl and a soft pillow. She placed him back inside, looked back and forth up the street then carried the precious pup inside with her.

Trust No Bitch 2

She sat the box down then picked the puppy back up. As she stroked under his chin she saw a collar with a tag that read *Trapstar*. Faydrah smiled and headed for her phone on the kitchen counter. It began to ring just as she reached for it.

"Hello," she answered.

"Hey you," he said real smoothly, causing a flutter in her chest.

"Hey you," she replied sweetly, with a huge smile on her face. "I am going to assume that you are behind the little surprise on my door step."

"I figured since I'm in the dog house I could have a little friend to talk to."

"You are so silly."

"I need to see you. Can we get together soon?"

"Maybe."

"Well you didn't say no so I'll take that. I love you."

"I know you do. Be careful."

"I will. And you keep me in that special place in your heart," he needlessly reminded her.

"Nothing can touch that Kiam," Faydrah said softly.

Kiam's heart thumped in his chest at the thought of how much she loved him and what he would stand to lose if he didn't do what he had to in order to make things right between them.

Sensing that he was struggling for words she eased his discomfort. "You better hang up before whoever is around you finds out you're pussy whipped," she teased.

"You better train that dog to attack because yo' ass is going to be in trouble when I finally get home," he smiled.

"Whatever. Bye."

"Bye baby." He disconnected the call.

JuJu looked over at him. "You want some tissue." He joked.

"You ain't talkin' about shit," said Kiam as they rode on.

"I'm just saying, I got some napkins from McDonalds."

Kiam had to laugh. JuJu laughed too then shook his head.

Kiam caught that. Now he had to teach. "Let me school you right quick, youngin. Every man, no matter how much of a beast he is in the streets, needs that one woman he can come home to at the end of the day and put his gangsta on the shelf. See, that justifies his existence and makes him feel human. You only get one woman like that, anyone else is just a consolation. So, if you find the one that makes you wanna rest your G when you're around her, do everything you can not to fuck it up. Gangstas love too otherwise their animals."

JuJu nodded his head in appreciation of the jewel.

Kiam turned on some music and flipped on his gangsta. "Enough of all this mushy shit," he said. "Let's go put some heat on these streets."

JuJu sat up in the passenger seat. That's the shit he was accustomed to.

Chapter 10
The Pick Up

JuJu sat waiting impatiently out in front of Bayonna's house. It was 10:00 P.M. and he had told her he would be there at 9:45 P.M. A scowl crept up on his face because he hated for a muhfucka to be late.

He twisted his hands on the steering wheel trying to keep calm. Just as he was about to hit Kiam up to let him know the business, Bayonna flew out the door with her cell phone pasted to her ear and her tote bag in the other hand.

She opened the door, threw her bag on the back seat and then hopped in the front, slamming the door after herself.

"Don't slam my shit," JuJu warned in a settling tone.

Bayonna looked over at him, rolled her eyes and continued her conversation with the person on the phone. JuJu took in some air in an effort to keep himself calm "Which way?" he asked as he pulled out of the parking space.

"Hold on," she said into the phone then looked at him. "Go jump on the expressway and take it to I-70," she said softly. "All this truck and no GPS?" She smiled looking at his dashboard, and then she returned to her conversation.

JuJu just looked at her and shook his head. He wanted to handle his business and get back to the city as soon as possible.

"Yeah LiLi, I'm back," he heard her say.

He did his best to block out Bayonna's conversation as he headed for I-75.

Once Bayonna hung up with Lissha she began fiddling around with JuJu's radio. He looked over at her with his eyebrows raised. "You need something else to do with your hands?"

"This is going to be a long ass ride, we gotta have some traveling music," Bayonna said as she reached in her purse and pulled out an Ace Hood CD and popped it in. When "Hustle Hard" came on she sung right along.

"Same old shit, just a different day. Out here tryna get it, each and every way." She slipped off her shoes then crossed her legs in the seat and began bopping her head and moving her hands as she used her cell phone for a mic.

JuJu looked over at her like she was crazy.

"Hustle, hustle, hustle hard." She turned to him singing in his direction. He wanted to keep his serious attitude but her antics tickled him.

Cracking a slight smile JuJu settled into his seat. When "Have Mercy" came on he started rapping along. "Have Mercy on a real nigga, 'cause I'm sinning every day, Lord," JuJu crooned, pushing the whip up to 80.

He hit cruise control and tried to enjoy the trip. Even though trafficking work up and down the highway was stressful, Bayonna made the first leg of the trip breeze by.

When they finally hit Route 78 JuJu glanced down at the tank then looked for the first exit to get off and get some gas. As he pulled into the station Bayonna stretched, threw on her shoes and got out.

JuJu reached in his pocket for his bank. When he looked up his eyes settled on Bayonna's fat ass in those tight ass skinny jeans. His gaze crawled up her body taking in all her beauty. She was little but all the right things were big: thick thighs, pussy print fat, D-cup breasts. Not only was she tight and right, she had a smooth pretty face. He usually didn't like short hair on women but hers was laying just right hanging over her right eye.

Bayonna walked around to the driver's side of the car and tapped on the window interrupting his little fantasy. "You want me to pay?" she asked with her hands on her hips.

"Nah, I got it shorty," JuJu said as he got out the car.

Bayonna looked up at him as he stood to his full height. He was only a couple of inches taller than her 5'5" frame but his short ass had a big presence about himself. *Damn* she thought as her eyes settled on his chest. He was thin but chiseled in all the right places. "I'll be right back." She spoke softly as she turned to walk away.

As she switched off JuJu's eye's settled before her waist. He wondered what was caressing all that ass under those jeans. "Nigga don't do it," he warned himself as he slid his Rush card in the slot and grabbed the pump.

When Bayonna came back to the truck, she had a pretty smile on her face and a bag full of snacks. "What you about to do with all that?" he asked, looking at her sideways.

"Eat it, what you think?" she replied giddily as she tore open her big bag of Twizzlers.

"I don't allow eating in my shit."

"Boy, we on the road," she said, grabbing one and biting into it.

"Don't drop shit. I just washed my car." His attitude was plain rude.

Bayonna cocked her head at him as he pulled away from the pump. "For real?"

"Fa muthafuckin' real," JuJu reemphasized.

Bayonna straightened up her head, reached into her bra and pulled out a Ben Franklin. She twisted her lips and stuck the money in the ashtray. "Here, cause I *will* be eating in this sexy muthafucka."

"You not afraid to defy me?" He asked with an undertone of playfulness.

"Uh— no," Bayonna sang.

"Shorty, you more 'bout it than I thought," he said as he pulled onto the entrance ramp.

"I'm the coolest bitch you'll ever want to meet *and* the wrong bitch to fuck with at the same time." She turned up the music and pulled her legs back into the seat.

Out the corner of his eye JuJu watched her look out the window and chomp away on her snacks. Again he smiled, he was enjoying her company and her cute, sassy attitude.

When they entered the tunnel, a sigh of relief passed his lips. "Damn, this ride long as hell," he said when they finally reached the other end.

"I know, we used to have to make it all the time. I was relieved when the pickup was moved to PA, that was only a five hour ride. I don't know how many of these I can do," she confessed, twisting in her seat.

"Where's the hotel. I just want to shower and go to sleep."

"Turn here," she directed.

Once they were checked in, Bayonna went to her room and showered. JuJu headed down the hall to his room to do the same. The water relaxed him and took his mind off the place it shouldn't have been anyway.

He had just laid across the bed and tucked the pillow under his head when he heard a knock at the door. "Ain't this a bitch," he huffed as he grabbed his whistle and headed to the door.

He looked out the peek hole and sighed. *Damn*, he thought that he was done with her for the night.

Opening the door he left only a small crack for her to state her business. Whatever she wanted, she needed to say it and be out so he could get back to his warm spot.

"Why you acting like I'm the Jakes?" She pushed past him and invited herself in.

"Little mama, I gotta get some sleep. I don't know these niggas so I gotta be well rested and on my toes when we fuck wit' them tomorrow," he said, closing the door. "Go back to your room. Damn."

"You ain't hungry?" she asked, ignoring his grouchy attitude.

"Not really. I can sleep through that shit."

"Well, I'm starving. Let's go get something to eat. And put that strap away before you hurt yourself," she said, moving to the bed and taking a seat.

"Why don't you go by yourself?"

"I didn't come here by myself so you're going with me." Bayonna crossed her legs and folded her arms over her chest.

JuJu looked at her small lips and those smooth sexy legs that were sticking out from under the skirt she changed into and he gave in. "We can't go far I need to get back and get some rest."

"Thank you," she sang as he went to put on his boots.

JuJu just shook his head. *What the fuck did I just get myself into?* he wondered as the stepped out into the unseasonably warm October night.

The whole ride JuJu was quiet while Bayonna was all out the window looking at everything like she was seeing it for the first time. When they got to *Time Square* she lit up. "Park in there," she pointed, all excited.

JuJu looked over at her with cold regard.

"Stop being antisocial, we're in the Big Apple." She was all full of energy.

He took a deep breath and pulled into the parking garage, "This shit gonna be two hundred dollars by the time we come outta here," he grumbled.

"I know you ain't complaining about green laces, you're Kiam's right hand—I know you laced," she said, jumping out of the truck.

"Not spending on stupid shit is how I'ma stay laced," he shot back, climbing out his seat and passing the keys to the attendant.

"Sometimes you have to live a little." She grabbed his hand and pulled him to the exit.

"You scratch my shit and I'ma scratch ya ass," he warned the young white boy as he was pulled away.

"Stop being grumpy and come on," Bayonna laughed as she damn near dragged him out of the garage.

Time Square was jumping. They weaved through the sea of people looking all around. It was actually JuJu's first time seeing everything up close and personal. He began to perk up when he looked up and saw the big screen and lights all around.

Bayonna gripped his hand sending a surge of heat through his body. "Ooh, look," she said when she saw a lady dressed up like Wonder Woman. She released her grip and handed him her phone. "Come take a picture." She walked over to the costumed woman and began posing.

JuJu snapped away; he was enjoying watching her bust crazy poses. When she stuck out her tongue and put both of her hands on the woman's breast his dick jumped. *Oh shit.*

Bayonna walked back over to him, laughing and smiling from ear to ear. "You didn't know you were going to luck up on a threesome, huh?" she joked as she reached for her phone.

JuJu just smiled.

They walked a little while longer then found an outside café. They got a table and ordered their meal. As they sat and talked and watched the sights he had to admit that he was glad he had allowed her to drag him out of the room. Being on the grind all the time could make a man's soul old and cold. He vowed to himself that he was would try to at least do something fun ever so often.

Arriving back at the hotel, JuJu walked Bayonna to her room. "Be ready in the morning. Play time is over," he said.

"Boy, you know you had fun." She giggled as she stuck her key card in the door. Turning back in his direction she said. "Life is short. Ain't no sense in living if all you have is bad memories and regret."

JuJu looked at her like she was speaking a foreign language.

Bayonna smiled at him. "Good night."

"Good night, shorty." He smiled back and walked away. Her words had mirrored his thoughts and he recalled his mother telling him that when God wants you to get a message he will tell you twice.

Back inside his room JuJu didn't even get undressed, he kicked off his boots and laid across the bed. In no time he was asleep.

At 10:00 A.M. the alarm on his phone went off, wakening him from a light sleep. JuJu jumped straight up and hit the shower, brushed his teeth and got dressed. As he threw his clothes in the bag he got into war mode. Grabbing his cell, he hit Bayonna's phone but didn't get an answer. He called back to back four times before his mood darkened. "That's just why I don't fuck with bitches," he said out loud, grabbing his shit and heading to the door.

When he opened it, Bayonna was standing there looking at her watch. She had on jeans, a t-shirt and boots, and her ratchet was tucked firmly in place. She closed her jacket to conceal it.

He saw a whole different woman than the one he had just walked and held hands with last night. "You late youngin. You might want to do something about that next time." She was sporting her game face. "Let's get it, time is money," she stated and headed towards the elevator.

JuJu shut the door and was hot on her heels. Once downstairs he popped the trunk, tossed the bags in the back and moved out.

Pulling up to Riz's apartment building, Bayonna went straight gangstress. "Look, when we get inside speak very little and pay attention. Don't leave shit to chance and if them niggas flinch the wrong way make them muthafuckas Swiss. But only when you are sure the deck is stacked against you. No premature ejaculation. Lastly, I'm a girl but none of that shit matters when we get up there. Don't hesitate to let your whistle twerp if the shit goes from sugar to shit. If I catch a hot one and you make it out you better come back and open up every one of these nigga's back or I'm haunting your ass," she promised then got out the car.

JuJu looked over at her with bewilderment and respect. Just a few hours ago she was wide-eyed and giggly, now she was wildin'. He had to admit that shit was a straight turn on. He grabbed the black duffle bag and headed to the door with a *do or die* bitch leading the way, ready to deliver a nigga to the pearly gates if he looked at them wrong.

They entered the building straight focused. Both of them had their bangers out and down at their sides as they climbed the steps leading up to Riz's apartment.

Their nerves were like live-wires by the time they reached the sixth floor. Knocking on the door Bayonna could feel her heart beating hard in her chest. Even though Riz was fond of her if he was on some payback shit they were walking into a death chamber. She took a deep breath and got ready for whatever.

She heard the door being unlocked, then it swung open. "Bay Bay." Bones reached out to hug her.

She moved into his embrace as she quickly scanned the room taking a head count. There were two more men present than normally.

"What's up?" Bones said to JuJu as he turned Bayonna lose.

"Ain't nothin'," JuJu replied. He wasn't sure how to take a warm greeting from a nigga whose face he had pressed a banger in.

Bones extended his hand out and JuJu bumped fists with him. "Sup?" he nodded.

"Everything is peace, young fella." Bones closed the door.

Riz came walking from the back with the two massive dogs on his sides. A huge smile came over his face. "Bay," he said, loving towards her. "If I had known they were going to send you, I would've robbed my damn self just to see that pretty smile."

Riz wrapped Bayonna in his grip and held her tight. JuJu was swelled up with anger watching this nigga handling her. Riz picked up on his heat and playfully kissed Bayonna on the neck just to fuck with JuJu's mental.

"Stop, boy," Bayonna said, gently pushing Riz back.

"You know I love you to death ma. Whatever you need you got it," he said, gesturing around the room with his arms. He had always craved her little sexy, quietly dangerous ass.

Bayonna wasn't going there with him. "Whatever. Just give me what I paid for, that will do," she said, checking her peripheral for any strange movement in case he had some Judas in his welcome.

When the two dogs moved towards them JuJu stepped back. They walked over to Bayonna and snuggled at her thighs. She reached down and began rubbing their heads and ears.

"Don't be scared youngin, they love Bay," said Riz.

"Not youngin'," he corrected. "JuJu."

"Oh, my bad," Riz chuckled. "Kiam did all the talking the last time so I never caught your name."

"Well, Kiam ain't here and I'll be taking care of this end so let's address each other like men," JuJu affirmed.

"Little man got a heart." Bones laughed in a condescending tone that Bayonna didn't miss.

She became very uncomfortable as the mood in the room quickly began to change. She had to do something before muthafuckas pre-ejaculated. "Stop all this muscle flexing. Y'all niggas fucking the mood up in here." She turned to JuJu and put her hand on the money bag and gave him the eye to turn it down a notch.

JuJu's look was acquiescing but inside he was turning up. Sensing his pulse, Bayonna turned back to Riz and applied her guile. "Come on, let's blow something." She sat the bag of money on the table.

"You know me I just like to make money and have a good time while I'm doing it," he readily agreed while keeping a strong eye on JuJu.

JuJu's hands were sweating, he was ready to pull out and let his gun eat their asses up. Bayonna was praying he would just calm down. Kiam had sent them on a mission, get the shit and bring it back and they damn sure couldn't do that if they were laid the fuck out.

Riz grabbed some weed and rolled up. He lit the end then signaled for Bones to go and get the package.

"Damn you gonna pass that shit?" Bayonna said aggressively.

"Say that shit Bay, you know I like it rough." Riz grinned.

"Riz. Behave."

"Come sit right here while they count and exchange." He patted a spot on his lap.

"I'ma sit down but you make your boy be good." Bay wiggled her butt a little as she sat on his wood.

"I can't make you no promises," he admitted, looking her over.

JuJu was on fire! *Be cool until we get what we came for,* he cautioned himself. After that he was going ham if that shit continued.

Bones emptied the bag and began loading the money machine. When the last dollar was counted he placed the money back in the bag and handed over the product.

Riz sat whispering shit in Bayonna's ear with his hand rested on her thigh. She giggled and puffed on the stick of loud until she felt things were peace enough to rise up.

"Thanks for the kick back," she said, lifting her butt up off of his semi-hard dick.

"Anytime." Riz eyes feasted on her heart shaped ass in those tight jeans. "When you gonna come see me by yourself?" he asked, standing up behind her.

"Riz please. I am not trying to be another trophy on your shelf." She turned him down with a snicker.

"If I could have you, I would tear that shelf down and build a baby room so we could fill it up." He macked hard.

Bayonna twisted her lips up. "Bye Riz." She turned and hugged him tightly.

"Damn, when the next pick up? A nigga wanna feel like it's Christmas."

"Boy let me go," She pulled back. "See you in a couple weeks." She used two hands to pick up the bag and pass it to JuJu who stood there with a face of granite and a heart to match.

JuJu slightly snatched the bag out of her hand.

"Tell your boy to relax," advised Riz.

"Why don't you tell me," JuJu broke in.

Bayonna knew JuJu was on the verge of doing something dangerous so she quickly responded. "He *is* relaxed. Usually he don't like traveling, you know how that drive is. JuJu is good people you don't have to worry about him," she said touching him on the chest.

"I can see that. Heart of a lion, look of a killah. If I had a few of him on my team I would be King of New York," replied Riz in a propositional tone.

JuJu took it as an insult to his loyalty to Kiam. He moved Bayonna's hand off of his chest and flexed his fingers. He was ready to kill them and her.

He quickly glanced around the room sizing niggas up for a wet melon. But they were on point, sizing him up for the same fate. He trained his eye on Riz and respectfully set him straight. "I'm happy where I'm at, but I appreciate the compliment." He extended his hand.

"No doubt," Riz said, dropping his smile and accepting the small jester. They bumped fists then Bones let JuJu and Bayonna out the door.

When they got to the car JuJu went in. He turned to Bayonna in full animal mode. "How the fuck you gonna put me in that kind of situation?" His nose flared wide as a bull's.

"Relax it ain't that bad." Bayonna blew him off but the youngin wasn't through.

"Fuck you mean it ain't that bad? You smoking and joking with that nigga then you gonna sit all on his dick! You fucking him or something?" he raged.

His outburst would've been cute had it not been ill-timed. Bayonna took a deep breath then tried to school him. "Those niggas were planning on killing us. The two extra men that were standing around looking stupid were Riz's cut men. They're the 'hide ya ass where nobody can find you' type niggas."

JuJu didn't wanna hear that shit. He was a 'smash everything moving' at him type nigga!

Bayonna turned in her seat and looked his young ass squarely in the eyes. "Yeah I smoked with him because it calmed him down. And yes, I sat on the nigga's lap because it would've been hard for them to shoot me without taking his head off too. I survive in this game because I think quickly on my feet not on my back."

JuJu still wasn't fully convinced. She had been too fucking comfortable on that ugly ass nigga's lap.

Bayonna was tight, she peeped his suspicion and quickly dissolved it. "You wanna know if I've ever fucked Riz? Hell no, but I use his desire against him. I was making these runs when yo' little ass was hugging the block, dropping nickels and dimes so don't come for me. I was Kiam's *first* choice to ride with you not his last. If you turn that raw ass gangsta of yours down a bit you might learn something from a thorough bitch like me," she said, fastening her seat belt.

"Watch your tone when you're bumping your lips shorty. Unlike Riz, I got dick control so your shit don't work here." He tried to save face.

Bayonna smiled then turned back to face him. "You was jealous up there, weren't you? You want me to sit on your lap so you can whisper in my ear?" She rubbed his leg.

"Don't touch me shorty." JuJu slapped her hand away. He was more mad at himself for briefly entertaining the thought of him and her to only have that shit smashed by the fact that she let that ugly muthafucka touch all over her.

Bayonna giggled, she could read his behind like his thoughts were written across the Goodyear blimp. "Go 'head, pull off and make a left at the light," she instructed. She was tickled inside that he had caught feelings over her little display.

JuJu was quiet all the way back home. Bayonna did her usual; she played her music, danced and snacked. She didn't pay his attitude any mind. When they reached Cleveland and had the work tucked safely away at a stash house, JuJu headed straight for Bayonna's crib to drop her off. He couldn't wait to get her out of his car.

"See you later angry man," she said through the window as she threw her bags over her shoulder.

"Go 'head so I can pull off," he grunted. His mug was all balled up like a paper bag.

Bayonna flashed him her thirty-twos. "You're too young to be so serious. You're gonna fuck around and have a heart attack," she kidded then turned and walked towards the house.

JuJu rolled up the window as he watched her walk inside. When her door closed he pulled off and called Kiam. He definitely was going to get in his ear about a replacement. He didn't wanna make another trip with Bayonna as his accomplice.

Chapter 11
Revenge Is a Sexy Bitch

"**W**hat you scared of, youngin'?" chuckled Kiam as he listened to JuJu while inspecting the work that had arrived from Riz. "You scared Bay is gonna cuff you and have you running around here singing love songs?"

"Nah dawg, it ain't nothing like that. I'm M.O.B. 'til these streets murder me face down or bury me face up. I just don't like how shorty handled that situation. Shit could've got real active," said JuJu, helping Kiam recount the bricks.

"I heard that slick shit," replied Kiam without looking up from the task at hand. He had no problem with the way Bayonna had handled the situation, his concern was with the way Riz and 'em confronted his peeps. That nigga acted like he wanted beef or something.

"Ju', don't let that cute face and fat ass fool you. Bayonna is 'bout this life. She played the situation with Riz proper and it should've shown you a side of him that you can use against him if the day ever comes where you gotta teach him some respect."

JuJu hadn't looked at it in that regard, but now it made sense. What Bayonna had shown him was that some situations called for guile more than guns. And she had opened Riz up for him to read the nigga while allowing JuJu to remain a closed book.

Kiam peeped that JuJu's mind was distracted. "You know what, lil' bruh?" he said. "I think you're feeling some kind of way because Bay sat on that nigga's lap. If you don't like her doing shit like that stake your claim. Put your name on that pussy." Kiam coached.

JuJu's silence confirmed his suspicions. Bayonna had his young boy caught the fuck up. He knew that she was much more polished and way more gangsta than the jump offs JuJu was used to, but he had no doubt that his lil' nigga could handle her.

Kiam continued dropping jewels on his understudy until he received a phone call that interrupted them. He pulled his cell phone out and looked at the screen. A sinister smile enveloped his handsome face as he accepted the call.

Kiam listened intently to what the caller was saying. His response was short and simple. "If this is a trap I'ma kill you and I'm gonna do it real slow so you'll suffer. Then I'm gonna R.I.P. your whole family." He hung up without allowing a reply.

Kiam turned to JuJu, school was over. Now he was all money, murder, and mayhem. "Strap up, it's killing time," he announced.

JuJu's eyes grew wide with excitement. Whenever it was time to ride he became amped. "Who we rolling on?" he asked though it didn't matter. All niggas' chests opened up with heat.

Kiam gave him the name and the game plan. Revenge was a sexy ass bitch that he could not resist.

JuJu smiled wickedly in anticipation of the surge of power that always flowed through his body as he took another man's life.

A half an hour later, they arrived at a barber shop on Euclid Avenue. The sun had moved aside to allow a dark grey sky to hover over the rotten city. The weather had switched up like an emotional ho, and yesterday's warm temperatures had bowed to a cold front that whirled in off of Lake Erie angry and cruel.

Kiam and JuJu ducked their heads against the wind as they made their way to the back door of the barber shop. Kiam's coded knock was answered and minutes later the door cracked open. Scooter, the owner of the shop put a finger to his lips and stepped aside so they could enter.

"How many customers are inside?" Kiam whispered.

"Just him. I've been closed for the last hour and like I told you on the phone, the other barbers have left for the day. He's in the chair waiting for me to finish shaving him."

With a gloved hand Kiam grabbed him by the collar and pulled him closer. "A'ight. Go back out there and act normal, and I mean you better win an Oscar, Bleed. Otherwise you'll win a tombstone," Kiam gritted.

Scooter looked at him confused. Something told him that he had made a big mistake, but it was too late to turn back now. Kiam and his junior assassin had their bangers out discouraging any thought of a flex move.

Scooter walked over to the small bathroom that was situated in a corner of the back room. JuJu was breathing on that nigga's neck, itching for him to pull out anything but his dick.

Scooter nervously unzipped his pants and relieved himself. He flushed the commode, washed his hands and headed back out to the front of the barber shop. Kiam had his hammer aimed at Scooter's back through a crack in the door as he strolled to his station.

The customer was still in the barber's chair with his eyes glued to the television mounted on the wall. A news reporter was saying, "In a heartbreaking story, a mother is accused of tossing her three year old child from a fifth floor apartment window after the child's father told her that he was breaking up with her."

"That bitch needs killing," remarked Scooter, reclining the customer's chair, preparing him for a hot shave.

"She gon' wish she was dead when they get through with her stupid ass. They gonna give that ho more time than Charles Manson. I wish one of my baby mothers would do some foul shit like that, I would bond her ass out of jail just to torture that bitch."

"I feel you. That shit don't make no muthafuckin' sense."

As Scooter began lathering the man's face with shaving cream, the man said, "Nigga, I hope you washed your hands back there. Don't be taking a shit, wiping ya ass then coming out here and shaving me with shit residue under your fingernails."

Scooter laughed.

"I ain't playing nigga. Let me find out," said Frank Nitti, cracking up himself. But in just a few seconds his laughter was about to turn to cries.

He closed his eyes and enjoyed the smooth stroke of the sharp blade gliding across his face, shaving him skin-close. He thought about how stupid Scooter was. He had been running dick up in the fool's wife for a month and the nigga was still blind to it.

Then Nitti thought about how stupid *he* was, letting a man whose wife he was fucking shave him with a muhfuckin' straight-razor! But the thought came to him too late.

"What up, Bleed?" The voice on the back of his neck belonged to the devil.

Nitti became paralyzed with fear.

"Go ahead, reach for your waist. I want you to. *Pleeeze*," begged Kiam.

JuJu walked around the chair and stood in front of Nitti with his whistle pointed at his chest. "Game over, Bleed," he taunted.

Kiam held the straight-razor firmly against Nitti's windpipe and leaned down close to his ear. "How it feel homie? Can you really see your whole life flash in front of you?"

"Fuck you, bitch ass nigga. I'm not gonna beg, I'm built for this shit!" Nitti snorted.

"Oh, yeah? You must think it's going to be over real quick. Is that what you think?"

"Suck my dick."

Kiam chuckled. "You tough, huh? Well, I'ma bring the bitch out of you." He reached over Nitti's shoulder and removed the heat off his waist. "You should've went for your gun, Bleed. You know— go out in a blaze of glory. That's how real niggas get down."

Kiam straightened his body back up and nodded his head. JuJu stepped forward, aimed his banger at Nitti's kneecap and sent some hot shit his way. Boc!

Scooter jumped at the sound of the fo-fifth. Nitti yelped and grabbed his knee. Blood seeped through his fingers as he winced in pain.

Kiam grabbed a fist full of Nitti's small fro and jerked his head back exposing his Adam's apple to the straight-razor in his hand. He pressed the sharp blade against Nitti's throat and whispered in his ear again. "When you bust your gun at a beast you can't miss or you'll find yourself in a situation like this. Was it worth it? Didn't you know when you didn't kill me that night that I would find out that it was you? You had to know that Nitti."

"I ain't telling you shit, pussy ass nigga. If you think it was me, quit barking and bite. I'll see your bitch ass in hell." He leaned his head back further and hawked a glob of spit dead in Kiam's face.

Kiam released his hair and gave him a short hard right in his face snapping his neck back. Kiam gave JuJu the nod as he wiped his face.

JuJu fired another shot, hitting Nitti in the other kneecap. "Ahhhh!" he cried out. Sweat beads popped up on his forehead as the heat from the gunshots soared throughout his body.

Nitti cut his eyes towards Scooter who was returning from the window making sure the blinds were closed. "This how you come at me about a bitch?" he grimaced. "Nigga, if the ho was really yours I couldn't have fucked her. You a fool, they're gonna murk you too."

Scooter looked at Kiam but Kiam's cold stare caused him to look away and swallow the question on his lips. His eyes cut towards a drawer further back where he kept his tool. He would have to get pass JuJu to reach it and the boy didn't look like he was in the mood to move.

Kiam slid the blade up to Nitti's ear. "Remember when you said you were hearing my name ringing in the streets?" He paused but Nitti didn't reply. "I told you that you were listening too hard, didn't I?"

In one swift motion Kiam sliced off his ear. "Try listening now mutha-fucka," he said as Nitti screamed, hollered, and squirmed to get away. His severed ear fell to the floor causing Scooter to cringe. "And you a nosy muthafucka," Kiam continued taunting then sliced off a huge chunk of his nose.

When it hit the floor inches from Scooter's feet he jumped back gagging.

In a panic stricken rage Nitti snatched away and tried to run, but with holes in both kneecap his legs didn't work. He collapsed to the floor, staring up into Kiam's diabolical face.

Kiam smiled down at him with no mercy. He turned to Scooter and barked, "Strip him!"

When Nitti was asshole naked they tied his hands together at the wrist and Kiam gagged his mouth with a towel. All the time he was humming a DMX song. When he finished stuffing the towel in Nitti's mouth to prevent him from screaming, he rapped, "I got things that make niggas spin, put niggas in the wind where you never see niggas again, I bless niggas with stitches the thin type, and this straight razor will put pen strips across your windpipe."

Kiam suddenly rose up and flashed the straight-razor in front of Nitti's eyes. "Fuck me, huh? You had the nerve to say that shit to a boss?" He grabbed a hold of Nitti's dick and cut it off in one gruesome swipe. Kiam threw that little shit next to the rest of Nitty's parts.

Nitti's screams were muffled by the towel. Kiam rolled him over on his stomach and shoved the razor up his ass turned it and pulled it out with his insides attached. "It ain't fuck me, it's fuck you nigga."

Nitti's whole body jerked in pain before he passed out. JuJu grabbed the alcohol and poured it all over him causing his eyes to jolt open.

Kiam then began cutting off different parts of his body as he talked shit.

They let Nitti suffer for a while then Kiam sent him where all bitch niggas belong.

JuJu was bouncing up and down. *Kiam is turnt the fuck up.* Beside him Scooter had pissed on himself. He looked at Kiam with pleading eyes. The look he got back caused his ass hole to tighten up.

"You don't have to kill me man. I'm one hunnid," he cried, staring down at the bloody razor in Kiam's hand and regretting ever talking to him about his beef with Nitti.

"Nitti was your sister's baby's daddy. That's like fam. If he couldn't trust you, how the fuck am I supposed to?" Kiam posed.

"Bruh…"

"Don't call me that shit!" Kiam growled.

When Scooter spoke again all the bass was gone from his voice and his words came out in a first tenor.

Kiam listened then rendered his verdict. "I'm a man of my word. I told you I wasn't gonna kill you when you first approached me with this. But you're gonna have to convince my man that leaving you alive isn't a risk. Good luck." He dropped the razor next to Nitti's body and headed out the back.

Scooter saw his fate in JuJu's murderous eyes a second before his brains splashed against the mirror.

Chapter 12
Spreading the Terror

In the days following the execution of Frank Nitti, Kiam didn't let up on Wolfman. He turned the heat up even hotter. Him and JuJu jumped out on one of Wolfman's runners on 123rd and Kinsman and left him slumped across the hood of his whip. The blood that stained the ground served as the only warning Wolfman would get that a shift in power was underway and if he didn't fold his hand Kiam would cut those muthafuckas off.

Others that wielded power in the game— particularly Money Bags Carter and Dontae— got their cards pulled too. "We're hitting every one of them, ain't no love for the other side. "Fuck 'em all," Kiam directed JuJu. "I got big plans and those niggas aren't part of them."

JuJu could barely sit still in the passenger seat of Kiam's whip as they rode pass the notorious King-Kennedy projects where Money Bags Carter held a stronghold. Any talk of murder sent a surge of adrenaline straight to JuJu's balls. He rocked back and forth with excitement as his eyes focused on niggas getting money on blocks that would soon belong to them.

Kiam looked over and saw his young wolf easing a banger off of his waist.

"Pull over boss man, let me hop out and make an example out of one of these lames," pled JuJu.

"Be easy. I'ma let you make an example out of more than one of them," cautioned Kiam as he bent a corner. "Right now we're just gathering info on how they move. When we strike we're gonna be on that mass murder shit real hard so these niggas will understand that we're not taking no for an answer. They're giving up their blocks or we're taking their lives."

"That's what the fuck I'm talkin' about." JuJu smiled sinisterly; he lived for that gangsta shit.

Kiam pulled over and they sat low watching for the slightest imperfection in the character of their enemy. JuJu could barely sit still, his right leg rocked back and forth and his heartbeat accelerated like a young cub waiting and watching for his chance to kill.

"There them niggas go," JuJu spat with heat rising from his tongue as he spotted Trigga and Bolo, a couple of dudes that held high rank in Money

Bags Carter's operation. "Them niggas dead and don't even know it," he gritted.

Kiam chuckled inside at JuJu's anxiousness. He saw that he needed to teach his young boy a lesson, one that would help him last in these streets.

"You hate them niggas, huh?" Kiam asked not taking his eyes off their prey.

"Hell yeah, my shit itching to make a coroner question his career path," JuJu answered as his eyes lowered and his grip tightened on his heat.

"Why?" Kiam asked in a deep calm voice.

JuJu thought for a minute then answered without missing a breath, "Sheeiit…them niggas in our way."

Kiam nodded his head then he dropped his gem. "Let me tell you something youngin, a nigga you can see ain't in your way. It's the mutha-fuckas you can't see that you have to worry about. Remember, stay calm in the face of your enemies that way you can see their every move. Anger will kill you both," Kiam cautioned then returned his full attention back on the street.

That piece of information calmed JuJu's nerves and steadied his body. He was now looking at them niggas in a whole new light.

Kiam sized up the area and the dark figures that faded into the background. There was no mistaking it, they were strapped and protecting Trigga and Bolo as they stood outside chopping it up with their workers. Once they finished talking and jumped in the car Kiam waited a cautious minute before slowly pulling out behind them. He had already peeped the weakness and their strengths, now he was about to unleash his terror.

They followed their targets inconspicuously until they reached a traffic light. As soon as their whip came to a stop JuJu was halfway out of the car with his *whistle* out, ready to make that bitch blow.

Kiam placed a hand on his elbow. "Fall back lil' killah," he hurriedly warned. "Look to your right, po po is parked in the gas station."

JuJu's eyes quickly found the police cruiser lurking across the street. He eased back inside the car, shut the door and nodded his head in respect for Kiam's keen awareness.

When the light turned green Kiam followed the two boys until they turned off. JuJu looked over at him with a puzzled expression on his face.

"You gotta always stay on point and pay attention to your surroundings," explained Kiam. "You see that green Monte Carlo two cars behind us?" he questioned.

JuJu checked the side view mirror and nodded his head.

"They pulled out behind us when we followed Trigga and his boy. Now, I know you're like 'fuck them niggas they can get it too' and you're right. But don't forget that *johnny* is only a few blocks back. As soon as they hear the gunshots they'll be all over us." He paused to allow his words to register while he checked the rearview mirror to see if the Monte Carlo was still following them.

Kiam didn't relax until he saw the car turn off. Then he drove on and resumed schooling JuJu. "Why you grilling? Those niggas not going anywhere. We can find them down here any day of the week. I just wanted you to peep their setup."

JuJu nodded his head as he took in the lessons Kiam was teaching him. He had to admit there was a chink in his armor. And he definitely needed to pay attention and sharpen his skills.

From there they rode over to where Dontae was regulating things. As Kiam pointed out one trap house after another JuJu tried to see what Kiam saw while controlling the beast within that wanted to hop out and cause some tragedies.

Kiam smiled at JuJu's unbridled gangsta. "Be easy fam I'm about to unleash you on these niggas but first I want you to put together a team of killahs just like yourself. When you've done that I'll give you the blueprint to cause terror."

That was music to JuJu's ears.

Kiam dropped his young boy off with instructions not to move too fast. When JuJu slid out of the car and shut the door Kiam watched him walk towards his condo with bounce in his step. The eagerness that JuJu displayed in his stride matched the eagerness Kiam felt as he made a call to the one that was his sanctuary away from the madness of the streets. Too much time had passed since he'd held her in his arms. For just a little while the streets would have to manage themselves.

Chapter 13
On Bended Knee

Faydrah moved around her office preparing herself for a big meeting she had to attend. As hard as she tried to push her feelings about Kiam aside the stronger they became. Once Kiam left her that night her heart ached from the distance she put between them. The reality of not being with him made her stomach sick which was confirmation that it was going to be impossible to live without him.

"Faydrah, you ready for the meeting?" Gina popped her head in the office with a huge smile on her face.

"Yeah, let me just grab my phone and I will be right there," Faydrah said without looking up as she reached in her desk to retrieve it.

"What's wrong Fay," Gina asked, picking up on Faydrah's mood.

"Nothing I'm good, I think I am coming down with a little something." She forced a half smile and rubbed her stomach.

"Well don't be spreading nothing I cannot afford to get sick, come on," Gina said as she turned to walk out the office.

Faydrah gathered her paperwork but needed to make a call before heading out. She stood by her desk listening to each ring and the brief silence that fell between them which felt like minutes. Her heart began to race with anticipation as she waited to hear his voice. When Kiam's voice mail came on her heart sank to her toes.

She quickly hit the end button pulled herself together and headed to the conference room. Faydrah sat in her chair trying to stay focused but couldn't. There was talking going on all around her but she didn't hear anything. Her mind was all over the place.

When her cell phone vibrated she jumped in her seat and scrambled to see who it was. Faydrah pulled the phone under the table and swiped left.

Hey you. The words caused an instant smile on Faydrah's face.

Hey you. What you doin? She quickly texted back.

Thinking about you.

I need to see you.

Come on.

I'm at work

Fuck that job. Come now. His request took her breath away.

Kiam. I can't just walk out of the meeting.
What I say? Hurry up and bring me something to eat.
I got something for you to eat.

Kiam closed the conversation with a smiley face and her coochie began to throb. She looked up at her boss who was deep into his speech. Faydrah took a deep breath then began to nervously gather her things. When she stood up all eyes were on her.

"Excuse me, I have a family emergency?" Faydrah moved to the door.

"Is everything alright Ms. Combs?" her boss asked with heavy concern on his face.

"I'm not sure but I have to go."

"Please keep me informed."

Faydrah didn't respond. She held a somber look on her face as she headed out the door. As she walked off the elevator her look turned into a smile. She was ready to reclaim everything she had ever wanted. She hurried to her car and headed to her King.

When Faydrah pulled in front of Kiam's house a sinking feeling hit the bottom of her stomach. The weight of going back on her promise to herself to walk away from this life along with the fear of losing Kiam began taking over her emotions. In that moment she realized that she would never be happy without him and by trying to force him to be disloyal to his commitments would cause him to be unhappy with her. She grabbed her purse reached inside the side pocket and slipped her ring back on her finger, smiled big then jumped out.

Standing on the porch waiting for the door to open felt like a million years, each second ticking by in slow-motion. When the door began to open her smile widened.

"What's up Faydrah?" JuJu asked in his relaxed tone.

Faydrah decreased her smile. "I'm good where is ya boy?" she asked as she proceeded inside.

"He upstairs." He said, closing the door.

Faydrah looked over at Bayonna who was getting up off the couch and putting on her jacket and anger rose in her gut. She knew exactly who Bayonna was and because she rolled with Lissha she was already on Faydrah's list.

Bayonna returned her stare with a colder one as she moved to the door.

90

"We on our way out. Kiam said for you to come on up. Lock the door right quick," JuJu said, grabbing a black duffle bag and looking back and forth at the two woman and feeling the vibe change in the room.

JuJu took Bayonna by the arm and led her out the door. "Catch up with you next time ma," he said to Faydrah as he closed it behind them.

Faydrah locked the door and set the alarm. She took off her shoes and headed upstairs.

"Bae, where you at?" she called out as she walked down the hall looking in each room. Stopping and entering the master bedroom she could hear music lightly playing but Kiam was nowhere in sight.

Removing her jacket she laid it across the chair and walked towards the bathroom. She turned the knob with caution and proceeded inside.

"Why you creeping through my house?" Kiam's bass boomed through the bathroom commanding her attention.

Faydrah turned the corner to see him standing in the tub with water dripping from his sexy chocolate frame. She was speechless as her eyes danced over his body taking in all of his splendor as if seeing it for the first time.

"I'm not sneaking," she managed to say a little over a whisper.

"Grab that towel and come dry me off," he ordered now letting his eyes roam over her body as she moved to the towel rack. The clingy material of her skirt hugged her ass deliciously and the sheer material of her blouse accented her breast causing his dick to semi rock.

Faydrah grabbed the thick towel and came to the side of the tub. She could hear Miguel playing from the other room and all of her emotion came rushing to the surface.

"I missed you," she uttered as she began to run the towel over his wet skin.

"How much?" Kiam asked, looking at her like she was his next meal.

"Enough to drop my guard and let you lead," she responded as she ran the towel between his legs and down his shaft.

"You sure about that?" he reached out and began unbuttoning her blouse, easing it off of her shoulders then letting it fall to the floor.

"Yes." she mumbled as she felt him unsnap her bra and free her luscious breast.

Stepping out the tub he pulled her in his arms. It was time to make her submit to his authority.

"Kiam we need to talk," she tried to protest as he walked her fast to their bed.

"I'm about to talk to you right now." He sunk his teeth into her neck and sucked as he pulled at her skirt causing it to fall to her ankles. A split second later her panties followed.

"Baby," she moaned as his mouth covered her nipple heating up her whole body.

"Yes," he answered between hot passionate kisses.

Kiam reached up grabbing a handful of her hair and pulling her head all the way back biting and sucking her neck and collar bone. Sliding his hand between her thighs he caused her clit to throb and her pussy to cream. Her pulsating lips was screaming for relief and he was about to give it to her.

Everything was moving fast even the room felt as if it was spinning. Faydrah rested her hands on his shoulders to keep balance as he continued to set her on fire.

When he looked down into the slits of her eyes he knew it was time. He pushed her back onto the bed, grabbed her ankles and guided her onto her stomach. He positioned himself behind ready to do damage.

"Baby be gentle," she moaned.

Kiam blocked that shit right out as he pushed all those inches in hard and fast. Each stroke had meaning and her deep moans confirmed she was getting the point. He pulled her back into his thrust sliding in and out of her wetness with familiarity.

Faydrah's moans filled the room caressing his ears. "I need you to ride for me baby," he grunted breaking down any resistance that may have remained.

"I'ma ride Kiam," she submitted.

"You gotta let me lead ma," he grunted, gripping her tightly and showing no mercy.

"Kiam," she cried out reaching back to slow his push.

"Move your hand." He lowered himself right on top of her back forcing her legs as wide as they would go.

Faydrah gripped the sheets as he stroked long and deep. "I need you to do what I tell you," he whispered in her ear as her thrusts punctuated his words.

"I will Kiam. I will," she cried as hit that spot that made her yield to his commands. Faydrah's body began to shake with each and every long, hard stroke.

From the pushup position he was in over her Kiam sucked on her neck and went deeper inside as Faydrah moved her waist intensifying their pleasure. She grinded her ass up to meet his power and the sensation that came over her mad her cry out his name. Faydrah came long and hard then lay flatly across the bed.

Kiam continued to stroke, bringing his long thick pipe out to the head then sliding it all the way back in nice and slow.

"Baby you gotta trust me, I got you," he spoke softly as he placed kisses on her shoulders. "You know I will love you forever." Kiam stroked from side to side guided by the moans that left her lips. "Didn't I tell you this pussy was going to be in trouble when you gave it to me?" he taunted picking up a little speed.

Faydrah was unable to speak she nodded her head and squeezed her eyes shut as she felt another orgasm coming on strong.

"What's that I'm hitting?" He pushed in and grinded deep inside her.

"Baby, that's my spot," she muttered.

"Mmmm. Wet this dick," he grunted in her ear. Faydrah released all her hot and sticky love.

Kiam looked down at his dick glistening with her juices as he pulled out. Flipping her over onto her back he climbed back in his favorite spot and gave her pleasure in the place of pain. He continued to please her from one position to the next until she couldn't take anymore. Kiam came inside of her then laid on his back with his arm around her. He was content, he had just made his position in their relationship clear. He was boss and she could follow but she wasn't going to be running shit.

Faydrah laid peacefully on top of Kiam with her head on his chest.

"Baby I think you broke your pussy," she mumbled, causing Kiam to chuckle.

"She'll be a'ight and you better be good."

"I don't have no other choice. You have me one hundred percent."

Kiam stroked her hair. "Don't worry I got you."

"I know you got me. And I got you. No matter what baby I got your back. But I will say this, I don't trust those bitches you roll with. And I promise you if they cause you any pain. I will hunt down and kill every one of those bitches and I won't lose no sleep."

"So you a killah now?" he teased.

"Only for you," she said and put her hand on his chest.

"Baby I need you as far away from this life as possible. But you're my eyes and if you see something coming for me handle your business and I got your back one hundred percent."

Kiam knew very well that Faydrah was not that bitch you fuck with. She had moved on up but had not forgot where she came from and he knew that if it came down to it she was just as dangerous with a gun in her hands as he was.

Faydrah laid in his arms as she began to fade to sleep. Her heart was with Kiam but her mind was still trying to come to terms with the fact that she had just surrendered her whole self, mind, body and soul.

Chapter 14
Cliqued Up and Dangerous

JuJu's mind, body and soul was invested in the game and the mission that Kiam had laid out for him. He stood in the center of the sparsely furnished living room looking back and forth at two faces that were identical. His arms swung out to the sides as if they contained adrenaline that moved through them like currents of electricity threatening to leap out the tips of his fingers like bolts of lightning. "I'm hyped like a muthafucka," he proclaimed. "With y'all niggas rolling with the team the streets are about to spread its legs wide open and get fucked raw dog!"

The twins, Isaiah and Isaac, sat on the worn down couch watching and listening to him intently. JuJu was the little cousin who had always had big dreams. They had heard him talk about ruling the streets from the time he jumped off of the porch at eleven years old and started pitching rocks.

The twins' mother and JuJu's mom were sisters. She had taken JuJu in after his own mother caught thirty years in the Feds for a string of bank robberies that her and JuJu's pops pulled. Though JuJu was their first cousin he was more like a little brother because the three of them had been raised up under the same roof.

Isaiah, who was 6'2, 235 pounds, and blueberry black with pearly white teeth cracked a half smile as he listened to JuJu talk like they had already accepted his offer. He knew that his little cousin was turnt up and ready to get to the money now but he needed a little more convincing before he'd take his tool off the shelf and cause mother's to weep.

Isaac on the other hand had already decided that he wanted to get down with the move. He had been hearing Kiam's name ringing all over town and he wanted to associate himself with a nigga of that caliber. He could hardly believe that his little cuz was offering them a chance to roll with an official ass team and all they would have to do to earn their stripes was put some niggas in the dirt. Sheeiit, that was like paying a dog to bark. Isaac thought to himself as he rubbed his thick Rick Ross-like beard; it was the only feature that distinguished him from his brother.

JuJu cut his eyes back to Isaiah since he was the one hedging on getting down and no matter what, the twins would move as one. "Like I told y'all, my nigga is about his business, *one hunnid,*" JuJu went on speaking about Kiam. "Ain't nobody starving on his watch, we all eating good."

He reached in his pockets and pulled out racks on racks then let his eyes roam around the apartment that the brothers shared. Besides the worn leather sofa there was a matching loveseat in equally tattered condition, a tired ass 54-inch flat screen, an X box, and carpet that was as thin as toilet paper. With both fists full of money JuJu spread his arms out and challenged, "Cuz, you like living like this? C'mon, Bleed, you can't bring no boss bitch up in this tore up muthafucka. It's time to step your game up. That little punk ass money y'all making selling weed ain't nothing compared to this."

JuJu tossed the bands in Isaiah's lap and folded his arms across his chest while he awaited his decision.

Those dea white men was calling Isaiah's name. He was a few weeks away from turning twenty-five years old and his pockets still weren't grown up. He looked around the room and wasn't impressed with nothing that he had accomplished so far. JuJu saw the hunger in his eyes. "And a child shall lead the way," he quoted from the Scriptures.

Isaiah nodded and looked towards his twin. "I'm down," Isaac replied without hesitation.

JuJu smiled and reached down inside the duffel bag that laid at his feet. He started pulling out black hoodies and gloves, tossing them to Isaiah and Isaac. Then he brought out those thangs that sent healthy niggas to the morgue.

Isaac's eyes lit up when JuJu passed him a Desert Eagle with a rubber grip. "This is that beast," he exclaimed, caressing the gun fondly.

JuJu handed Isaiah a fo-fo with a homemade extended clip. "Cause I know you like to squeeze that trigger non-stop," he said, recalling an incident a few years back where they had crushed two dudes on MLK. Isaiah had stood over one of their victims and dispassionately pumped sixteen shots in his chest.

He slammed the clip in the ratchet and looked up at JuJu with a killah's stare. "Lil' cuz I'ma ride but if your man ain't thorough I'ma pop his melon too. I'm not showing loyalty to no disloyal muthafucka," said Isaiah as he rose to his feet and began pulling the hoodie over his head. Isaac followed his lead.

96

JuJu chuckled, sounding just like Kiam when he felt disrespected. "Fam," he replied, "my mans is platinum baby. I put that on my life and you already know *my* pedigree. My moms and my pops serving three dimes and neither one of them would flip. You saying anything?"

Isaiah shook his head no. "I'm saying let's go show these fools that their time is up," he spat, holding his fist out for a pound.

JuJu dapped him and Isaac up, and then the three of them finished getting strapped. When they left out the door ten minutes later murder was the plan. Money Bags Carter's boys down in King-Kennedy were about to kiss the ground permanently. And their deaths were just the beginning of the massacres that he had devised for the streets.

Chapter 15
Forced Alliances

Wolfman sat at the head of the conference table in the office of his night-club with his hands folded atop the table. He looked around the room at the other men present. Money Bags Carter and his right-hand man, Crispy Jay, sat to the right of him. Young Dontae and his top lieutenant, Two Gunz, was on the left. Wolfman's newly elected street General Chino was posted by the door looking like a male model with his fair features and long ponytail that came down to the center of his back. Many had mistaken his pretty boy looks for softness and had gotten fitted for a casket as a result of underestimating his G.

Not only was Chino a pretty nigga, he was a stone cold murderer. He had added a half dozen bodies to his street resume since hooking up with Wolfman's team two years ago. Frank Nitti's demise had opened the door for him to move up in rank and he was anxious to prove that his promotion was a wise one.

As Chino looked around the room at the other men, he decided that anyone that bucked the agenda was getting carried out of there wrapped up in a sheet. He made eye contact with Wolfman and received the silent okay.

Sitting beside Wolfman, Money Bags Carter wore an expression of deep agitation. He unconsciously fiddled with his signature small diamond money bag earrings that hung from his ear lobes and released a heavy sigh. Four of his boys had gotten killed the other night and three others were laid up in the hospital fighting losing battles for their lives.

In addition to those problems he had a huge shipment due to arrive today and a feeling of angst had him by the throat. Normally he wouldn't be caught dead in the same room with Wolfman or Dontae but Kiam was making a power move that was a threat to all of them so this alliance was necessary. Money Bags Carter could barely hold his tongue as he sat waiting to see what the fuck Wolfman could tell him to calm his anxiety.

Dontae was seething too. Last night his nephew and one of his workers had gotten gunned down outside of a store on Hayden, then this morning one of his main runners stepped out of the house and caught a chest full of lead. Bodies were dropping all around the city and if Kiam was behind the killings he needed to be dealt with before he became an unstoppable force. Before today Dontae would've never considered joining forces with Wolfman or Money Bags Carter, he didn't trust either of their asses and neither of them could trust him.

Dontae stared at the bottles of liquor and the spread of cold cuts that sat untouched in the center of the table as he tried to comprehend why a muthafucka that he didn't even know and had never had words with would declare war on him. He didn't know the answer nor did he have time to search for it so he was going to send some heat right back at that ass. If this meeting was about any fucking thing other than killing Kiam, Wolfman was wasting his time.

Wolfman cleared his throat and all heads turned towards him. "Gentleman we have a problem," he began, leaving his hands folded on the table.

"You're got damn right we do," Money Bags Carter exploded as he shot to his feet, slamming his palms down on the table so hard that the liquor bottles rattled together.

Crispy Jay stood up next to his boss and slid his hand inside his jacket where his tool was tucked in a shoulder holster.

"Nigga sit your ass down before I shatter your muthafuckin' spine!" The voice on the back of Crispy Jay's neck belonged to the pretty boy assassin.

Crispy Jay let his hand fall to his side but remained standing in defiance. The only smell of pussy on him was on the tip of his dick. He had been through the battles and had the scars all over his body and soul to prove it. Five years ago a fierce rival in King-Kennedy had doused him with gasoline and set him on fire; Crispy Jay had lived through that to come back and torture the nigga in the same hideous fashion so a ratchet in the center of his back was nothing breezy to a fan.

Chino knew of Crispy Jay's reputation but he was not impressed. Yeah he had recovered and burned that nigga to death, but if it would've been him Chino would've eradicated that muthafucka's entire bloodline behind that shit. Every time he looked in the mirror and saw those scars he would've went out and killed another member of that nigga's family, he told himself as he waited for Crispy Jay to give him a reason to send his back flying out of his chest.

100

Wolfman shook his head, letting Chino know to turn it down. Chino nodded and backed away but he kept his stare trained on Crispy Jay's back.

"Gentleman, please be seated. This is exactly what Kiam wants to happen," said Wolfman in a calm tone.

Money Bags Carter reluctantly sat back down and after a pause Crispy Jay did the same. *I'ma have to let Chino kill him* thought Wolfman as he gauged the heat coming off of Crispy Jay's forehead.

Dontae sat quietly taking in everything around him. *He's a thinker. He'll choose sides with the stronger team* Wolfman quickly concluded. He hadn't ascended to the top without being able to read his friends as well as his foes.

He unfolded his hands and poured himself a glass of vodka, lifted it to his lips and tossed it back on one gulp. "Ahhhh," he let out as it burned the back of his throat.

He sat the glass down and rubbed his hands together. When he was sure that he held their attention he spoke with no preamble. "As we all can see Kiam is trying to take over the city. He's coming straight for the ones at top, and that's the three of us. So I would think it's in all of our best interest to come together and take him out," he said.

Money Bags Carter's eyes narrowed. "That's what Nitti was supposed to do and how did that turn out?"

"Not good," admitted Wolfman with a shrug of his shoulders that didn't sit well with Money Bags. He had lost seven souljahs to Kiam's guns.

"I told you if we missed he was going to come at us with all he has," he scoffed.

"Money Bags, there's no way Kiam could know that you were in on that because I'm the only one that knew. And what did Dontae have to do with it? Nothing. Don't you see that he's making a power play to supplant us all at the same time? It's a smart move. You sound like you're shook."

Money Bags Carter was offended but he hid it nicely. When this was over he was going to kill Wolfman. He suspected him of having one of his shipments knocked off. "I'm not afraid of no man. Let's send somebody after him that won't miss. I don't have time for this shit," he remarked, glancing down at his watch. In two hours he would have to meet his connect to receive the shipment and he needed to be out.

Wolfman looked over to Dontae. "You got something you wanna say?" he asked.

Dontae sat up on the edge of his seat. "I just wanna know who Kiam is and how in the fuck did he just pop up out of nowhere causing so much havoc? It's like one day this nigga's name just started ringing in the streets and the next thing I know he's killing muthafuckas."

"He didn't come out of nowhere, I found out that he was in the Feds with a muthafucka that I thought I would never hear from again," explained Wolfman.

Dontae lifted his eyebrows.

"Kiam was Big Zo's cell mate up at Lewisburg," Wolfman continued with a frown on his face. Even from the inside Big Zo was causing him problems. "You can bet he took Kiam under his wing and coached him to do everything that he's out here doing."

As Dontae listened he could hear the contempt in Wolfman's voice when he said Big Zo's name. He didn't know what that was about because he was still hugging the block when Big Zo got knocked. Something told him that Wolfman was holding back some information that could shed light on why his face got so tight when he uttered Big Zo's name but he knew that he would have to find that out on his own. In the meantime, he wasn't going to just sit back and let Big Zo's protege take what he had worked hard to build.

The three men discussed strategies on getting at Kiam. "We should go after Lissha, that would hurt Big Zo more than anything," suggested Money Bags Carter.

Wolfman agreed.

"But that won't take care of Kiam," Dontae pointed out. "Fuck snatching up bitches to make a nigga in the joint feel pain while his understudy is out here murking my people. Y'all can handle it anyway you want to but I'm going straight after Kiam." Dontae stood up and walked out the door with his boy, Two Gunz, on his heels. As far as he was concerned there was nothing else to discuss.

As soon as the door closed behind Dontae, Wolfman said, "Fuck it, we'll hit that nigga too."

"I'm down," Money Bags Carter co-signed. *And I'ma hit your ass last.*

Wolfman was thinking the same thing but his smile masked his duplicitous thoughts. He stood up and he and Money Bags Carter shook hands. "You work on Lissha while I work on getting to Kiam," he said, knowing that his Ace in the hole was DeMarcus.

"Don't miss this time," remarked Money Bags Carter as he and Crispy Jay stood and moved towards the door.

Crispy Jay and Chino eyed each other like a lion and a hyena. "Later for you, Bleed," said Chino as he stepped aside to let them out.

"Nigga, you better concentrate on Kiam 'cause this right here ain't what you want," Crispy Jay warned.

Chino put his fingers to his mouth and blew him the kiss of death. But somebody should have warned them both that Kiam would require all of their attention and he was not their only worry. One of the cruddiest niggas alive was in town stalking.

Ca$h & NeNe Capri

Chapter 16
Blood Trail

Wa'leek walked into Treebie's bedroom and just stared at her while she slept. A scowl enveloped his face; he had ordered her hard-headed ass back to New Jersey and she had disobeyed him and stayed in Ohio. What was her tie to Lissha and Big Zo that kept her so loyal to them? he wondered.

The thought that another muthafucka had more influence over his wife than he did plagued him and tasted bitter in his mouth. Knowing that he was the one that introduced her to the game and now she had more stake in it then he did wasn't the least bit palatable either. He had always known that she wasn't the average bitch, that's why he had wifed her, but he wasn't sure what she had become. Whatever she was doing had changed her.

Moving to the bathroom Wa'leek undressed and hopped in the shower, it had been a long day of digging and prying to try and hunt down Blood Money and their reasons for coming for Riz's crew. He thought back to the night of the attack and wondered why he was spared. Street legend had it that Blood Money's M.O. was always leave one standing to tell the story but they had left two, Jamaal and him.

Why?

It was a question he had asked himself a thousand times but the answer still alluded him. To think that it just wasn't his time to die explained nothing because that night Blood Money made sure that every nigga up in the house that they wanted dead stopped breathing. Allah couldn't have saved him from the carnage that Blood Money left in their wake. They had ran up in there and did exactly what they had come to do. There was no doubt in his mind that he was still alive simply because they hadn't wanted him dead.

Logic told him that the niggas up under those masks must've known him personally. Well, if that was the case then they should've known that it was a mistake to spare his life.

The irony was that Wa'leek wasn't supposed to be there that night, he was supposed to have picked Treebie up from the airport and gone back home to chill with her. At the last minute she had called to say that she had missed her flight. Wa'leek recalled hearing the lie in her voice but he had figured that she had changed her mind about coming because she feared he wouldn't let her return.

Treebie's decision had led to him going with Jamaal to the house that Blood Money invaded. Those blood red contacts haunted his day and night dreams and he could not rest until he had each and every head on his mantel.

Treebie began to stir when she heard the sound of the shower. Alarm set in and she jumped up and grabbed her gun from her purse. Moving carefully down the hall taking small quiet steps she held her gun firm in her hand as she peeked through the crack in the door. She was relieved when she saw Wa'leek's boots then heard him humming a rap from behind the curtain, something he always did when he was in deep thought.

Treebie lowered her weapon and entered the bathroom. She walked over to the shower and opened the curtain. Her man was lathering his hard body. "I almost blew you brains out," she said.

"I like it when you *blow* my brains out," he quipped as he soaped up the thick pendulum that hung between his legs.

"Shut up," she giggled staring down at *her* shit in his hand.

Wa'leek looked at her hungrily. "Why you just standing there?"

"Because it's 3:00 in the morning and I'm going back to bed," Her eyes wondered over his frame as the water and soap caressed all of her favorite places.

"Come here." He motioned with his finger.

"Nope." Treebie shook her head back and forth as her eyes briefly settled on that thick pole.

"You know if you make me come get you I won't be merciful," he warned.

"I'm not scared of you," she cooed as his eyes penetrated hers.

"You talking shit 'cause you got that gun. I got one too." He stroked his weapon. "Which one you think is more effective?"

"Both," she answered huskily as her body began to heat up.

"Let me hold yours and you come hold mine," offered Wa'leek.

Treebie considered making him beg for it but when she saw that dick jump her pussy tingled. She placed her gun on the sink and stepped in the shower.

"You miss me?" He grabbed her shirt, pulling her to him.

"I only miss you when you're not starting trouble."

Wa'leek ignored her comment as he enjoyed the way her erect nipples looked through the wetness of her t-shirt.

"Why you so quiet?" she asked as his intense stare quickened her breathing.

Wa'leek brought both his hands to the top of her t-shirt and ripped it down to the middle of her chest exposing her breast. "That shit was fucking up my flow," he said as his grey eyes brightened with hot desire.

Treebie took a deep breath as he grabbed a fist full of her shirt, pulled her closer and covered one of her taut nipples with his warm mouth. She grabbed the back of his head and gripped it tightly while his tongue slid over her breast causing her kitty to purr for attention.

"Wah," she whispered as he tore away at the rest of her shirt.

"Yes," he responded biting her neck and clutching her back with the tips of his fingers. He enjoyed the sound of each gasp that left her mouth as he tickled her special spots. Turning her quickly he pushed her forward.

Treebie placed her palms flat against the shower wall as his hands slipped between her smooth creamy thighs. "If you didn't miss me my pussy damn sure did," he said, playing in the wetness that began to ease down.

Treebie put her head down as she felt his thickness take the place of his fingers. The water rained down on her body as he grabbed her butt cheeks and pushed his way through her tightness, stroking her tenderly from the back.

"Ssss." A small hiss accompanied the rotating of Treebie's hips.

"You still mine?" whispered Wa'leek, pushing deeper and quickening his strokes.

"Yes." Treebie moaned. He was in that spot that rendered her incapable of common sense.

Commanding her body so that it moved to his desire Wa'leek enjoyed the sound of pleasure and pain that dripped from her vocals. When her legs began to shake he pushed her forward a little more to hit those baby making spots.

"Wah, wait," she cried out as he caused her to reach out for anything she could get her hands on.

"Didn't I tell you to bring it to me?" he taunted.

"Yes," she stuttered as his merciless stroke overpowered her ability to make full sentences.

"What did I say would happen if you made me take it?" His deep voice in her ear made her clit throb.

Wa'leek was in tune with his woman's body, his hand traveled down to her mounting passion and his finger tenderly slid back and forth over her hardening button of pleasure. "What the fuck did I say, Treebie?" he demanded an answer.

"No merc—" she mumbled.

"You want me to be nice to this pussy?" He teased, hitting her walls hard and precisely.

"Baby, please," she begged.

Her submission to his power bought her some time. Wa'leek pulled out and ran his hands up and down her back then bent behind her, gripping her ass in his palms he brought the pussy to his mouth and justified why she called him Daddy.

Treebie's cries went from pleas of mercy to moans of pure pleasure.

"Oh, my god Wah, do that shit Daddy," she cried out as she released from the depths of her soul.

Wa'leek rubbed his lips in her sweetness as she coated his tongue with liquid desire. Rising to his feet he slid back in and slow stroked her, enjoying her muscle play until he released deep inside her core.

After washing each other up and sharing tender kisses and firm touches, they stepped out of the shower, dried off, and climbed naked between the sheets. Wa'leek held her in his arms until she was fast asleep then it was beast time. Slowly he slid his arm from under her head and eased out of the bed, got dressed and was on the hunt again.

It took Wa'leek a day to locate who he was looking for but once he locked in on him he was like a GPS. As the sun settled behind the clouds and the whole city darkened, Wa'leek parked strategically so that he could keep Wolfman clearly in his sights. He noted that Chino appeared to have taken Nitti's place protecting the boss, but since Wa'leek was an equal opportunity killah it didn't even matter. This was Wa'leek's hour; he called it the hour of mayhem and confusion. The hour that made boys into men and changed the hearts of the righteous into soulless pits to fill with deceit and treason.

Reaching for his cell phone, he placed a call to Riz.

"Yeah, I got them niggas in my scope what's the verdict,"

"Nothing yet, let them niggas breathe but make sure it's short breaths."

"Got you," Wa'leek said as he watched Wolfman and Chino exit the restaurant, get into Wolfman's Benz and pull off. Wa'leek followed the two men until he knew where at least one of them rested their head then he posted up in a spot out of sight so he could begin putting together a schedule of how these niggas moved. It was hunting season and he was going to stalk his prey until they bit his bait and their head was mounted on his wall.

Wolfman had made the biggest mistake of his life when he had fucked over Riz and the only payment accepted was his life.

Chapter 17
Cold as Ice

Treebie always slept with one eye open even when they both appeared shut tight, so she had been aware when Wa'leek slid out of bed with her in the early morning hours. She had called him later in the day to keep track of him because Wa'leek's ass moved like a phantom. Her concern was that he might come home at the right time and see the wrong thing. Her heart pounded as she and her bitches prepared to move out.

Bayonna walked over to the iPod station in Treebie's basement and put her iPhone 5 on it and hit that *How I'm Raised* by Ace Hood. She stood still with her eyes closed nodding her head to the beat, when it got to her favorite part she grabbed her gun and sung along.

"I chase that money every day I wake. Though I keep my pistol on me yah, yah. And I just won't stop until my family straight. That's just how I was raised."

She turned in Treebie and Lissha's direction and watched as they loaded their guns and passed a blunt back and forth. Her heart began to ache as her eyes settled on the empty chair where Donella once sat. The small twinge quickly turned into anger then rage. Her hand trembled around the handle of her Glock as she fought back tears and the urge to blow the back of Treebie's head off.

"What's up, Bay?" Lissha asked, noticing the flare of her nostrils and the whites of her eyes turning red and glossy.

Bayonna blinked back the tears and took a deep breath. "I'm good. Just getting into character," she said then moved to Lissha's side and took the blunt from her hand.

Treebie snatched the bottle of 1800 by the neck and took it to the head. Looking up into Bayonna's face she gave her a hard stare that was more like a warning. Breaking the gaze she looked at Lissha and spoke clearly. "We gotta be on point tonight. Them niggas ain't 'bout no bullshit. They gonna be on their 'put a nigga down' game. We need to move like it's four instead of three."

"I know what needs to be done," Lissha asserted, taking the bottle to her mouth then slamming it down on the table. She then picked up her contacts and placed them in her eyes. "It's Blood Money bitches, let's do it."

"Indeed," Treebie chimed, placing her contacts in then pulling her mask around her face.

Bayonna tucked her anger away as she too placed the contacts in and put her mask firmly around her face. She knew very well that she could not make this move with any hatred in her heart for the women whose hands she had to place her life in. If nothing else she understood that hesitation could be the death of them all.

As they proceeded out the door, Treebie quickly glanced up and down the street for any sign of Wa'leek's return. She didn't even want to think about what she would do if he popped up right now. Pushing that thought from her mind she climbed in the car and they backed out of the driveway and drove off. The car was silent as they focused on the job they were about to pull.

They drove down on Kinsman and parked a few houses down from their intended target. The night wind whistled outside the car as they waited patiently for the nigga to show up. Minutes turned into to an hour and just when they were about to give up on the lick, a car turned onto the street and drove pass them.

Lissha ducked down in the driver's seat, Treebie was on her right and Bayonna sat in the back seat getting into murder mode. They all peeked over the dashboard watching Bolo park in the driveway then move towards the house. He was carrying two big black duffle bags and quick stepping while looking in all directions.

When he was in the door they saw the porch light flicker twice then a car that was parked a half block in the opposite direction pulled off. They all got lower behind the tinted windows as the black Chevy Impala drove slowly pass them.

Once the tail lights were out of sight, Lissha picked up her cell phone and summoned her accomplices. Within thirty minutes Jocelyn, Che Che and Brielle arrived in a cherry red Infiniti. They parked in the driveway behind Bolo's ride and strutted up the walkway, weaves swaying, heels clacking and asses bouncing. When they got on the porch Jocelyn knocked on the door and waited. Seconds later the door opened and Bolo stepped out slightly with a slick smile on his black face.

When the last woman was inside, Treebie looked down at her watch, they were giving them thirty minutes to get them niggas relaxed and comfy.

Bayonna sat in the back seat getting her thoughts right as she battled with visions of Donella. Lissha tapped her feet to the beat of murder that played strong in her mind while Treebie pulled on a pair of biking gloves.

Thirty minutes on the dot they checked their guns looked around in all directions and jumped out moving stealth close and low. Slowly they slipped down the side of the house headed to the back door. As soon as they got to the back yard a dog in the next yard went off sending alarm through the neighborhood.

"Shit," Lissha cursed under her breath.

They stood frozen in place as a light came on in the house next door. The curtain opened and an old woman darted her eyes around the darkness. When she was satisfied that nothing was amidst she yelled out for the dog to hush but he continued to bark and scratch at the wooden fence.

"I'ma shoot the muthafucka," Treebie whispered as she raised her gun ready to blast. The silencer that was attached would muffle the sound.

"Hold up," Lissha said, grabbing her arm.

Just as Treebie was ready to squeeze the old lady came out her back door and pulled the dog inside. "Hush all that fuss dog," she gripped as the door slammed shut.

Inside the house that they were targeting Bolo had heard the commotion. "Why that bitch ass dog acting up? Go check that out Murph," he said as Jocelyn gave him sloppy head.

"Nah nigga, I wouldn't move if I could," Murph replied as Che Che rode his dick slowly while nibbling his earlobe and whispering something hot and nasty in his ear.

"Nah, we good plus he quiet now," Trigga slurred as he also enjoyed some neck action. Brielle's jaw grip had a nigga shaking his leg.

The dimly lit living room was in full orgy mode.

Treebie, Bayonna and Lissha moved slowly up the steps. Treebie turned the door knob and the door opened effortlessly. She eased the door open enough to peek through the kitchen to the living room. The light from the television caused shadows to form in different parts of the room. Treebie carefully stepped inside the door with Donella close behind and Lissha taking up the rear. They moved up behind the couch with guns pointed directly at the back of Murph and Trigga's heads.

Bolo had his head back on the verge of busting all over Jocelyn's tonsils. When he brought his head forward to grab her hair he saw black hoods and red eyes.

"What the fuck?" he shrieked as panic accompanied his nut.

"Make the wrong move nigga so I can circumcise that little muthafucka for you," Treebie barked at Bolo, lowering her gun.

Murph and Trigga froze in place.

"Y'all punk muthafuckas put your hands up where I can see 'em," Bayonna ordered. Both men raised the arms above their heads. Bayonna pointed her banger at one of the girls and said, "You, raise up off that dick bitch."

The girl did as she was told and Bayonna turned to her friends and barked, "And you two hos get the dick out your mouths and get over in that corner."

The girls moved with the quickness as the stared at the gun in her hand. Bayonna stepped over to Trigga and put her heat right on his forehead.

"What the fuck is this about?" Murph asked with a little too much bass in his voice as his eyes settled on the handle of the sawed off shot gun that slightly stuck out of the cushion under Bolo.

"Shut the fuck up," Lissha smacked him across his head.

"You ain't gotta do all that," Bolo barked.

"You're right," Lissha said then blew the back of Murph's head off, spraying his blood all over Trigga.

Over in the corner, the three females gripped each other tight as they looked on in fear.

"Now let's start this shit over," Lissha enforced. "You muthafuckas ain't in charge. So any request will be denied. Next, I need those two bags your pussy asses walked in here with."

"We aint got shit fo you bruh," Bolo spat, giving Lissha a hard glare.

"You hear this nigga?" Lissha's distorted voice boomed in Treebie's direction.

"Yeah, I heard him but his words don't mean shit." Treebie blasted him in the ankle damn near severing his foot from his leg.

"Ahhh!" Bolo yelped.

"How is your memory working for you now?" she taunted.

Bolo bent over, clutched his ankle and writhed in pain as blood seeped through his fingers. When he came up his hand shot under the cushion pulling the gun from under his seat.

"Fuck you niggas," he belted and squeezed off several errant shots in Treebie's direction.

As bullets whizzed past her head, Treebie reacted like the boss bitch that she was to the core. She ignored the threat to her life and sent some heat right back at Bolo. Her aim was better than his and two shots caught him high in the shoulder causing him to drop his tool. His arm fell limply to his side and he grimaced in pain.

Treebie quickly spun her whistle towards Trigga and blasted him in the stomach. *Boc! Boc!* "Y'all bitch niggas think this is a game?" she chortled. Through the voice distorter she sounded like the grim reaper, and tonight she was exactly that.

Trigga doubled over and whimpered out a plea for mercy. Bayonna gritted and filled him with hollows. "Didn't we tell y'all all request would be denied?" she spat mercilessly.

Lissha held her gun on a dying Trigga in case he wanted to act up on his way out.

Jocelyn vomited all over the wall and floor next to them causing Che Che and Brielle to crawl to an opposite corner.

"Y'all muthafuckas better up those duffel bags," Lissha barked.

"It's in the upstairs bedroom on the right," Brielle yelled covering her head as tears ran from her eyes. When she agreed to set up this lick she hadn't expected anyone to be killed.

Across the room Trigga took labored breaths as his lungs filled with blood. Realizing that he wasn't getting any mercy and that his life was seeping out through his fingertips he summoned up some testosterone. "Fuck y'all bitch ass niggas," he mumbled as blood bubbles formed on his lips.

"No, nigga, fuck you," Bayonna corrected right before she blew his forehead all over the coffee table and TV screen.

"Oh, my god!" cried Jocelyn when a clump of brain matter landed by her foot. Horrified, she squeezed her eyes shut and scooted away from the gory evidence of cold blooded murder. Never had she expected shit to go down like this. It was supposed to be a jack move not homicides. A panic attack seized her and she let out a shrill cry.

Treebie leveled the gun down at her. "Bitch shut the fuck up! Che Che go run me those bags," she ordered.

Che Che jumped up and took the steps two at a time. Lissha listened hard as a few bumps and bangs resonated through the ceiling. When they looked up Che Che was dragging the big black duffle bags down the stairs.

Che Che stood behind Bolo's dead body as her eyes settled on the grotesque figures that were slumped around the living room.

"You two hos get up," Treebie commanded, aiming her banger at them.

"These bitches shaking like jello. You know what this is. And you know Blood Money only leaves one witness. You decide," Lissha said, playing with the last bit of sanity they had left.

"Please I don't want to die. We did just as Spank asked. You got what you wanted," Brielle cried out for mercy.

"I don't do begging bitches," Treebie announced as she put one between Brielle's eyes sending her crashing into the wall. She slid down slowly, landing into the pile of blood and vomit that lay at her feet. Without hesitation Treebie turned and blew a hole in Che Che's the chest.

"Why?" Che Che cried, grabbing her chest and collapsing to her knees.

"Because I can, trick ass bitch," Treebie spat.

Che Che's eyes glossed over and she fell face forward. Her head smacked the floor and she toppled over on her side.

Lissha grabbed the bags and turned to the back door. Bayonna held her position next to Treebie as Jocelyn stood half-dressed and trembling staring back at them.

"You like sucking dick for money?" Treebie asked

"No," Jocelyn answered with her eyes fixed on Treebie's cold steel.

"Yes you do bitch go ahead and get some," she pointed at Bolo's body. "Step to your business ho."

Jocelyn cried harder as she went to kneel in front of Bolo's dead body. "Suck it bitch," Treebie yelled.

Jocelyn took his flaccid penis into her hand, her stomach turned at the sight of blood and semen that covered his shaft. She tightened her eyes, lowered her head, and began to suck.

I would rather die, thought Treebie. "Bitch, you nasty," she derided her.

Bayonna was tired of Treebie toying with the girl. She reached in her pocket and pulled out a five dollar bill walked over to Bolo and rubbed it in his blood. "Open your mouth and let's get this over with," she ordered Jocelyn.

"Please don't," the girl pleaded.

"Open your mouth." This time Bayonna spat each word singularly but with more force. Jocelyn's lips slowly parted. Bayonna stuck the money in the terrified girl's mouth and took a step back.

Treebie stepped forward placed the tip of her gun in the center of Jocelyn's heart and made sure that it never beat again.This time they couldn't leave one behind because the girls knew their true identity.

As they left out of the house, Bayonna stopped and looked back for Donella. With tears welling up behind her contacts Bayonna realized that her girl was not coming because she was already gone.

Chapter 18
Heating Up

JuJu could tell from the tone of Bayonna's voice that something was bothering her but when he asked what was wrong she told him that everything was gucci.

"A'ight, lil' mama, just make sure you have your game face on when I come through to scoop you up, we gotta make that trip up top again," he informed her.

"Yeah, I know," she confirmed. "I spoke with Kiam earlier so get your face out of whatever little ratchet bitch's pussy you have it in and let's get on the road. Okay lil' daddy?" she teased.

"Whatever shorty," he shot back. "You got life fucked up. Ain't nare bitch ever got none of this head. Straight up."

"Mm hmm," Bay giggled, thinking that she would turn his young ass out. "Just get over here and don't have me waiting all damn day. Handle your business playa." She hung the phone up and began counting.

By the time she reached four her phone lit up. "House of beauty. This is Cutie," she answered playfully.

JuJu wasn't amused. "Don't be hanging no phones up on me," he chastised.

Bayonna folded her legs up under her on the bed and giggled at his remark. "I'm sorry lil' daddy," she cooed. "Am I going to get a spanking?"

"Stop playing and have your ass ready when I get there."

This time it was JuJu who hung up.

He tossed his phone down on the console between the seats and shook his head. Isaiah who was in the passenger seat laughed. "Whoever shorty is she got you open," he said.

"Picture that," JuJu denied. "Money over bitches."

"Yeah, in a rap song but lil' mama got you sprung. Nigga you was blushing like a bitch."

In the back seat Isaac was cracking up.

"Fuck y'all. This shit is official," JuJu boasted as he steered the whip down the block.

He parked outside of one of their trap houses on 114th and Miles Road and waited for the twins to go in and collect the money and return. A few dudes on their squad didn't like the fact that Isaiah and his brother had ascended past them so quickly in terms of rank but to question it would've gotten them a brand new suit.

JuJu kept his eyes trained on the block until his fam returned with the dough. They made a few more stops collecting and making sure that business was on point, then JuJu dropped his people off at their new apartment out in Bedford Heights and headed over to pick up Bayonna.

As he waited for her to come out to the car, he dreaded having to make this trip with her again.

As soon as JuJu and Bayonna arrived in New York, they went straight to Riz's apartment made the pickup then got on the road to head back. Again the interaction with Bayonna and Riz left him heated.

JuJu drove in silence as Bayonna bopped and crunched on spicy Doritos. He looked over at her with a wicked glare. He knew that she was only playing the role but to know that a woman would compromise her body like that bothered him. She seemed intelligent and was damn sure beautiful which made him wonder what could have happened to get her caught up in the game.

Bayonna's voice interrupted his thoughts. "JuJu I'm tired. We need to stop," she said, stifling a yawn with her hand.

"Go to sleep I'm good."

"No I want to take a shower and lay down," she pouted.

"You can do that when we get back." He kept his eyes focused on the road.

Bayonna sighed, crumpled up her bag, pulled her legs up in the seat and turned her back to him.

JuJu drove on for about an hour simply ignoring her. Bayonna finally fell asleep but her head kept bobbing and almost hitting the window. When he saw how uncomfortable she looked, he got off on the first exit that advertised a hotel.

Bayonna didn't open her eyes until JuJu was walking out of the registration office. When he hopped in the driver's side she lit up. "You're so sweet."

"No I'm not. We gonna chill for a few hours then we back on the road."

"Can I have something to eat first Father?" she asked with her hands together like she was begging.

JuJu looked over at her with his mouth tight. "Don't play with me."

Bayonna poked her bottom lip out. "Pleeeese."

JuJu had to chuckle on the inside because she was so silly.

He looked to the left and spotted Micky D's. "You can have something from the dollar menu." He shot back.

"Oh shit, can I get a toy too?"

"Can you get a toy?"

"Yeah, you can give me the one that comes in your kid's meal," she teased.

"Yo' ass ain't funny."

"No?" she begged to differ. She looked at him with childish playfulness dancing in her eyes then began poking her fingers in his side.

"Stop, shorty," he said as he tried to keep her fingers from moving up and down his side.

"Oh, you talking shit and you ticklish?" Now she was going in with both hands.

"Stop." JuJu slightly yelled through his laughter and grabbed ahold of her wrists.

Bayonna smiled at how cute he looked when he was laughing. "See laughter doesn't hurt that much."

"I wasn't laughing." He threw his mean mug back on.

"Whatever, Mr. Crabby."

They pulled up to the drive-thru and JuJu ordered three Big Macs, a large fry and a strawberry milk shake. "Damn where you putting all that?" Bayonna asked as she slid her hand under his shirt and rubbed up and down his abs.

"Keep putting your hand over here I'ma give you something to touch," he warned

Bayonna twisted her lips. She started to say something else but the cashier asked if there was anything else they wanted.

Bayonna leaned over, purposely damn near climbing in JuJu's lap. "Let me have two fish and cheese and a large fry, a cheese burger, a medium coke, three cookies and a vanilla ice cream cone."

JuJu put his head to the side and looked at the bump in her jeans. His mouth watered as he pictured himself standing behind all that ass making her reach and grab. Instinctively his hands did what his mind entertained. He reached up and smacked her ass. "Why you got all of this in my face?"

"Keep it up and you're going to be putting more than food in your mouth," she said as she crawled back to her seat.

JuJu just gave her a slight smile.

When they pulled up to the window the girl had her eyes all over them trying to see who the freaky couple was that boomed through the order box. Passing them the food she kept smiling at JuJu.

"I think old girl got a crush on you, try to get us some free shit," Bayonna joked.

"She might be smiling at *you*."

"Well, shit, let me smile back so I can get three more cookies." Bayonna sat up. "Thank you sweetie." She threw on a smile as she reached for her ice cream cone.

JuJu burst out laughing. "You a fool."

"I don't do pussy but I'll smile my ass into an extra meal any day." Bayonna sat back, licking her ice cream as he drove away.

Bayonna sat across from JuJu at the hotel's table tearing her food up. JuJu was staring at her biting into that fish like she hadn't ate all day. "That shit stink, yo," he said, wrinkling up his nose.

"You don't eat fish?" she asked, licking the tartar sauce.

"Hell no. Why girls always eating food that make their breath stink?"

"I have something to fix my breath but what do you have to fix your grumpy ass attitude?" She sucked on her straw while looking at him.

"Yo tongue too slick."

"You know you love it," she teased.

"You don't want nothin' from over here," he spat back.

"What I would give you, you can't handle," she continued to sip her drink.

Seeing that things were going in the wrong direction, JuJu quickly deaded it. "I thought you were sleepy?" he asked, getting up and throwing his trash away.

"I thought so," she teased as she got up and collected her empty containers.

JuJu went to the bathroom and hopped in the shower and changed his clothes. When he came out he grabbed a pillow and posted up in one chair and propped his feet up on the other. He watched Bayonna move around getting herself together then she disappeared into the bathroom. He grabbed the remote and flipped the channels.

Bayonna came out the bathroom smelling like something edible. JuJu's senses heightened as her perfume rose in his nostrils. His eyes followed her as she moved from one spot to the next when she bent over to go in her bag. He could see her leopard print G-string right through her white stretch pants. He grabbed his dick to keep it calm as his fantasies again took over.

Bayonna stood up combing her hair then glossed her lips and moved to the bed. "Why you in the chair?"

"Don't worry about me I'm good."

"I won't bite you boy. You can lay at the bottom and I'll lay up here. You gotta drive you need to get some rest."

JuJu thought about it for a minute then he gave in. "You better not try nothing, my mother taught me about good touch versus bad touch," he said, placing his pillow on the bed and lying on his stomach.

"You act like I'm a rapist or something," she giggled.

"Stay on your side," he said, tucking the pillow under his head and closing his eyes.

"JuJu?"

"What, Bayonna," he answered with a slight attitude

"Can you tell me a bed time story?"

"Go yo ass to sleep before you get fucked up, how's that?"

"I love you, too," she said then tucked the pillow under her head and closed her eyes.

Before they knew it the sun was piercing through the openings in the curtain. Bayonna opened her eyes and looked over at JuJu who as stretched out. He had her isolated to a small section of the top of the bed while he dominated the rest.

"How this nigga gonna tell me to stay on my side when he had me sleeping on top of the head board." She mumbled then slid out the bed and moved to the bathroom. When she returned he was on his back lightly snoring like he was at home. She tiptoed to the bed and eased into it. Once she was in the standing position, she began jumping up and down snatching him from his dreams.

"Wake up sleeping beauty," she sang as she caused him to bounce all over the bed.

"What the fuck?" he woke up pissed off. "Get yo ass down."

"Nope."

JuJu reached up and grabbed her by the waist and pulled her down by his side. Since she was in a playing mode he decided to humor her. Bayonna laughed and giggled as he began tickling her. She squirmed and kicked as he showed no mercy.

"You gonna stop playing?"

"Yes." she cried out, trying to catch her breath.

JuJu let her go and got off of the bed. But Bayonna wasn't done. She hopped up and ran over and jumped on his back.

Her playful spirit brought out things in JuJu that his gangsta had suppressed. They tussled around for about fifteen minutes then fell on the bed laughing and out of breath.

"See, I told you laughter is fun."

"Maybe," JuJu conceded as he sat up. "We gotta go."

"Okay," she said with a little disappointment in her voice. "But you gotta promise to have more fun," she put her pinky finger out.

JuJu looked at her with the side eye. Bayonna raised her eyebrows and extended her arm.

"What are we five years old?" he asked as he extended his pinky.

Bayonna hooked his pinky with hers as she looked at the scare that was left behind from that night. A little regret settled in her chest, she brought his hand to her mouth and kissed it. "See, all better." She gave him that irresistible smile.

"You a'ight shorty," JuJu said as he locked eyes with her.

124

"Don't try to butter me up, I'm still eating in your car," she joked to break up the tension between them.

"Let's go, lil' mama."

They gathered their things and hit the road. Pulling up to Bayonna's house, they both felt a small amount of remorse not wanting to see the trip come to an end.

Bayonna grabbed her things and jumped out the Rover and headed inside. "See you soon," JuJu yelled out.

"Remember our promise." She held up her pinky.

JuJu just smiled. When she was safely inside he dropped the smile from his face and went into street mode. The streets was waiting for that Schizophrenic and he had bricks on deck.

Ca$h & NeNe Capri

Chapter 19
Trepidation

DeMarcus sat the phone down on the bar top in his den and let out a long frustrated sigh. The news from his runners wasn't good, trap money was coming in slower than ever and he knew exactly why. Kiam was dropping that Schizophrenic on the blocks with a potency and at a price that he couldn't compete with. Niggas on Kiam's team were eating so good several of DeMarcus' workers had defected over to his camp and that wasn't the half of it.

To make matters worse, sales at the car dealerships were at an all-time low causing DeMarcus' money to look real funny. He glanced at himself in the mirror behind the bar and saw a face that showed a whole lot of stress on it ever since Kiam had touched down. He wished like fuck that the hit that Wolfman had put out on the nigga had been successful. *No Kiam. No problems,* he concluded. But he knew that getting at Kiam could be hazardous to a nigga's health.

Wolfman was pressing him to set Kiam up but DeMarcus damn near shitted in his pants every time the subject came up. He didn't even want to think about what the consequences would be if he tried and failed. Something had to be done though, and he had multiple reasons for wanting to see Kiam lifeless.

As he stood there trying to pump his nuts up to participate in some shit that would get him killed, DeMarcus poured himself a stiff drink. His cell phone rung with a call from Chino asking him if he was coming to the club tonight to help welcome Wolfman's girl, Xyna, home from prison.

"Yeah, I'm getting ready to leave in a few," said DeMarcus as he headed upstairs to check on Daphne.

Daphne sat on the edge of the bed and battled with her demons. Her false claims had caused the death of an innocent woman and now she had some vicious females on her ass. And if Kiam ever found out her role in feeding him bogus information he would put a bullet in her without hesitation.

As she slid into her jeans, her hands began to tremble from fear and anxiety. She hadn't been out the house much lately because she could sense that death was hiding in the shadows ready to pounce on her the moment she walked out the door. She was totally against going out with DeMarcus to this party but she knew she had to leave the house sometime and if she rejected his offer he would think that it was about Xyna.

It was that bitch too but not really.

"Damn, you ain't dressed yet?" he remarked, walking into the room with a full glass of Jack Daniels and the phone plastered to his ear. He was dressed in crisp dark blue jeans, a dark grey button down and a pair of dark grey Gianni Monk-Strap Loafers.

"I'll be ready in a minute," she replied dryly as she moved to the closet to grab her sweater.

DeMarcus looked at her strangely so she quickly faked a smile to throw him off. "You a'ight?" he asked accusatorily.

"Yes, baby, I'm fine." Her tone was deceptively sweet. DeMarcus swallowed it like a candy morsel.

As Daphne pulled the sweater over her head, she thought about how fucked up her life was. She had never planned to end up in the bed of a punk ass underling, she had been aiming for the boss. But that's what happens when you fail to make niggas respect you.

In a moment of impulsiveness and seeking revenge on Wolfman for his infidelities, she had fucked Xyna's brother. When it came out Wolfman discarded her like yesterday's fashion. It hadn't mattered that he had been running up in different bitches behind her back, when it came to shit like that niggas had double standards.

Xyna had been Daphne's bestie but it turned out that she was the ho that had ran and told that. Afterwards she became the bitch in Wolfman's life that Daphne had sought to become. And now that she had done a bid for the nigga she had cemented her position.

Daphne almost choked on the envy that rose up in her throat. She didn't know if she would be able to stomach seeing the next bitch sitting on her throne. That had been the motivation behind all of her recent treachery. To be honest she really just wanted to get enough money to carry out her revenge but instead she had dug a deeper grave for herself. Now time was on her ass and ready to be the foot that would push her into the shallow hole.

She put on her brown Fendi riding boots and jacket to match and fluffed out her curls. She applied a little more lipstick and was ready to go.

When she hopped in the car DeMarcus seemed to be on cloud nine. This was his type of shit—show up and show off.

Daphne just shook her head.

"Don't kill my fucking buzz," he said as he pulled out of the driveway.

"Ain't nobody trying to kill your buzz. I told you I ain't feeling going out tonight," she stated as she fastened her seatbelt.

"Well cheer the fuck up. I need you to be smiling on my side tonight. Fuck Wolfman and his bitch; you ended up with the prize."

"I'm not thinking about them, baby," she half lied as she cut her eyes over at him with contempt in her heart wishing she could erase his nothing ass from the pages of her life.

Wa'leek sat comfortably in his rented black Mercedes Benz GL Class peeping all who entered the back door of club. When he saw DeMarcus pull up and walk inside with Daphne on his arm he deaded his engine and got out. He moved swiftly across the street wearing his stiff blue jeans, black V-neck t-shirt, fresh Timbs and black leather jacket. Approaching the back door he reached into his back and secured his heat.

Knocking on the door, adrenaline coursed through his body. He was on the hunt for answers and was prepared to get them any way possible.

The door eased open and a smirk came on Chino's face. It had been a while since he'd seen Wa'leek and he couldn't say it was a pleasure to see him now. The last time Wa'leek graced the city with his presence blood poured into the street at an alarming rate.

"What's up, Wah?" spoke Chino, gangsta to gangsta. He extended his hand and brought Wa'leek in for a friendly embrace.

"You know me, just trying to have a little fun while I'm in your great city," Wa'leek stated as he pulled back giving him a stern look.

Chino gave him a suspicious eye. "Don't have too much fun. I know you want to make it home safely."

"Don't worry about me, you better start worrying about some other muthafuckas. I'm good," he returned, looking Chino in the eye giving him the silent warning to back the fuck up.

Wa'leek knew all about Wolfman's new enforcer's get-down but he wasn't fazed.

Chino threw his hands up in a slight surrender, moved back and watched as Wa'leek headed to the bar and ordered himself a drink.

After Wa'leek had a drink in hand, he made his way upstairs and stood watching the room trying to pinpoint his mark. His eyes beamed in on the roped off VIP section where DeMarcus was just now joining Wolfman's party. They were over there poppin' bottles and stunting like there was peace in the streets.

Wa'leek took a seat at a table and waited patiently for an opportunity to pounce.

"What's up, my nigga?" DeMarcus shouted over the music as he walked up to where Wolfman was sitting and extended his fist. "The king of the muthafuckin' city," he jeffed.

Wolfman stroked his thick beard, smiled, and touched fist with De-Marcus even though he didn't respect his punk ass. "What's good? I'm glad y'all could come out and join us." His natural deep bass boomed. He looked from DeMarcus to Daphne and smirked, she had just sucked his dick and swallowed yesterday.

Daphne looked down at him with a fake smile plastered on her face and fought back the impulse to claw the skin off the bitch's mug sitting next to him.

"Welcome home, Xyna. I see the time was good to you," offered De-Marcus.

Xyna was looking radiant, like she had just stepped out of a photo shoot instead of out of prison. She was not the typical hood rat. She was half black and half white which gave her that high yellow olive tan, and she had long brown wavy hair that she wore straight and parted down the middle. She stood at 6'1 and her rail thin frame was accented with a high booty and breasts that looked like they were hand sculpted by God on one of His most creative days. The only time she smiled was when Wolfman occasionally whispered in her ear; other than that she wore a seriousness on her face that read *I wish a bitch would.*

DeMarcus tossed so many compliments her way he might as well have dropped to his knees and ran his tongue up the crack of her ass. Beside him Daphne bristled.

Xyna felt the heat coming off of her former bestie but she was not worried about little Miss Daphne. She could wipe the floor with that trick without even spilling her drink. She looked up at DeMarcus and smiled. "Thank you, my man took good care of me while I was away." She leaned over and slid her tongue in Wolfman's mouth. He grabbed the back of her head and tongued her down.

When they broke their lip lock, DeMarcus and Daphne joined them and other members of Wolfman's crew in the large booth. As the men talked loud and boisterously Daphne and Xyna eyed each other with undisguised contempt.

But while Daphne was all in her feelings about some backstabbing shit, outside of VIP a bitch much more dangerous than Xyna was seconds away from breathing up her ass.

Chapter 20
A Fatal Mistake

Bayonna stood across the room peeping Wolfman and his crew's whole playing card, them niggas were sloppy. It was just a matter of time before all of their asses would be laying in polyester and pine. What really stirred her fire was the chic who was the center of attention. *When did that bitch touch down?* she wondered, recognizing Xyna immediately.

The cutthroat ass trick sat on her perch like a trophy on a shelf and Wolfman strutted around like a proud peacock.

When Bayonna's eyes settled on Daphne she saw that the girl had a pain and anger in her face that was borderline suicidal. She tried to mask it but every time Wolfman touched Xyna, Bayonna could see Daphne cringe. She didn't know what the beef was about but she knew that whatever it was paled in comparison to the problem Daphne was about to have out of her.

Bayonna watched and waited; she just needed a small window of opportunity to get Daphne away from the herd and then she would get out of her what Kiam obviously couldn't. The funny thing about the hunt was even the hunter could become the prey, each one of them had a stronger and more evil eye on the other and the race was on to see who got to who first.

Wa'leek shooed one thirsty bitch after another away as he bid his time and waited for the perfect opportunity to make his move. He was still nursing the same drink, keeping a hawk's eye on Wolfman's whole squad. Finally he saw DeMarcus and his girl get up and drift away from the entourage and walk over to the main bar. Now was the time to step to the nigga and apply some pressure. *Attack the chain by going after the weakest link*

DeMarcus jumped when he felt the strong hand clamp down on his shoulder. He turned and looked up.

"Dismiss this bitch so I can holla at you real quick." Wa'leek said as he brought his glass to his mouth.

"Excuse you?" Daphne sat up looking at him with an evil glare.

"Bitch, you betta save all that attitude for one of these fag ass niggas, 'cause I'm good. Hurry up and get the fuck outta here." Wa'leek took a seat shooting daggers through those icy grey eyes.

Before she could say anything else DeMarcus put his hand on her leg and whispered something in her ear. She looked at him and shook her head. Sucking her teeth she slid past DeMarcus and stormed to the bathroom.

DeMarcus returned his attention to Wa'leek. "I never expected to see you back in Ohio," he said with a hint of surprise in his voice. "And I see you haven't changed one bit, you're still disrespectful as hell."

"Yeah, and I see you haven't grown any balls since I last saw you," Wa'leek jeered.

"Why are you here?" DeMarcus asked as sweat formed in the pit of his arms.

"Why you hiding behind that nigga Wolfman when he's the one that had your grandmother killed?" he asked, holding eye contact.

"I'm just tryna eat."

Wa'leek looked at him like he wanted to slap the fuck out of his bitch ass. "Nigga you're pitiful. You might as well put on a muhfuckin' thong and learn how to make it twerp," he said with distaste.

DeMarcus dropped his head.

Wa'leek stood there scouring at him. There was nothing that he despised more than a pussy ass nigga. "Fuck you scared of another man for? You got your weight up now, grow some balls and avenge that shit."

"I'ma handle my business," claimed DeMarcus, but even to his own ears it sounded empty.

Wa'leek shook his head. "I hear your people is with Big Zo. Why don't you rock with them?" He continued to try to sew dissension as a means to divide and conquer.

DeMarcus looked at him curiously. "I thought you were against Big Zo?" He sat back feeling safe surrounded by witnesses.

"I'm my own man. I don't give a fuck 'bout none of them niggas. But I see you let Kiam come home and fuck you in the ass with Big Zo's dick. How's that working out for you? Maybe I should have brought you some Vaseline." Wa'leek chuckled. "At any rate you owe me. And I'm going to be on your ass until you pay me what you owe."

"Owe you for what?"

134

"For keeping my mouth closed tight about your little secret. In return I need you to feed me any upfront info you have on Wolfman's moves. Also, I need for you to find out who those Blood Money niggas are affiliated with. And *no* is not an option."

DeMarcus drew back. What Wa'leek was asking him to do was dangerous to even think about. Wolfman dealt with treason ruthlessly and Blood Money's rep was warning enough for him to stay out of their lane. He shook his head no. "You know I'm not no snitch."

"I don't give a fuck what title you give yourself. I'ma give you two weeks to bring me back some answers and if I don't hear from you I'ma pay your daddy, Kiam, a visit. I think he will love my honesty."

DeMarcus sat looking at Wa'leek like he was the devil. "I need more time than that," he said as his eyes darted around making sure the wrong set of ears wasn't passing by.

"Two weeks, not a day longer," Wa'leek repeated. "I'll stop by your car lot."

All of the color drained from DeMarcus' face.

Wa'leek looked up and saw Wolfman and a few of his boys headed past them. He leaned his elbows on the bar counter and ducked down out of sight. Before he eased on he gave DeMarcus a final warning. "Just remember muthafucka your bitch ass is in this shit deep. You think Kiam is on your ass you ain't seen shit yet. Get me the information I need or I'ma make the rest of your days a living hell."

Wa'leek stood watching Wolfman until he returned back in VIP before he moved to the door.

DeMarcus rested his head on his hands as fear filled his chest. Every way he turned a muthafucka was breathing on the back of his neck. Maybe it was time that he manned up, he thought as he ordered a drink and waited for Daphne to return.

Daphne stood at the sink with the water on blast fumbling through her clutch. She was so angry at DeMarcus that her hands shook and she dropped her lipstick into the sink. Quickly she fished it out and dried it off then began applying a fresh coat. There was no way she was remaining with his weak ass another day.

At the sink next to her two noticeably drunk women stood side by side chatting about which nigga they wanted to leave with. Their silly banter almost made Daphne throw up. And to think she had been just like them. Ugh!

She wondered which one of the chics was a snake like Xyna, willing to tell all of her girl's dirty little secrets in order to steal her man. The friends ended their conversation with a high five and left out to pursue a come up. The door closed behind them and Daphne dabbed a speck of lint that was on the corner of her mouth. Her eyes bulged when she saw the reflection behind her in the mirror.

"You're a hard woman to catch up with," said Bayonna, her voice had the effect of fingernails scrapping across a glass window.

Daphne shuddered then quickly regained her poise. "I don't know why. I ain't got no reason to hide," she said, turning to face her in an effort to not miss anything that was coming her way.

"I can see right through you. Who made you set up Donella?" Bayonna asked, staring her in the eye.

"I didn't set up anybody. You saw the evidence for yourself," she said, clutching her purse tightly under her arm.

"Bitch, don't play with me. You know good and got damn well that shit was bogus. My girl wasn't fucking with Gator like that and she would've never betrayed us to Wolfman. You cost an innocent woman her life. And I think the only exchange for such ratchetness would be your life in return," Bayonna responded ready to pull out and blast her right in her face.

"I told the truth." Daphne maintained.

Bayonna's hand went inside her bag and her lip curled up. "Now I'ma ask you for the last time who put you on my girl?" she hissed.

"Look, I don't know what you're talking about. I didn't lie on your girl. What can I say? Sometimes the truth hurts." She continued to stick to her story even though death was knocking on her door with both hands.

Bayonna knew the ho was lying, she bared her teeth and spat, "I wanted to have sympathy for you because I know that you are the piece of shit of the crew. You know, the bitch they pass like spliffs. But a grimy bitch like you deserves whatever is coming to you and I hope my hand is the one to serve it. How does it feel watching another bitch get all the glamour while you end up with fool's gold?" Bayonna hurled, trying to anger her into blurting out the truth.

"You don't know me," Daphne's voice trembled as the pain of Bayonna's words cut into her heart.

"I know you're on borrowed time and the longer you hide the bitch responsible for my sister's death, the more painful yours will be. That's a fuckin' promise."

Just as Daphne felt the urge to divulge a small piece of truth to save her soul, two girls fell through the door clawing, kicking and cursing at each other. "Bitch I saw you all up in my baby's daddy face. I'ma fuck yo thirsty ass up!" screamed one of the girls. She had a handful of the other girl's hair and was punching her in the face.

"Ho, let go of my hair!" cried the other. She reached up ripped the girl's shirt and her titties popped out.

A crowd spilled in behind them hooting, hollering, pushing and shoving to get a better view. "Beat that ho's ratchet ass!" someone yelled.

"Knee her in that stank pussy!"

Niggas was waving money over their heads tryna place bets on the fight. The two girls were breaking each other off. Daphne was pressed up against the sink while Bayonna was caught up between two stalls. Daphne used the opportunity to escape from Bayonna's grasp. She squirmed her way through a sea of bodies and dashed out of the bathroom.

Bayonna was in hot pursuit but a second crowd of drunken onlookers bum rushed through the door and she got swept back inside. "Dammit! Get the fuck out of my way!" she screamed at a half-drunk man who was blocking her path.

"Yeah, talk dirty to me," he slurred and pulled her into his arms.

She pushed away from him and whipped out her piece. "Fuck off of me nigga," she spat.

Old boy saw that big ass burner in her hand and he sobered up real quick. He threw his hands up in surrender and moved aside.

Bayonna slammed one in the chamber and held her gun chest high. "Make room muthafuckas," she bossed and the crowd moved like a bald bitch's hair line.

As soon as she realized Bayonna was no longer on her heels, Daphne headed straight for the stairs. Fuck DeMarcus, he would find a way home. Descending down the stairs in a hurry, she turned sideways to keep from brushing up against partygoers that were headed up. When she got to the bottom of the stairs she glanced over her shoulder to make sure that Bayonna wasn't behind her. Seeing that she wasn't, Daphne thanked her guardian angel and kept it moving.

"You leaving already?" Chino asked, lowering his eyes and licking his lips. "I was hoping to put something big and fat in your mouth tonight."

"Put it in your mama's ass." She pushed past him and flew out the door.

The nighttime air felt cold on her bare arms and for all she knew Bayonna was hot on her ass. Daphne wrapped her arms around herself and quickened her step. Again she glanced back over her shoulder. Not looking where she was going she bumped into someone and her purse fell to the ground. "Excuse me," she apologized as she bent to retrieve it.

"It's cool. Why are you running?"

The familiar voice caused Daphne's eyes to shoot up. "Ooh shit!" she muttered and slowly stood straight.

"What's up?"

Daphne didn't answer right away, she took off for the car. Her co-conspirator moved in step with her barely able to keep up. "What the fuck is you running for?" she asked, hurriedly catching up to Daphne.

Daphne was running out of breath and outta time. Panicking she turned and looked back towards the club's exit. "Your girl Bayonna is inside and the bitch cornered me off and started asking questions about who paid me to lie on Donella." The stress in her voice caused her to stutter.

This bitch will break, concluded the woman at her side as she coyly slid her hand inside her purse.

Bayonna searched the club for Daphne but the bitch had disappeared like smoke. She saw DeMarcus posted up at the bar entertaining a couple of rats, but his ho was nowhere around. On a hunch Bayonna decided to check outside.

She moved through a crowd that was standing by the dance floor and took the stairs in double time. Stepping out of her heels at the door she picked them up and hurried outside.

Three gunshots cackled from a distance, alerting Bayonna's senses. The sound of squealing tires on gravel came from the rear of the parking lot. Bayonna pulled out her tool and raced barefooted towards the sound. Looking up she saw just a glint of a car's taillights as it zoomed out of the rear exit.

Her eyes darted around in search of Daphne. Then her legs began to move and she weaved through parked cars, headed further towards the back. Bayonna moved low and careful as she tried to regain her breath. When she reached the well-lit area she saw a body sprawled on the ground several parking spaces away.

"Fuck! Fuck! Fuck!" Bayonna uttered as she re-quickened her step. She knew what she would find even before her intuition was confirmed.

She stood over Daphne as others began to run in their direction. "You dumb bitch," she sneered, looking down at her twisted form. Blood ran from a hole in the back of her head and two in the center of her back.

Bayonna shook her head but she felt no pity. *Karma is a heartless bitch and I bet her real name is Lissha or Treebie.*

She looked to the sky. "I'm going to find out which one it is Nella," she said then moved back as the crowd formed around her.

Chapter 21
Subtle Signs

In the days immediately following Daphne's murder, Bayonna didn't have time to figure out anything because she had to make another run with JuJu. Lissha left to go visit and report to Big Zo, leaving Kiam and Treebie alone to watch each other's backs. Though their relationship hadn't begun smoothly they had quietly earned each other's respect. Treebie knew that Kiam wasn't nothing nice and he acknowledged to himself, if not to her, that even though she didn't have a set of balls her gangsta was dick hard. Whatever retaliation Wolfman and them decided to send his way for the ongoing assaults on their teams, Kiam felt confident against it with Treebie by his side bustin' her gun. And if things got real hectic the Twins were always primed to put in that kinda work that left blood stains on the ground.

After being introduced to Isaiah and Isaac several weeks ago, Kiam had seen the proof of their sick murder game up close and personal. His mind flashed back to an incident a week ago.

Kiam and JuJu were coming out of a restaurant called the Shrimp Boat, headed back to the truck where the Twins waited. The nearly empty lot quickly became a small battle zone when two fools rolled up and hopped out of a car bustin' at them. Kiam dashed right and JuJu darted left, taking cover both of them snatched their whistles off their waists and rose to their feet with those toys going the fuck off.

In the face of return gunfire the two sloppy gunman quickly retreated to their car but never reached it. Isaac and Isaiah was out of the whip in a split second, running up behind them, guns blazing. They Swiss cheesed one gunner and treated the second one like a paper target. As both ill-trained hitmen lay on the ground dying Isaac stood over one and crushed him while Isaiah put a half of a clip in the other man's torso.

"Pussy muthafucka," Isaiah spat, breathing like an angry bull.

Kiam smiled at the memory of how quickly the brothers had reacted that night and how cool they were afterwards. Yeah, Wolfman and them could bring it on, Kiam had some killahs on his squad that craved that body bag shit and some of them rocked stilettos.

Rain drizzled down on the windshield as Kiam cruised down Treebie's block pulled in front of her house and called her to come outside. Treebie thanked God that Wa'leek had just pulled off minutes before Kiam's arrival; she definitely hadn't wanted to find out what a meeting between the two of them would result in.

She grabbed her jacket and a hat and ran to the car trying to avoid getting wet. When she jumped in the truck she took off her hat and shook her hair. "You know you must be pretty important 'cause I don't fuck with the rain," Treebie said, going in Kiam's glove compartment looking for napkins.

"Don't be all in my shit." He closed it and reached to the back and grabbed a hand towel from the pocket on the back of the seat.

"I don't want no shit you use to clean up after your hoes." Treebie gave the towel the side eye.

"I'm a boss nigga I get to nut all up inside my woman we don't waste shit," Kiam responded, putting the car in gear and pulling off.

"I don't need all that extra information but thanks," she said, wiping off her hands and dabbing at her clothes. "So what's up?"

"Look, I know we never really talked about it after that shit happened with Donella. Nevertheless I respect your get-down. I know that it had to be hard for you to lay your girl to rest but a boss bitch makes decisions now so there won't be mistakes later." Kiam came to a stop and looked over at her.

Treebie watched the wipers go back and forth as she filtered Kiam's words through her mind. By the time he was ready to pull off she had formulated exactly what needed to be said.

"First of all I didn't do that for you. My reasons for doing anything I do is for self-preservation. I understand that this game is like a ticking time bomb; you gotta get yours and get the fuck out the way before shit blow up. You walked in and sat on a thrown with many thorns. I just hope you don't get stuck in your ass before you decide to get up," she said then looked out the window.

"And you said that to say what?" His brow was furrowed.

"You're a smart man Kiam and when all the pieces are out in the open you will know what I am saying."

"Don't talk in riddles, if there's something I need to know spit that real shit."

"No, there's no big revelation, I just know that don't nobody love you more than they love themselves."

Kiam backed up a little because he could see that Treebie's words was more of a caution than slick words or a dry snitch. On the real she had just given him a coded warning and he had to respect her for that. In that moment he realized he needed to keep her close to him. Not only was she official, her gunplay was ridiculous and if nothing else she would have a nigga's back.

In regards to her statement he replied, "I'ma leave that alone for now." He would allow time to reveal its hand.

Treebie nodded in agreement.

"I want you to do something for me," said Kiam, moving on to the subject that was heavily on his mind. "Put your ear to the streets and find out whatever you can about those niggas that call themselves Blood Money."

"No problem," Treebie said, looking over at him watching for any sign of a set up.

"Why you looking at me like that?" he asked.

She looked in his eyes and quickly deduced that he didn't know anything. "You know I owe yo ass for feeding me dead muthafuckas," she played it off, yet she was serious.

"My bad. That shit was just so gangsta I couldn't help it. I'll make it up to you." The smirk in his face revealed his arrogance.

"Nah, I'm good. Just make sure my paper is longer than the rest of them niggas and we even." Treebie threw her offer on the table.

Kiam tossed her words around for a few minutes, he knew that what she was asking for was fair and not greed. "I'll up your pay two g's but you can't make more than my right hand."

"That's cool 'cause the left hand has a purpose too."

"I hear that slick shit."

"Don't just hear it, believe it. Let a bitch ass nigga come at us sideways and watch how fast I make his wife a widow."

"What if he ain't married, ma?" Kiam joked.

"Well, I'll make his mama mourn."

Kiam put his fist out. "You a bad bitch."

"You already know." She hit his fist and they both chuckled.

"Let's go see what wet money look like," Kiam said as he headed to check on the traps.

Chapter 22
Crossing the Line

"Hello," JuJu answered his cell with a groggy voice.

"Why you sound like that," Bayonna teased as she whipped her silver two-door 2012 BMW M6 around the corner heading to his house.

"I just got back from the gym. I was about to take a nap, what's up?"

"Nothing. I left my CD's and bag in your car." When they got back from the New York run last night she had been so tired she just got out the car and left everything.

"Can't you get 'em later? I'm laying down." He was stretched out on his bed in a towel and not trying to move.

"No. I need my shit and I don't trust you. You'll be done let somebody take my stuff. Just come open the door, I'm already out front."

"Damn, you a brat."

"Are you going to open the door or what man?" she whined.

JuJu sighed then sat up. "Alright, hold up," he relented.

Before he could get to the door she was ringing the bell and knocking. When he opened it he just looked at her like she was crazy.

"Why you just standing there? You got a little hottie up in here?" she asked, looking down at his towel.

"Come get these keys so you can be out and I can get some fuckin' sleep," he growled.

"Eww. Aren't we pleasant today?" She walked past him.

JuJu closed the door then limped to the kitchen counter.

"What happened to you?" Bayonna asked like a concerned parent.

"Ain't nothing, I was balling and pulled a muscle in my leg, but it's all good." He grabbed the keys off the hook and passed them to her.

"Aww, you gotta be careful." She reached out and took them then headed to his garage. Bayonna popped the locks and fumbled around collecting her music and her Louie bag.

When she came back in JuJu was sitting on a stool with a look of pain all over his face. "You gotta hit the streets tonight?" she asked, passing him his keys.

"Yeah, I'll be a'ight I just need to rest it for a little while." He stood up and grimaced from the pain that shot up the back of his leg.

"Nah, I got you. Go lay down."

"Huh?" JuJu looked up at her with suspicion.

Bayonna's expression revealed nothing conniving but her thoughts were a whole 'notha story. "Just go lay down and let me hook you up real quick. Before I got caught up in this fast life, I went to school for muscle therapy." She sat the CD's on the counter, her bag on the floor, threw her jacket on the couch then took his hand leading him to his bedroom.

He looked at her again to reassess her intentions but saw nothing different in her eyes than he had seen moments ago.

"You got some baby oil or something?" she asked with innocence that disguised her true intentions. She had been sizing JuJu up for a minute and now was the perfect opportunity to turn his young ass out.

"Yeah, the baby oil is under the sink." He pointed towards the bathroom.

"Alright, lay down."

JuJu got on the bed and laid on his stomach. Bayonna returned, placed the oil on the dresser then began taking off her pants.

"Yo, what you doin' shorty?" JuJu questioned.

"Stop being so scary and relax. I don't want to get this on my clothes." She pointed to the bottle then pulled her shirt over her head. She grabbed her cell, tuned the Pandora to the R. Kelly station and sat it on the dresser. *Seems Like You're Ready* boomed through the room as she moved slowly preparing herself.

Temperatures rising,/And Your body's yearnin' for me./Girl, lay it on me,/I place no one above thee,/Oh, take me to your ecstasy./It seems like you're ready (seems like you're ready)./Girl are you ready,/To go all the way?

JuJu watched as she walked over to the bed in a hot pink thong and tank top which lay perfectly over her hot pink lace bra. He couldn't resist glancing down at that camel's toe that was on display between her thighs; it had her thong on swole.

Bayonna climbed on the bed and began working her magic. "Okay breathe in and out and relax," she directed him.

146

"Fuck," he yelped as she got deeper into the muscle. He grabbed a pillow and buried his face in it to muffle his cries.

Men are always tough until they get sick or get hurt then they bitch up. "Stop crying and man up." she giggled.

"Fuck that shit, it hurts. You're tryna punish a nigga."

"Trust and believe if I wanted to punish you I could put some real pain on that ass."

"Shorty, you ain't talking about shit. I can withstand whatever. C'mon, do what you do." He issued a challenge.

"No, you're the one who's not talking about nothing." Bayonna slid her hands up and down his leg, purposely getting close to his inner thigh.

"You better be careful something might jump up at you," he joked as he began to feel relief.

I hope so. She poured more oil in her hands and began to work his lower back.

"Why you all the way up there?"

"I have to work the whole side or it will seize up somewhere else," she explained as she climbed up his body and moved her hands all over his back.

JuJu closed his eyes and enjoyed the precision of her touch. "Damn," he mumbled as she rested her pussy on the small of his back and worked his shoulders. His dick boned up as he felt the heat that came from between her thighs.

"You like?" she asked softly.

JuJu didn't know if she was talking about the massage or that plump pussy that was pressed against his back. All he knew was that if he didn't stop her he damn sure wasn't gonna be able to stop himself. He lifted his face out of the pillow. "I'm good ma," he said, trying to end her unintentional foreplay before they crossed the line.

Bayonna ignored him. "Relax, I'm almost done. Flip over."

"Huh?"

"Why you always say *huh* when you know you heard me?" She lifted up slightly. "Turn over."

"I'ma turn over but don't be tryna touch shit that'll lead to trouble," he warned as he slowly turned onto his back and rested his hands behind his head.

147

"No put them straight out." She sat on his waist and met the steel that he carried in his pants while guiding his arms where she wanted them to rest.

JuJu looked into her eyes. "A'ight, shorty, I'm warning you. Keep playing around with a nigga and something gon' pop off."

Bayonna poured oil in her hands and rubbed his shoulders and neck then up and down his arms. As she slid her hands down his chest she locked eyes with him and sucked in her bottom lip very seductively. "You got all this dick and trying to be all stingy with it." She slid down his length sending heat through his whole body. "Break a bitch off." Her voice was thick with lust.

"You ain't ready for all this dick. And you damn sure ain't ready for what comes with it."

"Is that what you think?" she asked a little over whisper as she reached for the opening of his towel.

"That's what I know."

Bayonna ignored him and grabbed him firmly in her hand and began massaging up and down his length. *Damn little nigga holdin' like a mutha-fucka.* She caressed him, allowing the oil to guide her strokes. "Why don't you stop playing and fuck with a bitch?" She laid his dick up on his stomach and rested against it.

"I don't fuck with friends like that," he said, placing his hands back behind his head.

"I'm not your friend." She leaned down closer to his mouth as she rocked gently back forth on his pole causing it to swell to full potential. "Can I kiss your lips?" she leaned in resting her breast on his chest.

Normally JuJu would never kiss a female in the mouth but it was something in her eyes that said, *I'm yours.* His dick screamed, *Nigga get that pussy.* He licked his lips then responded. "Gon' get you a kiss then fall back."

Bayonna heard that boss shit but she was a boss too. She wasn't letting his young behind turn her down. She traced his lips with the tip of her tongue then slid it in his mouth and took his breath away. "I wanna ride this dick," she whispered then kissed him deeply.

JuJu gave up trying to front and surrendered to what he really had been wanting the whole time. He reached up and pulled her thong to the side. "Lift up," he commanded.

Bayonna did as he said.

Grabbing his dick firmly at the base, he said, "Handle ya business."

She smiled impishly and slid down his length nice and slow. "Ssss," he hissed as her tightness caressed every inch of him. He placed his hands behind his head and watched her do her thing.

Bayonna moved gracefully up and down as small moans slipped from her lips. When she dropped her head and began rotating her hips he closed his eyes and bit into his bottom lip. She lifted her head and rose to the top of his dick allowing only the head access as she squeezed her muscles tightly each time he moved in and out.

"Damn baby," he mumbled and grabbed her ass cheeks.

"Open your eyes," she moaned, continuing her tease.

JuJu opened his eyes a little as he tried to get deeper inside her. Bayonna held her position causing him to crave her every movement.

"I want you to be mine," she whispered heavily and kissed his lips.

"Stop playing with this dick and let me make you mine," he responded as anxiety rose in his nuts.

"I'm not sharing you," she said, laying down the foundation of their new unspoken relationship.

"Same here," he confirmed. JuJu grabbed her around her back and pulled her to him taking over. With her chest firmly against his he planted his feet into the mattress and stroked up fast and hard causing her to climb his chest.

"Baby wait," she moaned breathily.

"I thought you wanted to be mine?" he taunted and continued to handle his business.

Bayonna tried to escape all those inches but he held her down so he could make her walls regret the offer. Bayonna knew that it was an advantage and a disadvantage of fucking with a young boy. The disadvantage was most were half man/half rabbit, although they could rock up often they couldn't last very long. But if you could train them to slow the fuck down that young dick was to die for.

Pushing herself up she tried to gain back control. "Wait baby, I wanna come, let me do it." She looked down into his hungry eyes, leaned back and grinded on him just right to hit her spot.

"Relax baby so you can enjoy your pussy," she moaned as she reached for his hand putting his fingers on her clit. "You work that and let me work this." She leaned her head back and moved skillfully on his dick.

The room filled with their passion as they moved to the beat of their hearts. JuJu watched his pole get juicier as she came for the second time. Shaking and moaning his name, Bayonna leaned forward and grabbed his hands locking his fingers with hers.

When she regained some of her composure he flipped her over, threw her legs over his shoulders and made her know she was indeed his.

When he finally came he laid between her soft thighs and kissed and sucked her lips and neck. Bayonna had him making love to her when normally he just fucked a female and sent her on her way before her panties could get cold on the floor.

"Damn you feel good," he muttered.

Bayonna was spent. All she could do was moan. When she felt him rock back up inside her she just closed her eyes and held him tightly.

JuJu was charged and way past ready to go. When he finally stopped she turned over, covered herself with the blanket and fell fast asleep.

JuJu kissed her shoulders and smiled, and then he got up and placed a call to Kiam. They spoke briefly then he hopped in the shower and got dressed. He sat on the bed laced his boots then leaned over and kissed Bayonna on the forehead. Her eyes opened slowly and a smile came across her face.

"You can't hang," JuJu teased.

"Whatever." She nudged him with her foot. "You about to leave? You want me to leave with you?"

"Nah, I want you right in that spot when I get back. The towels and wash cloths are in the hallway closet and my t-shirts are in that middle drawer." He pointed at the tall dresser. "I'll see you when I get back." He kissed her again then got up, tucked his gun, threw on his leather jacket and was out.

Bayonna turned over and fell back into a slumber with her pussy throbbing and a smile in her face.

150

When JuJu popped out his door Kiam was sitting out front scoping out the block. Missing nothing he noticed that Bayonna's car was parked in the driveway.

When JuJu got in the front seat and slid down with a peaceful look on his face he had to fuck with him. "You good youngin?"

"Yeah I'm straight," he slurred like he was high.

"You sure?"

"Yeah I'm sure, why what's up?"

"Bay put that pussy on you," Kiam teased.

JuJu looked over at Kiam and shyly chuckled. "Fucked up my whole gangsta."

"I thought so, jumping in my shit smelling like new pussy."

"Oh shit." He burst out laughing.

"Nah, on the real, that's what's up. Bayonna is a boss chic and a woman like that will have you feeling like your whole world only exist between two slippery lips."

JuJu nodded his understanding as he soaked up the game that Kiam spat.

"Just remember youngin love is good, but tuck that shit when we hit these streets. You can't bring it with you. When you're with your woman you can be all heart, but when we hit these streets you can't feel shit but survival. These niggas will pounce on your ass if you bring love out here on the block with you." He paused allowing him to process the information.

"Never that, Bleed," JuJu vowed, pussy nor paper could put that sucka shit in him.

"In the streets it's beast season 24/7, 365. Then when you get home you make your pussy remember why it missed you," Kiam reiterated as he hit the radio and pulled off.

JuJu nodded his understanding and quickly flipped his feelings and got beastly. Ruling the streets by force felt just as good as bustin' a nut.

Chapter 23
No Betrayal/No Regrets

Bayonna couldn't believe that she had actually gone there with JuJu's young ass but the way her body was feeling she couldn't say that she regretted it. She hadn't had any dick in weeks and JuJu had definitely handled his business.

As she laid there in the after-glow of having gotten some good dick, it made her think about Gator for just a split second and she realized that she didn't really miss him at all. His sex game had been top notch but he had been seriously lacking in the boss department. No real nigga would've allowed Kiam to step in and just take his throne.

Bayonna shook her head at her own stupidity. Had she really been that hard up for a nigga? Her allegiance to Blood Money didn't allow her to permit outsiders to get close to her so maybe that's why she had fucked with Gator? she told herself.

Yep, he had just been convenient dick. In the end she had lost respect for him anyway though she hadn't admitted that to herself until this very moment. *It's a good thing his soft ass is dead.* Her thoughts echoed her soul. In order for Bayonna to truly love a nigga his gangsta had to be above reproach. That was just the way she was built. If a man didn't have no balls he might as well have a pussy and Bayonna damn sure didn't fuck with coochie.

She opened her eyes and looked around JuJu's bedroom and instantly saw the evidence of the young boy's gangsta. Choppas and all different types of artillery was scattered about. It looked like he was preparing to go fight a war in Iraq or some got damn where.

Bayonna smiled, nothing turned her on more than a nigga who didn't hesitate to crush everybody in his way. She preferred her men older and much more seasoned but in JuJu she sensed a young boss in the making. Whatever he lacked would come with the passing of time. At the very least it would benefit her to keep him close because he was tight with Kiam. He would be her ears without even realizing it.

While Bayonna was at his condo feeling satiated and assessing the benefits of hooking up with him, JuJu was riding shotgun with his mentor listening attentively as Kiam gave him the game plan.

"We're hitting Money Bags Carter's spot over in Garden Valley. I got somebody on the inside setting it up. This time we're killing in a way that will make the whole city tremble. We're letting muthafuckas know that opposing us will get them murdered in the most gruesome fashion," said Kiam, delivering the directive that him and Big Zo had agreed on during one of their late night strategy sessions when they were cell mates.

"Impose fear in the opposition and you'll force them into making many mistakes," Kiam passed on to his understudy.

When they pulled up to a hardware store JuJu was literally rubbing his hands together and bouncing around in his seat like a kid about to be turned loose in Toys R Us. Kiam backed into a vacant parking space and they got out and went shopping for all the things that were needed to make their enemies shimmy and shake at the mention of their names.

An hour later they came out of the store with what they had gone in after. They put the objects in Kiam's backseat and headed back to JuJu's house.

Kiam's cell phone rung with a call from Faydrah. "What's up baby?" Kiam answered.

"Missing you."

"I miss you, too, but I promise we'll spend some time together real soon a'ight?"

"Okay. I guess you have to go now. I can hear the dismissal in your tone."

Kiam chuckled. Faydrah didn't miss anything. "Yeah ma, I'm in the middle of something. Let me hit you back in a few," he said.

"That's what I need you to do, *hit* me. Your garden needs to be watered," she cooed.

"I got you," he promised.

"Okay, baby. Be safe."

"I will. Bye."

Kiam ended the call and without missing a beat went right back to plotting murder. He stopped at a traffic light and looked over in the passenger seat at JuJu. "Tomorrow night we're gonna change the way street wars are fought."

JuJu peeped the instant switch. *In the streets it's beast season 24/7, 365. Then when you get home you make your pussy remember why it missed you.*

He nodded his respect and Kiam went on. "Ain't no mercy and ain't rules to this shit besides loyalty to one another. You feel me souljah?"

"You already know how I do, Bleed. Loyalty or death fuck the other side. Straight like dat!" JuJu vehemently exclaimed.

"That's the only way niggas like us can survive in this dirty game. Without loyalty there's nothin'. When a nigga falls it's usually a muthafucka in his own crew that brings him down."

"Never dat!" JuJu vowed. He would rather be beheaded than go out like a bitch.

"Nah youngin, I'm not questioning your officialness. I'm speaking on this lil' nigga, Kato, who's down with Money Bags and 'em. I flipped his bitch ass for fiddy stacks." Kiam let the window down and spat on the ground. Kato's name tasted like shit in his mouth.

He rolled the window back up and continued to school JuJu. "Complacency breeds betrayal. That's why it's better to be feared than respected; fear never sleeps. You're my street general, it's imperative that you inflict fear in all those under your command so that they'll never entertain the thought of betraying you," Kiam went on.

JuJu clearly understood what he was saying. It meant that tomorrow's show would be a warning to their own crew as well as to the enemy.

When they arrived back at JuJu's condo, Kiam helped him unload their purchases and carry them to the door. He saw that Bayonna's whip was still parked out front. He sat the items at the door and held his fist out to his protégé. "Tomorrow night," he reminded him. "Now go in there and engrave your name in that pussy."

"I'm all over it, fam."

They touched fists and JuJu went inside to tat his name on Bayonna's ass.

Once JuJu carried everything inside and put it away in the hallway closet, he went into the bedroom and smiled at the sight of Bayonna's sexy body positioned in the middle of his bed. She stared at him seductively and gestured with a finger for him to come join her.

"Let me take a shower right quick," he said.

Bayonna had showered while he was gone but she followed him into the bathroom and joined him under the water. This time JuJu didn't hesitate to get that pussy. He pinned her against the wall and took what he wanted.

"Go deep," Bayonna urged as her arms went around his neck and her legs wrapped around his waist. "I've been playing in this pussy waiting for you to come back and fuck the shit out of me again. Do you feel how wet it is?"

"He'll yeah," he growled, pushing balls-deep inside those tight wet walls.

"Oh, my god!" moaned Bayonna, opening completely to him and moving her hips in perfect rhythm with his. "Hit that shit nigga. Make it talk to you." She breathed heavily in his ear.

JuJu was brick hard and turnt all the way up. She was making mad fuck noises in his ear and throwing that pussy back at him like she was the one doing the fucking. That wasn't how it was going down though, she needed to understand that he was in control. He pressed her securely against the wall and brought her legs up around his neck. "Baby don't drop me," she whined.

"I got you shorty. Now shut up and take this dick like a grown ass woman."

"Oh, yes, I'ma take it," she cried out in pleasure as she felt him hit her bottom.

The water cascaded over them intensifying their pleasure and making their sex slippery and wet. JuJu's powerful strokes had Bayonna coming so fast and hard she thought it might blow the top of her head off. And when he shot his cum up inside of her a second after her juices poured down, it came out like a jet spray.

156

"Boy you're a beast," she praised him as he lowered her back down to her feet. He had to hold her up because Bayonna's legs were weak and her breath was short.

JuJu smiled. He had put his stamp on that ass for real. He lifted her chin up so that their eyes were locked into each other's. "You see this right here?" He pounded his chest with his fist. "This that grown man shit."

Bayonna couldn't even refute it, he had that ass wobbling.

Later that afternoon, they hit Maggianos in Beachwood Mall and ate a late lunch then he dropped her off to go holla at the Twins. Kiam's words played in his mind, he needed to have a strong beautiful woman by his side but he needed to keep his feelings in check so his mission would always be in focus.

"Bye, babe," Bayonna said as she leaned over and kissed his lips.

"Can I come play house with you later?" JuJu joked as he pulled back looking in her eyes.

"Sure can," she responded, giving him her innocent school girl eyes.

"I'll hit you when I'm on my way."

"Okay. I was supposed to meet up with the girls but you wore my ass out. I'ma take a hot bath and jump in bed," she confessed, grabbing her purse. "I need my car too," she reminded him.

"A'ight, tomorrow. I want that ass in the house for a couple days," he said, cracking a semi smile.

"Oh, so you Daddy now?" She sat to the side with her lips twisted.

"I guess so you said that shit about twenty-five times this morning,"

"Shut up," she giggled and hit his arm. "See you later. Be careful babe."

"Always," he responded as he watched her get out and head inside. When he thought she was safe he pulled off and hit that switch that turned him into a stone cold killah.

Bayonna stripped out of her clothes as she moved to her laundry room. She quickly threw in a load then headed to the bathroom to run herself a nice hot tub of bubbly water. She threw her iPhone on the docking station and hit the R. Kelly channel and reminisced about the many hot moments that her and JuJu had just shared. A feeling of peace and teenage crush rushed through her veins as she replayed the way he touched her, the slight sparkle in his eye when he looked into hers and the slick shit that came out his mouth when he stroked deep.

"Damn, boy you tried to fuck me to death," she said aloud, shaking her head as she felt a slight soreness between her legs with every step.

She had to admit they had crossed the line but she had no regrets. The only thing that tugged at her heart was not having Donella to share it with. Normally she would run straight in the house grab her phone and give Donella every detail then listen to her many opinions as they laughed and swapped their experiences. She could hear her girl's voice loud and clear.

"I hear you Bay, give that young nigga all the pussy he wants, but every time his dick swells your pockets better inflate."

Bayonna chuckled at the thought but then a lump formed in her throat and she fought back the tears. She moved to the linen closet grabbed a fresh towel and washcloth then headed to the bathroom. As she slipped into the hot bubble bath, she tried to relax her mind and fill it with happy thoughts because the reality of the situation was getting real. She was not any closer to answers and time was ticking by without justice or revenge for Donella's death.

Bayonna put the cloth down in the water then placed it over her face. She slid down until the water was up to her neck and allowed her head to fall back against the headrest. She didn't know how things we're going to play out but she knew that when it was all said and done a bitch was going to be laying at her feet, blood leaking on the ground. She just hoped she wouldn't have to lay JuJu next to them.

Chapter 24
Demented

Kiam felt the warmth of Faydrah's body pressed against his; she had an arm and a leg draped across him and her head rested on his chest. He looked down and saw that she was asleep with a smile on her face and he hadn't even sexed her down. They had watched television and cuddled then they had gone to bed. Faydrah had practically moved in and that was all good with him because he liked knowing that his woman would be at home waiting for him when he came out of the streets at night. What he didn't like was having her worry about him when he had to get out of bed in the middle of the night to handle his business. But that's exactly what he had to do.

Tonight was the night. In a few hours the niggas whose heads he was going after would realize that he was something out of their worst nightmares. He looked over at the clock on the nightstand and saw that it was just a little before midnight. Time to get up and go strike terror in the whole dope game, he thought wickedly as he eased out from under Faydrah's leg and tried to slide out of bed without awakening her.

Faydrah stirred and reached for him, letting out a small whine when she felt the absence of his body. "Bae, come back to bed," she mumbled with her eyes still closed.

"Go back to sleep ma. I gotta leave for a minute," said Kiam, moving to the closet and pulling out his gear.

Faydrah grabbed at the comforter pulled it to her neck and snuggled with his pillow. "Be careful baby," she whispered and began to drift off.

Kiam stepped into a pair of black jeans and pulled on a black t-shirt, he strapped on a bullet proof vest and covered it with a hoodie. Grabbing his black Timbs from the back of the closet, he turned around and walked over to a chair across the room. Kiam sat down and pulled on a pair of wool socks then put on his boots and laced them real tight before grabbing his fo-fo and his Nine off the nightstand.

He looked up and saw Faydrah sitting up in bed staring at him. Her eyes held the familiarity of having seen him strap up many times before and knew what it meant. But that had been a long time ago.

159

She saw the serious set of his jaw, the darkened hue in his eyes, the quiet purposefulness in the way he moved, and she could easily discern that he was going out to kill someone tonight.

Now came the test of her mettle.

She had promised to play her position and to let him do what he had to do without complaint. But it was very hard to love a man and just sit quietly by while he strapped up to go out on a mission from which he wasn't promised to return. Faydrah's worst fears were that the next time she saw Kiam he might be on a coroner's table or behind bars. Either reality would crush her to the core.

"What's wrong?" he asked, picking up on the expression on her face.

"Nothing." She tried to keep her fears from resonating in her tone but she lost that battle.

Kiam walked over and sat down beside her. He gently took her in his arms and kissed her softly. Pulling back to look into her eyes he said, "Baby, you don't have to worry I'll be back. That's my word to you."

Faydrah blinked back tears and her voice cracked. "You promise?"

"Yeah, ma, I promise. I'll be back," he repeated.

"I pray that you will," she said, dropping her head under the weight of her worries.

Kiam used a finger to raise her chin. Looking into her eyes he replied, "It's not me who's gonna need a prayer." He planted a quick kiss on her cheek and tasted a tear that had escaped from her eyes. "Try to go back to sleep. I'll wake you up when I get in." He stood up to leave.

Faydrah stood up with him and followed him to the door. "I'm gonna wait up for you. Please be safe," she pleaded as he left out.

Kiam turned and winked at her then he hit that switch that was imbedded in his heart and turned into a beast.

When Kiam pulled up in front of the twin's new townhouse, JuJu, Isaiah and Isaac was already out front loading the last of the special items they would need tonight in the back of a Durango. The large truck had been purchased for this one mission and would be torched afterwards.

The night chill of approaching winter was accompanied by a strong wind that whistled around him as he met his men at the rear of the truck where JuJu was just closing the back door. They locked fists and bumped chest. "You ready?" Kiam asked his most trusted.

160

JuJu smirked. "It's just another day in the hood fam."

Kiam turned and dapped Isaac and Isaiah, studying their expressions to see if they were in that killah zone too. What he saw in their eyes confirmed what he needed to see. "Let's roll out," he said, leading the way.

They climbed inside the truck without anyone saying a word. JuJu got behind the wheel and blasted the heater. Isaac and Isaiah were in the backseat pulling on leather driving gloves. In the passenger seat Kiam went over the last details of the mission.

"Did you make sure y'all have everything?" Kiam asked his right-hand.

"Yeah, fam, everything is in the back," JuJu vouched.

"Let's go and handle this then," said Kiam.

There were very few words spoken as they drove down to Garden Valley. When they got close Kiam directed JuJu to turn into a small shopping plaza that sat on their right. A dark colored truck was parked there as expected. "Let me get the money," said Kiam, slipping on a pair of gloves.

"Here you go, boss." Isaiah passed a shoe bag to him from the backseat.

"I'll be right back." Kiam opened the door and slid out. The twins click-clacked their bangers and climbed out too. Kiam put a hand up. "Wait here," he said then walked over to where Kato was parked.

The front driver's window slid down and Kato smiled showing gold teeth. "Sup Bleed, you got that?"

Kiam answered by tossing the bag of money in his lap. The boy opened the shoe bag and gawked at the sight of the fifty bands. It was the easiest money he had ever made and the most costly.

He looked up at Kiam. "Them niggas in there chillin', smoking weed and drinking. Just knock on the door and say *It's time to eat,* that's the code we're using today. They'll ask who sent you, just say *the devil.*"

Kiam chuckled. The irony was not lost on him. *That's the only real shit that ever came out of your bitch ass mouth.* "Anything else?" he asked.

"Nah, they'll let you right in. There's six people inside the house, all of them are strapped but the one you gotta take out first is Ty. He's a little stocky nigga with dreads and he's 'bout it. He's not gonna give up shit, and if you slip on him he's gonna put you on your back."

Kiam nodded and tried to keep the revulsion that he felt towards Kato from showing on his face. But a man knows when his actions are foul without having to be told. The guilt of his betrayal forced a half-assed explanation off Kato's tongue. "Fuck those niggas I don't owe them no loyalty. You feel me?" he blurted

Kiam couldn't feel that sucka shit even if he had ten pairs of hands! His arm came up and he aimed his fo-fo at Kato's head and shot him straight through his gold grill. Kato's head snapped back then bounced forward. Boom! Boom! Two more shots sent his whole head splattering all over the dashboard.

Kiam snatched the door open and reached in and grabbed the money, being careful not to get that bitch ass nigga's blood nowhere on him. With the shoe bag securely in hand he raised up and pumped another shot in Kato. "That's the price of disloyalty," he gritted then calmly walked back to the Durango.

The stash house looked like any other one on the street. Only two cars were parked in the driveway and no one had come or gone in the twenty minutes they sat watching it. Kiam checked his bangers. "It's that time," he announced.

JuJu was the first one out of the truck. Isaiah and Isaac got out and strapped the special hardware over their backs. Kiam slid out last. He glanced up and down the block and saw no pedestrians moving about at this hour of the night. In a few long strides he caught up with JuJu and 'em.

Together, with their tools out and their backs pressed against the side of the house, they crept silently. When they reached the backdoor Kiam knocked lightly then stepped to the side in case Kato had pulled a double cross.

A minute or so passed then someone called out, "Who is it?"

"It's time to eat."

"Who sent you, Bleed?"

"The devil." Kiam smiled demonically.

On both sides of him his assassination squad stood ready to air shit out. The door opened a crack and Kiam's foot sent it flying inwards. A big

Debo-looking dude stumbled back and raised his arm. The overhead light in the kitchen bounced off the chrome whistle in his hand. Kiam squeezed the trigger of his fo-fo and sent something lethal all up in big boy's chest, sending him flying back into the refrigerator.

Boom! Boom! Boom! The fo-fo roared angry and loud.

JuJu dashed around Kiam and ran into the living room spraying niggas, tearing wood off furniture and paint from the walls. The twins were on his heels joining in the rat a tat tatta. An older gray-haired man bounced up off the couch and tried to grab a Glock .50 off the cocktail table. As soon as he rose up Isaiah opened up his chest with a sudden blast from his Desert Eagle. Pops staggered back like a Saturday night drunk. The Glock slipped from his hand and fell to the floor as he put his hand over his heart. Blood seeped through his fingers and he sat back down heavily.

Kiam stepped in the room and shot the old man in the face. Boom! Pops slumped over on his side with half of his crown missing.

"The next muthafucka to move is gonna join him," Kiam barked.

He looked around the living room. Including old dude, three bodies were sprawled out. Half smoked blunts, dirty glasses and half empty Ciroc bottles littered the end tables and Lil Wayne's The Carters III CD played from an iPhone that was plugged into a 60" flat screen. A dark skinned pretty female and a little stocky dude with shoulder length dreads sat on a loveseat side by side. JuJu had his banger shoved against the broad's forehead and Isaac had lil' man guarded.

Kiam walked over and smiled at them menacingly. Lil' man threw his arm around shorty and glared up at him defiantly.

"I know all about you Ty," said Kiam evenly. "You 'bout it, huh?"

"You muhfuckin' right so do what you came to do."

"Oh I'ma handle mines, that's a given." Kiam aimed his gun down and shot him in the stomach. Boom!

The girl screamed.

"Shut her up!" Kiam told JuJu.

JuJu slapped her across the face with his steel and she whimpered against Ty's shoulder.

Ty clutched his stomach and winced.

"Just remember you ain't running shit," Kiam said.

"Fuck you, bitch ass nigga!" Spittle flew out the corners of Ty's mouth splashing over Kiam's forehead.

When Kiam wiped his face Ty pushed the girl forward and reached under the loveseat for the choppa that he kept stashed there. Kiam reacted quickly, he kicked the AK-47 out of Ty's hand and fired a shot in his side.

The chic was on her knees scrambling after the assault rifle. She grabbed it but Isaiah dived on top of her and wrestled it away from her. She fought him tooth and nail, biting down on his forearm with the vicious lock of a red nose pit. Her teeth cut through the sleeve of his hoodie and dug into his flesh.

"Bitch!" yelped Isaiah, drawing back and punching her in the jaw.

She grunted but wouldn't release the lock on his arm. Isaiah flipped her over on her back and pounded her in the face with his gloved fist until she unclenched her teeth. "Fucking ho bit the shit out of me!" He stood up and aimed the choppa down at her. "You're gonna pay for that," he spewed.

"Not yet!" Kiam cut in.

Isaiah eased his finger off the trigger and calmed his breathing. Five minutes later they had Ty and the girl duct taped and bound. Kiam gave a nod and the twins unstrapped the large backpacks from off their backs and sat them down at their feet. When they went inside the backpacks and brought out chainsaws the girl's eyes grew large with fear.

Kiam looked from the girl to Ty to see if the sight of the chainsaws had diminished his gangsta. Excruciating pain shot through Ty's body as blood poured from the gunshot wounds. His body was weak but his heart remained strong.

"Where does Money Bags Carter rest his head?" Kiam asked. He bent down and ripped off the strip of tape that covered Ty's mouth.

"Nigga, suck my dick," he spat.

Kiam kicked him in the face. "Learn how to talk to grown folk."

He stepped over to the chic and asked her the same question he had asked Ty. When he removed the tape from over her mouth he got the same response. "Suck my dick too," she echoed Ty.

Kiam chuckled. "Cute. But watch how wickedly I play the game." He nodded his head and the twins plugged the chainsaws in an outlet and powered them on. The loud gnashing of the metal teeth sent shivers up the girl's spine but Ty remained stoic in the face of impending torture.

"I'ma start with you first tough guy," mocked Kiam. He placed the tape back over Ty's mouth then took the chainsaw out of Isaac's hand. "It's like cutting up chicken," he said dementedly as he began severing Ty's arm from where it connected at the shoulder.

Ty's muffled cries damn near blew the tape from over his mouth. The girl turned her head away from the gory sight as the contents in her stomach threatened to come up. JuJu stepped forwarded, covered her mouth with a fresh strip of tape in case she screamed, and forced her to watch Kiam dismember her man limb by limb.

By the time he was finished, Kiam was covered in blood and body parts were laying at his feet with ligaments hanging out. The girl had fainted and had to be slapped awake. This time when Kiam removed the tape from over her mouth she told all that she knew. She didn't know where Money Bags Carter rested at but she told them about several of his top men and the location of the stash upstairs.

Isaac got ready to head upstairs. Kiam grabbed his arm. "Fuck that nigga's little bit of money," he spat. He turned back to shorty and said in a low frightening tone, "Bitch you could've saved yourself all this pain and torture you're about to experience."

"Please, I gave you what you wanted," she cried as she looked at the darkness in Kiam's eyes.

"Nah, you want me to suck yo dick," Kiam reminded her. "Next time stay in your fucking place. Do this bitch dirty," Kiam barked. He handed the chainsaw back to Isaac and turned and walked out of the house.

Kiam felt no remorse as he climbed in the truck and waited for JuJu and the twins to leave a message that would reverberate all over the city when the dismembered bodies were found in the house. He drummed his fingers against the dashboard as he waited for his ruthless young boys to carry out his instructions.

When they were finished with the mutilations, JuJu and Isaac picked up an arm and a leg of each victim and placed the severed limbs in a black plastic garbage bag and tied it tight. They gathered up the chainsaws and slung the bags over their shoulders and headed out to the truck.

Kiam was waiting behind the wheel when JuJu and them reached the vehicle. They hopped and he pulled off to carry out the last part of tonight's mission. He was about to deliver something to his victim's people's doorsteps that they would never forget.

The chic had given him several addresses on the same side of town. Kiam parked at the end of each block as his henchmen delivered the body parts one by one. After they had dropped off the last bag of gruesome contents they rode back to the twin's apartment in silence. Kiam was confident his message had been sent. From now on niggas would scramble like roaches to stay out of his fuckin' path.

It was almost three o'clock in the morning when Kiam walked in the house. He was all cleaned up and he wore no signs on his face of the atrocities that he had committed an hour ago. Faydrah met him at the door with a relieved smile on her face and Trapstar in her arms. As she stroked the puppy's back she stared up into Kiam's eyes lovingly.

"I told you I was coming back," he said as he took her in his arms and kissed her, squishing the little dog between their bodies.

Trapstar barked.

"Shut your little ass up before I turn you into a pair of house shoes," said Kiam.

"Leave him alone," Faydrah said setting Trapstar on the floor.

As Kiam led Faydrah back to bed, she tried to pretend that she hadn't seen the specks of dried blood on his face.

Chapter 25
Mad Confusion

Just as Kiam predicted, as soon as the dismembered bodies were discovered and it was reported on the news, the streets went wild with innuendos and rumors. Niggas that were not in the know speculated that the murders were a message sent by the Columbian Cartel or maybe Jamaicans because both nationalities had reputations for committing brutal drug related killings.

Money Bags Carter knew exactly who had committed the gruesome murders and Kiam's message rung loud and clear. Inside, Money Bags Carter was shaking like a stripper but outwardly he swore revenge. He ran to Wolfman and Dontae pleading that they pool all of their resources together to eliminate Kiam immediately.

For the second time in little more than a month, the three men and their lieutenants had a round table to discuss what to do about Kiam. Also in attendance was Xyna, she sat at the head of the table on Wolfman's right to serve notice to those present that he now had a boss bitch on his team who was more than a pretty face.

Before the discussion could begin, Money Bags Carter looked from Xyna to Wolfman and asked, "Why is she here? This is men's business. With all due respect can't you send her shopping or something?" He looked haggardly and stressed as he rubbed his forehead and pulled on a Newport.

Wolfman was about to reply when Xyna put her hand up to stop him. "Baby let me answer that?" she said.

Wolfman nodded his consent and Xyna turned in the swivel chair and looked Money Bags Carter straight in the eye. "You want him to send me shopping?" she repeated his question, pausing while her stare burned like hot coals on his face. "A'ight nigga, what size casket should I get you while I'm out?" She brought out her pearl handled .380 and placed it flat on the table with the business end aimed at his chest.

Money Bags Carter stared at the tattoo of the deadly Black Mamba snake that wrapped around her entire wrist. Feigning calmness he blew smoke towards the ceiling while wondering if he could whip out the Nine on his waist and do her before she could do him.

"Play pussy and get fucked," spat Xyna, reading his mind.

Crispy Jay, Money Bags Carter's personal protector, had already slipped his banger off his waist. The air in the room became thick with tension. "Everybody just calm the fuck down," shouted Wolfman.

"I'm calm baby," replied Xyna sliding her gun back and resting it in her lap but keeping her eyes locked on Money Bags Carter who started going the fuck off.

"You just gonna let her disrespect me like I'm some lame ass nigga with no name in this game? I don't give a fuck how loyal she's been to you I'm not bitch ass nigga, she needs to know her muhfuckin' place," he railed.

"You disrespected her first," Wolfman pointed out but Money Bags Carter wanted an apology.

Tempers flared up again because Wolfman refused to command Xyna to do that. The argument became very heated and turned to the real reason everyone was so unnerved. Kiam was murking muthafuckas in an unmerciful manner that gave them nightmares.

Money Bags Carter had been the one to discover the dismembered corpses in the house. The ghastly visual of all that blood all over the living room and the mutilated torsos lying on the floor had him afraid of his own shadow. He lit another Newport and pulled on it hard.

Wolfman was livid; his newly clean-shaven face twitched as words spewed from his mouth hot as acid. "If y'all muthafuckas would've taken this threat seriously when I first brought it up we wouldn't have this got damn problem. Now Kiam is really feeling himself, running around cutting people up and shit, making it hot for everybody, and I got a feeling he's just getting started." He used a handkerchief to wipe the sweat that had beaded up on his forehead.

From the door where he stood posted, Chino noticed Wolfman's uncomfortableness. He walked over to the control panel on the wall and turned the heat down.

Money Bags Carter frowned at Wolfman. "It sounds like you're blaming everybody but yourself, but let's not forget that it's you that Big Zo suspects of putting the heat on him to get it off yourself. That's why he unleashed Kiam on us in the first place," he accused.

"You calling me a snitch?" gritted Wolfman.

"I'm not calling you nothing," Big Zo called you that."

Dontae hadn't uttered a single word the whole time. His head ping ponged back and forth between Wolfman and Money Bags Carter. This was the first time he had heard the accusation.

"Little punk ass boy, I've been in this game since you was on titty milk and my reputation stands for itself. Don't let your mouth get your ass killed up in here," Wolfman threatened Money Bags Carter who shot up out of his chair.

"Who the fuck you think you're talking to?" he snarled. Next to him his lieutenant Crispy Jay rose up. "Y'all muthafucka ain't runnin' shit," he continued to rant taking the temperature in the room way past boiling. When his hands went inside his jacket he got the back of his cabbage blown to pieces and the front of his chest wet up at the same time. He crashed down on the table face first sending glass flying.

Chino stood over his body with his banger poised to bark again. "Didn't I tell you to sit your ass down the last time you were here?" he snorted.

"Bitch ass nigga!" added Xyna, popping two more caps in Crispy Jay. She turned and looked at Money Bags Carter as if to ask did he still question her presence.

"What the fuck?" he cried, looking down at his second-in-command sprawled across the table with his brains leaking out.

"You brought that on yourself," said Wolfman. "Don't come up in my place talking disrespectfully. Now have a seat."

Money Bags Carter could feel Chino breathing on the back of his neck, and he now knew that Xyna wasn't that bitch to underestimate. He knew that there was no chance of him winning if he pulled out so he let his whistle remain on his waist and sat back down. But murder was prevalent in his mind as he watched Chino drag Crispy Jay's body over in a corner and discard it like an old rug.

Xyna stood with her gun firmly in Money Bags Carter's face praying he would make a move. When Chino returned she slowly sat back next to Wolfman and crossed her legs, resting her gun on her knee.

Dontae still hadn't uttered a word, he looked at Money Bags Carter whom he had lost all respect for and felt like snatching those little punk ass diamond money bag earrings out of his ears and squashing them. A nigga didn't deserve to floss if he allowed another man to handle him like a bitch. As for Wolfman, Dontae didn't respect him either. *I don't know if this nigga is the folks or not.*

Dontae had already decided what he was going to do and it damn sure wasn't going to be joining forces with them. The way he saw it they didn't stand a chance against Kiam.

Wolfman said exactly what Dontae was thinking. "I don't have time to protect anyone but my own people. From this point on it's every man for himself."

Dontae and Two Gunz stood up to leave. "Good evening gentlemen," Dontae said and they headed out the door.

Wolfman looked at Money Bags Carter trying to decide whether or not to stack his ass over there in the corner with his dead lieutenant. Chino was anxiously waiting for the signal.

Money Bags Carter stood up and walked towards the door on shaky legs, half expecting a bullet in the back. Wolfman called out his name. He stopped and slowly turned around ready to face Chino and Xyna's guns.

Wolfman saw the expression on his face. "I'm not gon' have you killed nigga, but if you try to come for me you'll regret it," he warned.

Money Bags Carter turned back around and walked out without replying.

"Send somebody back to dispose of your trash," Wolfman called out.

When the door closed behind Money Bags Carter, Wolfman pulled out a cigar, lit it and put it to his lips. Chino took a seat at the table only inches from the pool of blood and brains. "You know we gonna have to take care of that nigga right?" he said, ready to strike with force.

"It's already taken care of," Wolfman replied blowing out smoke and pulling Xyna onto his lap. He looked back up at Chino and added, "Money Bags Carter is weak. I left him alive to give Kiam somebody else to gun after. The one we have to watch is Dontae. A quiet man is always plotting."

Chino nodded.

Wolfman looked at Xyna. "Your job is to go after the bitches that are down with Kiam but don't sleep on them because they'll bust their guns, that's a known fact. Especially Treebie. Try to touch that nigga where it really hurts; every man has some woman that he cares about. Find out where Kiam's heart is and cut that muthafucka out."

Xyna smiled. "I'm on it baby. I'm going to show you how a real bitch operates. Watch me give that nigga a funeral to attend," she promised.

Wolfman grinned wickedly. Soon it would be Kiam's turn to mourn.

Chapter 26
Put that Shit in Check

Kiam was laying low, letting things cool down before he struck again because the Jakes were everywhere, questioning everybody. He took this time to do things with Faydrah and she was loving it. He had been so sweet and attentive to her needs lately.

Faydrah knew that it wouldn't last forever but she was enjoying it while it did. The night that he had come home with traces of blood on his face were all but forgotten as she got caught up in his tenderness.

Faydrah had been fumbling around in the closet for the last half hour trying to see what she was going to put on. It seemed like nothing she picked out fit right. She pulled on several pairs of jeans and shirts and tossed them to the side one by one. It was Friday night and they were going out to dinner.

For some inexplicable reason Kiam had invited JuJu and Bayonna out with them. Faydrah was totally against the idea and it was eating her up not to let it be known. She tried to swallow her displeasure as she prepared to get dressed.

"Babe, I can't find nothing to wear," she shouted from the walk-in as she fingered the clothes in their closet.

"Baby, please come on. We gotta pick up JuJu and Bay in like twenty minutes," Kiam hurried her.

Faydrah couldn't contain her feelings any longer. "To be honest I don't like that little girl. JuJu is cool but you could miss me with this double date situation," she yelled back in his direction.

Kiam walked out of the bathroom and into the closet where she was standing in her bra and panties with her hands on her hips. "Why you trippin'?" he asked as he looked her up and down.

"I'm not trippin'. I just don't like to be in those bitches face. You know I don't do phony well, I will fuck around and say something."

"Do it for me and stop cursing," he ordered.

Faydrah sucked her teeth then turned back to the clothes and grabbed a pair of leggings and a long shirt. She walked past Kiam and threw them on the bed with attitude.

Kiam had to smile. He could see she was trying to pick a fight so he would let her have her way. "So now you mad?" he asked, coming up behind her.

"Does it matter?" She turned around and looked up in his eyes.

"No." He looked down at her and her pouty lips was telling him she needed something only he could give her.

Kiam reached in his pocket and pulled out his cell and hit JuJu real quick. "Y'all can relax, I'ma be a little late," he said then disconnected the call.

He grabbed Faydrah around the waist, walked her to the dresser, and placed her on top with purposefulness then stepped between her legs. "You talking shit cause you need some act right." He unzipped his pants and pulled out that steel.

"Kiam wait." Faydrah held his shoulders and looked up in his eyes as he pulled her panties to the side.

Taking his dick in his hand he stroked it just right until he had it at *shut the fuck up and do what I tell you* mode. As he forced himself inside of her and stroked deep, he told her exactly what he needed her to do.

"This what you needed. You wanted daddy to touch these walls," he grunted as her wetness covered his length.

"Yes. Right there," she moaned as he found her spot.

"I need to you act right tonight."

"I'ma be good baby."

"You better." He picked up a little speed as he felt her muscles tighten.

"Baby, baby, baby," she mumbled as she felt her orgasm coming on strong.

"Get that shit, ma," he moaned, gipping her ass tight he brought her to the edge of the dresser and drilled her spot.

As soon as she released, he felt himself weakening and within seconds he was coming too. "Got damn. Shit. This pussy been crippling a nigga lately," he confessed as he rested his body against hers.

"Maybe *you* needed the act right," she teased as she tried to catch her breath.

"If it's going to be like this, I'ma fuck up on purpose." He slid out and pulled her to her feet.

They hit the bathroom cleaned up and got dressed. When they hopped in the car they both had silly grins on their faces like they had just stole something precious. "I love you baby."

"I love you, too," he said as they pulled off.

Once they picked up JuJu and Bayonna, they headed straight to the sports bar. Everything was jumping. Football was on all the big screens and the music was loud and on point. They took a seat at the bar until their table was ready.

"Who's your team, Kiam?" Bayonna leaned over JuJu and asked.

"I'm bout those Browns you already know. Dog Pound for life."

"You about losing then," she shot back.

"Oh, shit," JuJu said, moving out the way.

"Who you fucking wit'?" Kiam asked ready to talk shit.

"Sheeeiit. It's all about them birds."

"The Falcons?"

"Yep."

"Man fuck them dirty birds." Kiam stood up getting all excited.

"You wanna put some money on it?" Bayonna did a little dance in her seat.

"Hell yeah."

"Man both y'all gonna be broke when them Cowboys take the field," JuJu started up.

"Shut yo ass up nigga. Y'all gonna be home again just like last year." Kiam spat back pulling money from his pocket.

"Oh, boy, here we go," Faydrah said, shaking her head.

"Baby, you supposed to have my back," he said then leaned in and kissed her lips.

"I got you, baby," she said affectionately then turned to JuJu and Bayonna. "Man sit y'all asses down. Both of y'all teams are booty. Get ready to pay my man. Make them run they pockets baby," she said, grabbing Kiam around his waist.

Kiam began counting off those green laces in JuJu's face. Not to be outdone JuJu pulled out his knot and started counting back.

"You ain't said shit." Bayonna went in her bra and pulled out a few hundred.

When they saw her go back in the other side everybody busted out laughing.

"JuJu damn y'all can't afford a safe? You got shorty walking around with the bank roll in her push up bra." Kiam joked.

"Don't be hatin'," Bayonna said and they fell out laughing again.

"Combs table of four," they heard come over the PA system. They moved to the hostess and was seated.

Over the next two hours they laughed and joked and ate several trays of wings and fries and tossed back a few drinks. Faydrah had to admit she was having a good time. Bayonna was actually cool. Nevertheless, Faydrah kept a certain amount of caution up just in case she had to step to that ass.

Kiam was leaned back in the booth with Faydrah in his arms whispering some later action in her ear when he looked up and saw Lissha and Treebie coming their way. He immediately tensed up.

Faydrah picked up on it and looked up to see what had changed the atmosphere. When she saw Lissha she sat straight up. Recalling their confrontation at the hospital, Kiam pulled her back close to him knowing Faydrah would be quick to tap that ass. And with Lissha's propensity to start shit he knew one wrong word could fuck the night up.

"What's good, Chief?" Lissha said, standing dangerously close to Faydrah.

"Ain't shit just enjoying some down time," replied Kiam.

"I hear you," she said to him but kept her eyes on Faydrah. She turned slowly in Bayonna's direction and started her shit. "Hey Miss Bay, I see you out playing house with your young boy."

"Bitch don't start," Bayonna warned.

"*You* need to find somebody to play house with. These seats are taken" JuJu said.

"Oh shit, I done rolled up on honey moon lane, everybody all edgy and shit. My bad," Lissha lipped, throwing her hands up in surrender.

"Why you always starting shit?" Treebie asked. "Let's go get a drink and let the boss enjoy his night out." She pulled at Lissha's arm. "That bitch ain't even on our level," Treebie mumbled.

"Yeah you right, this the sensitive section. Let me move before I come on my period up in this muthafucka." Lissha agreed.

"You's a messy bitch," Faydrah hurled.

"Eyez!" Kiam said sternly.

"Excuse me?" Lissha said, turning back around.

"You heard me." Faydrah pulled away from Kiam and was up in her face.

"Eyez!" he repeated forcefully.

"You hear your daddy calling you. You better listen before you get fucked up," Lissha clowned her.

Kiam looked at Lissha then looked at Faydrah. *Fuck it, shorty can handle herself.* He sat back and let happen what needed to happen. Otherwise Lissha would continue to take his woman for a joke.

"You just mad cause every nigga you fuck with make you suck dick and get on," Faydrah smirked.

"What's your prediction for when I finish sucking your man's dick?" Lissha spat, feeling full of herself.

Treebie grabbed her drink and sat down on a bar stool. Bayonna's mouth dropped to the floor and JuJu was over there silently praying that Faydrah let loose on that ass.

Lissha continued to mouth off but Faydrah was done talking. She turned and looked at Kiam and when he nodded his consent she balled up her fist and knocked the shit outta Lissha. Before Lissha could respond she was all over her like a size 6 on a plus size woman, allowing her no room to wriggle or run. She did a little Floyd Mayweather like bounce and said, "Yeah bitch I've been waiting on this day!" She hit Lissha with a combination that snapped her head back.

Lissha rocked back on her heels then quickly regained her balance. "That's all you got? You hit like a bougie ass white girl," she taunted.

"Oh yeah?" This time Faydrah caught her in the eye.

Lissha wobbled but she didn't go down. She shook the cobwebs out of her head and got her Laila Ali on. "Bitch you're too pretty to fight," she spat, charging at Faydrah with both fists flailing. She landed a few punches high on Faydrah's forehead then it was on and cracking.

Faydrah backed up and rushed Lissha picking her up and slamming her to the floor. Faydrah was connecting from the top and Lissha was throwing hammers from the bottom. Wasn't no hair pulling or scratching going on with these two hell cats. Faydrah was from the hood and Lissha was from a place called all over a bitch's ass. "Fuck up off of me," she gritted as she connected with Faydrah's jaw.

A bitch couldn't fight if she couldn't take a punch. Faydrah wasn't that bitch, she shook of Lissha's blows and slammed her fist in Lissha's mouth. They rolled around on the floor giving it as good as they took it. When Faydrah ended up back on top she hammered Lissha's head into the floor with blow after powerful ass blow.

Kiam jumped up and JuJu was right behind him. Treebie and Bayonna began helping them pull the two apart but every time they got them semi-separated they found their way right back to locking blows.

"That's enough ma," Kiam said, picking Faydrah up in the air and moving her to the other side of the bar. Treebie and Bayonna grabbed Lissha and JuJu stood in the middle. Glasses and trays were all over the floor. Both of their shirts were wrinkled and torn.

"Fuck you, bitch," Lissha shouted as she tried to break away from her girls.

"Try sucking his dick through that bloody ass mouth. Trifling ass," Faydrah shouted back, tossing a bottle from the bar in her direction.

"Eyez calm down," Kiam yelled at her. "Go get the car yo," he ordered JuJu and tossed him the keys. JuJu was out the door and to the car in seconds.

"Please, we need your party to leave. I don't want to have to call the cops," a bald white man said behind Kiam.

When Kiam turned to see his beet red face he quickly tried to calm the situation. "That won't be necessary." Kiam calmly stated then went into his pocket and pulled out a band of money and handed it to the man. "No harm intended. This should take care of the meal and the damage. And give everybody a round on me. Keep the change." He took Faydrah by the arm, ready to drag her out to the car.

"Yeah, you better get her up out of here," shouted Lissha.

Kiam whipped his head around and stared at her with steam rising out of his collar. "We need to meet tomorrow. Twelve o'clock and don't be late. I'll deal with you then!"

Lissha didn't even respond. She stood there breathing heavily and looking at Faydrah through beady blood shot eyes. "I'ma see you again."

"You can see me again right now," Faydrah reached around Kiam and punched Lissha dead in her face.

Lissha charged at her but Kiam blocked her path. "Get the fuck outta my way tryna protect that bitch," Lissha huffed.

"Let them fight, Kiam," intoned Treebie. She didn't want Faydrah to have the last lick on her girl.

Kiam continued to keep them separated but he saw Treebie balling up her fist like she was about to get froggish and leap. "Do it and I'll break your fucking neck," he warned.

Treebie started to test his G but this wasn't all that serious so she fell back. Kiam turned back to Lissha. "Twelve o'clock," he ordered. The vein in his temple was pulsating. "Make sure she's on time," he said to Treebie.

"Uh huh," she mumbled half-heartedly.

"Think it's a game," Kiam warned them both.

They both stood there shooting missiles at Faydrah.

Kiam took Faydrah by the arm. "Let's go shorty," he said. "Bay you coming or what?" he asked Bayonna.

"Yep," she said feeling trapped in the middle. She hurriedly kissed her bitches on their cheeks and followed Kiam out to the car.

Driving home everyone was quiet as they tried to gauge Kiam's mood. He hadn't said a word to any of them since they left the restaurant. He had to admit to himself that it was about time Lissha got that ass checked. It was crazy seeing Faydrah throw them thangs like she used to back when they were hugging the block and she used to knock bitches out on command, but he knew that Lissha wasn't just a shit starter she was a killah. What he could not have was her gunning for Faydrah. He would rather put two in her head and fall out with Big Zo than risk her getting at his woman. Tomorrow, when he meet with her, he was going to put all that shit in check.

The morning after...
Lissha stood at the makeup counter in the mall trying on a pair of Tom Ford shades. She turned her head from side to side to see if they could hide the evidence of a rough night.

"I see somebody finally tapped that ass." The familiar blood curdling voice came from her left.

Lissha turned her head in the direction of the words and got an instant headache as her brow creased tightly in the middle of her forehead.

"Bitch, if you don't get away from me I'ma make some furniture move up in this muthafucka," she hurled back at the woman who was feeling the same disdain.

With a chuckle the woman continued. "Bitch, please. You may run your mouth but you damn sure don't run me," she hurled back.

"Why don't you go back to the hole you crawled out of? With your broke ass I'm surprised they let you through the door." Lissha balled her fist up tightly as she tried to stay calm.

"You ain't the only one that has pussy with value. Or is Daddy still controlling what you do with yours?" the woman responded with an evil grin on her face.

"Didn't I whip your ass good enough at the gas station to keep you away from me or do you need a reminder?"

"I don't need shit from you. I hope your black ass die."

"Fuck you."

"No fuck you, bitch," the woman spat then began moving away from the counter stopping to give a few final words. "Remember one thing: your loyalty to him is going to be the death of you and I'll be saving some spit to toss on your grave," she warned then walked away as fast as her legs could carry her.

Lissha was seeing a dozen shades of red. If looks could burn she would have brought the whole building down.

"Lissha, you good?" Treebie asked, placing her hand on her shoulder.

"Yeah, I'm straight," she responded.

"Who the fuck was that?" Treebie asked as she could see her girl was on fire although she had only caught the woman's last words.

"Nobody," Lissha said then grabbed her keys from the counter and headed to the register to pay for the shades.

Treebie stood there trying to process everything she had witnessed. Whoever the woman was she had made Lissha very uncomfortable and Treebie wondered why. She knew that she would find out the answer if she followed the trail of shit that Lissha kept leaving behind.

Chapter 27
Deadly Loyalty

Treebie pulled up in front of Lissha's house five minutes before twelve. During the whole ride she had not spoken a word. She looked over at Lissha who appeared to be defeated; the crease in her forehead gave away the fret that she felt inside. Lissha knew Kiam was going to get all in that ass and she was not looking forward to it.

"A'ight, get yo scary ass in the house." Treebie teased.

Lissha looked over at her with heat coming up off her brow. "Tree don't do that."

"This shit is your fault. You could have just kept it moving but you had to mess with Miss Corporate America," Treebie joked.

"Don't say shit else to me," Lissha grabbed the door handle and jumped out of the car.

Treebie rolled down the window and gave her some more of her own medicine. "You should have ran away from ol' girl like that and you wouldn't be in trouble." She continued. "And have yo ass ready for tonight we getting fucked up," she chuckled as Lissha walked in the house and slammed the door.

Treebie hit the satellite radio and prepared her some traveling music. Just as she was about to drive off JuJu's Rover pulled up next to her. The window came down and Kiam was in the passenger seat with a half scowl on his face. "What's good?" he asked from his reclined position.

"Nothing much about to go handle some business. You need something?" Treebie asked.

"You good on last night?"

"Yeah, my girl held her own. Don't worry we're not plotting on your boo."

"Don't, because that would be real hazardous to your health." He gave her a hard stare to emphasize his seriousness.

"I told you I'm good," she replied, not even sweating his tone because if she wanted to slump his chic it would take much more than a fierce look to quiet her gun.

"A'ight, park your car. I want you to ride with JuJu to make the rounds," said Kiam.

"Why you ain't ask Bay to do it?" she asked.

"Because I told you to do it," he said ready to get in that ass. He hopped out of the truck leaving the passenger door open indicating that the subject wasn't up for debate.

Treebie rolled up her window, deaded the engine, grabbed her piece and got out. As they passed she shot him some heat. Kiam didn't respond to her slight attitude. He pushed on and walked up on the steps and rang the bell.

"Don't be driving like Miss Daisy, let's go," Treebie turned her smart remarks to JuJu as she closed the truck door, but the young boy's wit was as quick as his trigger finger.

"A'ight, fuck around and you'll be jogging next to this muthafucka," he warned. "Sit back and tuck that smart shit."

Treebie waved her hand and put the seat back.

"Who is it?" Lissha called out when she approached the door.

"You know who it is," Kiam said with extra bass in his voice.

Lissha took a deep breath and opened the door. She held it open for a minute and looked Kiam up and down. Even in sweats and a hoodie the nigga was still sexy.

He raised one brow at her. "You letting me in?" He quickly eyed her body in her short sleeveless body dress that clung to her curvy figure and pronounced her nipples.

Lissha twisted her lips and moved to the side. When Kiam passed, his cologne slid up her nose causing her heart to flutter. *Lord help me.* She closed the door and followed him into the living room.

Kiam took a seat on the couch with his hands in the pockets of his black hoodie. Lissha sat across from him and pulled her legs up in the chair. The silence was thick with uncertainty. Lissha was waiting for him to tear in to her but he kept quiet and just stared at her making her fidget in her seat.

When she couldn't take it any longer, she spoke first. "Look, I know I was wrong. Being who I am I should show more restraint and being who you are to Daddy I should show more respect." Each uttered word hurt worse than a toothache. She wasn't used to apologizing and on the low she was slick jealous of Faydrah.

Kiam looked at the bruise below her eye and a part of him felt bad for her. He could see that her pride was injured but he would injure her ass if she went after Faydrah. "Lissha," he said, looking at her with lowered eyes, "I accept your apology but I can see that you're still angry and I know how you get down."

"What is that supposed to mean Kiam?" she rested her elbow on her thigh and propped her chin on her fist.

"C'mon, shorty, I know how you're built but you need to check that shit. Eyez is my girl. If you touch her, you touch me. And if you touch me, I touch back. You need to stay the fuck out of my personal business and focus on the mission at hand. This little catty shit you got going with Eyez is over immediately. Do you understand?"

"Did you give that bitch the same sermon?" asked Lissha, twirling a strand of her hair around her finger and looking at him defiantly.

Kiam chuckled, he could see straight through her smart mouth re-marks. "Shorty, keep it one hunnid. What's this really about?" he asked.

Lissha let her hands fall in her lap lifelessly and she stared at him deeply as if what she had been holding in for months threatened to shoot out of her mouth like flames. She unfolded her legs from under her and sat up on the edge of the chair with her palms on her knees.

"Spit it out," he urged.

"Oh, believe me it's not what you wanna hear."

"Try me, baby girl."

That was all the encouragement Lissha needed. "A'ight *baby boy*, you want me to give it to your ass raw?" She sat straight up with her head slightly tilted to the side.

Kiam didn't have the opportunity to answer before she let it spew.

"You real loyal to a bitch that left you hanging for eight years. Where was she when Daddy had me sending you money and keeping your books straight?" She lightly tapped her fist in her palm. "Where was she when you needed shit behind the wall and I was out here busting my ass to send it to Daddy so he could make sure you were straight? And with a straight face you come to me and threaten to kill me if I put her in her place." She threw her hands out to the side and her lips trembled with fury.

Kiam just listened and let her go in ranting.

"You got this shit twisted. I was the one looking out for you and Daddy. That bitch ain't send you a postage stamp and yet you put her on a pedestal like she don't bleed once a month like the next bitch. That trick was sitting in a hair salon while my ass was out here taking penitentiary chances so that you and Daddy could live like kings behind those walls." She folded her arms across her chest as her body began to flood with jaded emotion.

Kiam was shocked by the intensity of her anger and the sight of tears pouring down her face. "Come here shorty," He lowered his voice.

Lissha caught the next tear that tried to roll down her face and toyed with his invitation. After a few more seconds of staring intensely in his eyes she rose to her feet and took a seat next to him on the couch.

Kiam put a consoling hand on her arm and asked. "What do you want? What's repayment for all that you've done?"

"I want you to give me the same respect that you give *Eyez*." She elongated Faydrah's pet name derisively but Kiam let it ride.

He sat up further on the couch and took her hands in his. It touched him to see her show her vulnerable side. "Lissha, never think that I don't respect you because I do to the utmost. But I gotta be hard on you because you'll try a nigga, and with everything we got going on in the streets the last thing I need is an unstable team."

"You don't respect me and you don't care nothing about me. It's all about the money and the power, that's how y'all are." She slid her hands away from his and held his gaze. With so many emotions coursing through her body she did not trust her hands being that close to him.

Kiam was taken aback by her statement. He looked into her eyes and shook his head. "Nah, you're wrong. I'm not that nigga and I do care about you. I love Big Zo and by extension I love you too. I don't just do what I do for the cheddar, I do it for the love. For the loyalty that I have for Pops. If you want out just say the word and I'll make it happen. I'll take care of you like you took care of me when I was bidding. Just tell me what you want."

Lissha lowered her eyes and mumbled a response that Kiam didn't quite hear. "Play that back," he said.

"I said *I want you*." Her eyes met back with his but this time it was her that was sending an invitation and Kiam heard it loud and clear.

A silence came over the room as Kiam processed her response. Lissha tried to blink back the tears but lost the battle as they fell slowly down her face. Catching them at the bottom of her chin she continued. "I want you baby. I've wanted to be you from the moment I first saw you in person. I love you Kiam and I'm tired of fighting this shit."

Kiam took in a deep breath then released it slowly. Her confession was a weight on his shoulders heavier than the sins of men. He gently guided her closer and held her in his arms, placing soft kisses on her forehead. "Shorty, if things were different I would love to make you mine. But my heart belongs to someone and I can't do her like that. And even if Eyez wasn't in my life I could never be with you without your father's blessing."

"He would never give it," she sobbed.

"It's okay, Li. I can love you like a brother."

Lissha pulled back and twisted her face up at him. "I don't want you to love me like no damn brother," she frowned and they both laughed at the thought of that.

"Can you just make love to me one time? Please, I promise not to ever ask for anything else." She put her hands together like a little girl begging to watch one more show before bedtime.

Kiam chuckled but didn't waver. "Nah shorty, if I was to do that I wouldn't be the man I claim to be," he stood firm.

Lissha smiled at him through her tears. "I respect that, but I still love your scary ass," she joked.

"I love you too, shawdy, but let's keep it between us." He held his fist out and she touched it with hers.

"Loyalty is all or nothing."

"All or nothing," she echoed then hugged Kiam tightly around his neck. He allowed her that to keep her pride intact. They exchanged a few more friendly words then Kiam was ready to bounce.

As he stood up to leave Lissha looked at him and realized that she had more respect for him than she had for anybody in the world.

Including Daddy.

Ca$h & NeNe Capri

Chapter 28
A Critical Slip of Tongue

Wa'leek was running out of time and patience; DeMarcus had seemingly disappeared since Daphne's murder, he had not been to his car dealerships in weeks and he wasn't answering his cell phone. Wa'leek didn't know if the scary nigga was somewhere hiding up under a bed or floating at the bottom of Lake Erie with a slab of concrete strapped on his back. With the bloody drug war that Kiam was waging in the streets the latter was definitely a possibility. That nigga was smashing fools and taking names.

Wa'leek planned to handle his business and get the fuck out of Cleveland before the Feds came swarming down on everybody and he got caught up in some shit that didn't involve him. And this time when he left Treebie was bringing her ass back to the Brick with him even if he had to tie her up and put her in the trunk like drug money.

Fuck! He had been in Cleveland too long and his hands were itching to deliver death notices to the doors of his enemies and be out. He had run into a brick wall and his last resort was to pull some help from an old friend. He wasn't in the habit of involving people in his murderous plots but he wasn't going back home until he beheaded every member of Blood Money. The only hope he had left of finding them was the one he hadn't wanted to explore because the nigga he would have to holla at was the type of cruddy muthafucka that would sell his own mama out for a grip.

Wa'leek shook his head and resigned himself to doing what he had to do as he made a right on 131st and Harvard headed to Garfield Heights where Spank lived.

He pulled up in front of Spank's crib and took a second to assess what he was about to do one last time before getting out of the car. There was no way of telling what Spank might be involved in. He was the type dude that dipped in and dipped out of the game and it was also suspected that he set up jack moves. Thus he had enemies like a dog has fleas.

Wa'leek checked his heat then slid out of his whip and went to pay Spank a visit. He reminded himself to be in and out, he didn't want a muthafucka to blow Spank's house up with him up in that piece.

"Hi, Wa'leek?" Spank's girl, Jewel, said as she opened the door.

"Hey, little mama." Wa'leek opened his arms and gave her a half hug.

"Your boy is down stairs, please make yourself at home. Can I take your coat and offer you anythingyo?" she asked as she closed the door.

"No, thank you," Wa'leek said as he headed towards the basement.

By the time he got to the door, Spank was standing there with no shirt on and a .9mm in his hand. "What's up my nigga?" he said, putting his free hand out towards Wa'leek.

"Damn, nigga, that's a hell of a hello you got in your hand."

"You can never be too careful. I got my girl up in here." He gave a half smile.

"Baby, you gonna be long? I need you for something," Jewel said softly as she headed upstairs.

"Nah, I'll be up in a minute. Make sure your tiny security team is on knock out mode," he joked.

Jewel threw him a sexy smile and was out.

Wa'leek observed their interaction, it still amazed him that Jewel was still with Spank after five years. The dude that she was with before Spank had spent a few seasons in the NBA playing with the Cleveland Cavaliers. That had to be a long fall for a broad like herself. Jewel was beyond thirsty, she was dehydrated.

"Come on, nigga," Spank said, heading down the basement's stairs. "Catching a nigga in a romantic moment."

"Sheeeit. At least your wife is home giving you a romantic moment. Mine run the streets harder than me."

"Damn," Spank forced a laugh. Knowing what he knew, he did not want to discuss Treebie at all. It was too close for comfort. He took a seat in his oversized red suede recliner and pushed it back. Reaching over in the ashtray he lit up a blunt.

Wa'leek took a seat in the other recliner and organized his thoughts. He needed Spank to come up off some information but he damn sure was not going to reveal his whole hand.

Spank took several deep pulls then offered it to Wa'leek. "Nah, I'm good. I can't chill when I'm in another man's city. I gotta keep my eyes wide open."

"You sure? This that *strong*."

"I'm good," Wa'leek declined once again.

188

"I hear you. More for me," Spank said, pulling it back to his mouth. "So what's up, Bleed? I know you're not here just to chop it up, that's not your M.O. What can I do for you?"

Wa'leek heard a trace of nervousness in Spank's voice but couldn't figure out what was up with that. Spank was grimy but he wasn't bitch-made. "I'm not here to do you dirty yo. You know me, if I was on that type of time I wouldn't have knocked."

The statement seemed to put Spank at ease, he closed his eyes and inhaled the smoke. He knew Wa'leek was a real nigga. When he was in Ohio years ago he had gave refuge to one of Spank's lieutenants when the city was in a full war. He sat his banger on the small round table on his left, "Anything for you Wah. Just tell me what you need."

"Your city has been plagued with a cancer. And that cancer has spread all the way to my house." He looked over at Spank to gauge his reaction. "What does that have to do with me?"

"Not sure yet but I know you stay on point with what's going on. I traced them here and I need to have their heads before I leave."

"Who you looking for?"

"Some stick up niggas that call themselves Blood Money. I'm sure you heard of them, every hustla from here to New York has." Wa'leek watched for any change in Spank's demeanor.

Spank picked up his drink from beside the ashtray and took a swig to relax his lying tongue. "Yeah, I heard of those boys. They jacked a lil' spot of mine over there off Quincy Road. Left everybody dead but one. I wanna find those chics and murder them myself," he said. "I ain't got shit right now but when I know you'll know," he responded, taking the last of his drink to the head and sitting the glass down light.

Wa'leek stood up to leave. Since Spank had no information about Blood Money that concluded their business. "A'ight son, keep your ears pressed to the streets and as soon as you hear anything hit me up."

"Bet dat," replied Spank as he walked him to the door and let him out.

Once Wa'leek was inside his car, he replayed everything in his head. His well-honed street instincts told him that Spank had been deceptive. But why? he asked himself. What would make that money hungry ass nigga deny knowing Blood Money if it wasn't true? And why had he called them *chics*?

Wa'leek tossed the idea of that around in his head for a minute then concluded that it had to have been a slip of the tongue. There was no way Blood Money were females, their reps was just too vicious for that to be true. He dismissed the thought, started his car, and continued his search for their true identities.

Spank stepped away from the window and closed the blinds as soon as Wa'leek pulled off. He hurried down in the basement, picked up his phone and called Treebie.

"What's up?" she answered, sounding happy to hear from him. His voice always sounded like a money machine. "You got another lick set up for us?"

"No. I would have called Lissha if it was that."

"Then why you on my phone?"

"Because I had an unexpected visitor a minute ago."

"Damn, nigga who was it? Spit it out. Was it po po?"

"Nah, a whole lot worse. It was your husband." Spank picked up his glass and sat it in the sink.

"Wa'leek?" she asked in disbelief.

"Yeah. And he's asking questions about Blood Money."

"Oh shit," Treebie gasped, sitting straight up in her bed.

"Yeah, you better tighten up. If shit gets too close I promise you I won't get caught with my dick out." Spank disconnected the call, hit the lights and headed upstairs.

Treebie put her phone down next to her on the bed as her mind ran a 5k trying to figure out what all Spank could have let fall out of his mouth. One thing she knew for sure he didn't reveal his true role or she would have gotten a call *about* him and not from him. But had he gave any of them up to save his own ass?

The more she thought the more she realized she needed to get Wa'leek's ass back to Jersey as soon as possible. She grabbed her phone and quickly dialed his number to see where he was at. Treebie's fears were confirmed, he was on his way and closer than she expected. She jumped out of bed hit the shower and threw on something that would make Wa'leek spit from more places than his mouth.

By the time Treebie had dimmed the lights and put on something to set the mood, Wa'leek was walking through the door.

190

Trust No Bitch 2

"Hey, babe," Treebie said from her seated position on the couch. Wa'leek's eyes traveled up her smooth legs and rested on that fat print that sat plump and juicy between her thighs. "Yo ass ain't slick," Wa'leek said placing his keys on the table then removing his gun from his waist.

Treebie's heart dropped to her feet when she heard those four words slip from his lips. She swallowed her spit and took in a little air. "What is that supposed to mean?" she asked as she uncrossed her legs thinking of how fast she could get up off the couch and into the kitchen to retrieve her gun from the kitchen drawer.

"You know yo ass been depriving a nigga so you all up in your fuck me panties trying to act like you miss me," he said real smooth still with his gun firm in hand.

"I do miss you, baby," she cooed and opened her legs wide. "Come here and let me show you how much." She motioned with her finger.

Wa'leek sat his gun down, took off his jacket and pulled his shirt over his head. Treebie's eyes rested on his tool as she wondered if he was friend or enemy. Had Spank sent her man home with death in his eyes or was the intensity she was picking up coming from that heat that hung damn near to his knee?

As Wa'leek walked over to where she lay, he used only his eyes to communicate that tonight the only business he was trying to handle was "putting that ass to sleep" business. He accepted her offer and climbed between her legs with force and purpose. Within seconds he was totally out of his clothes and he had her totally out of hers. The living room was filled with his deep grunts and her sexy moans. Wa'leek was turnt all the way up. Treebie had the type of pussy that made a nigga fuck hard and long.

Treebie held him tight with every hunch of his back and when he began to whisper how good she felt in her ear she knew that the only thing he was planning to kill was between two slippery wet lips. She relaxed and allowed him to have her any way he wanted her. Time seemed to stand still when Wa'leek put in that work. It was the only time that things between them were in perfect rhythm. She needed to let him feel as powerful as possible so she could get him to move how she needed him to.

"Shit," Wa'leek said as he released deep inside her womb. "You be making a nigga bring that shit from his toes," he hissed as he pulled out.

Treebie looked back at him from over her shoulder and smiled. "This your pussy Daddy. I make it do whatever you need it to do," she purred as she felt his seed running down her inner thigh.

"I didn't really hear you." He smacked her on the ass. "Come speak into the mic." He said, standing behind her stroking himself back to life.

Treebie got into position and took him into her mouth and made his eyes roll into the back of his head. She sucked him so good she rearranged all his thoughts. When he released to the back of her throat he fell back onto the couch with his eyes low and breath heavy. "Damn, ma," he panted.

Treebie rose to her feet and straddled his lap. "You can't do nothin' wit' ya girl?" she teased, biting and sucking that sweet spot under his chin.

"Sheeeit. You know I can hang. But when you do that tongue trick," he shook his head side to side, "you have a nigga ready to turn his mother in for snitch money."

Treebie giggled. "You so stupid."

"You already know." Wa'leek closed his eyes and enjoyed her soft body against his.

Treebie knew that this was her small window of opportunity so she seized it. "Baby I'm ready to go home."

"We are home." Wa'leek slurred.

"No, baby, I mean I want to go back to Jersey," she said and kissed his lips.

Wa'leek's eyes came open and locked with hers. "What brought this on?"

"I just think it is time. Ain't shit here for me. And I need to let my man lead as I fall back," she said in a low tone.

Wa'leek could hear her words but he was trying to find the honesty in them. He had been trying to get her home for months and all of the sudden she submits? "Nah we good for a little while longer. You got shit to do and so do I. Let's handle our business then we can leave this muthafucka and not look back."

"Baby, I understand all of that but I don't want to have to lose you to the pen or the grave. I see that shit is getting crazy. Kiam is going ham on niggas and after we lost Donella things just ain't the same." She lowered her eyes and voice.

Wa'leek pulled her head to his chest. "Don't worry. I just need a few more days and I'ma kill everything that threatens our peace and anyone who stands in my way will regret it. Just ride with me for a few more days."

"I will always ride with you," she confessed as she stared at the wall across from them. If he knew anything he was doing a damn good job at hiding it and if he didn't, she needed to do whatever it took to keep him from finding out. She listened to the sound of Wa'leek's heart and wondered just how long it would remain beating.

Ca$h & NeNe Capri

194

Chapter 29
Real Nigga's Shit

Kiam tightened the fur hood of his thick butter soft leather jacket around his face and stepped out of the truck into the blistering cold. Winter had come in with a bang depositing six inches of snow on the ground and the temperature had dropped to a freezing 2° below zero. His hands were shoved deep down in the pockets of his jeans, wrapped around the butt of that thang that could melt the grease in a nigga's hair.

Lissha slid out of the passenger seat rocking a 3/4 length mink coat, six inch stiletto boots, and a mink hat that she wore cocked stylishly on her head. The Gucci bag that was slung over her shoulder packed enough heat to change the weather forecast from frigid to extremely hot.

Beside them the twins exited Isaac's brand new Escalade with their burners on their waists and their heads on a swivel. The first nigga that walked by or rode up looking suspect was getting left in a bed of snow. Shit had gotten real serious. Last week Dontae had hit one of their spots and killed two of their workers. They had struck back with swift retaliation, bodying five of his boys.

In the middle of the back and forth bloodshed, Dontae had reached out to Kiam for a meeting. What the fuck he wanted to discuss Kiam didn't know but he surely didn't trust that nigga.

Everyone's eyes were alert as they made their way across the street to the restaurant where the meeting was taking place. JuJu and Bayonna was waiting for them just inside the door. Treebie was chilling at a table with Dontae and his main man Two Gunz, making sure that the only thing in those nigga's hands was a fork.

The owner of the small family diner had closed the establishment for the evening to accommodate this meeting between the two bosses. He rushed up to Kiam and shook his hand then ducked back off in the kitchen to mind his business because theirs was a deadly one.

"Everything is cool, boss. We checked the whole place," whispered JuJu, taking Kiam's coat and hanging it on the coat rack.

Lissha and Bayonna briefly touched cheeks before Bayonna took Lissha's mink and hung it next to Kiam's coat. Lissha clutched her bag and glanced down to make sure that it was unzipped for easy access. The twins moved around them and posted up on both sides of the room.

Kiam stood in place for a minute as he looked across the small dining area to where Dontae was seated. He had a mind to pull out and go ham up in that bitch but he fought back the urge to do so. At the very least he had to respect Dontae's gangsta, it took a lot of heart to murk a nigga's people then arrange a sit-down with him before the bodies were even cold.

If the shit had been a movie, Kiam might've liked Dontae's character but in real life he was out to smash that nigga. He had already decided that if Dontae didn't make him an offer he couldn't refuse he was gonna leave him and his goon's faces in their plates before he walked up out of there. *Fuckin' with me!*

Kiam quickly stemmed his anger and prepared himself to hear Dontae out. When he stepped, it was with a stride of confidence and his team moved behind him like a small platoon. Dontae and Two Gunz saw him approaching and respectfully stood up to greet him. There was head nods and grunts but no handshakes. No one was under the illusion that they were in the company of friends.

"I see you showed up in full force," said Dontae, acknowledging Kiam's numbers but not in fear of them.

"That's how we rock," Kiam let it be known.

"I see." He looked Kiam in the eye like a man does. Two Gunz was beside him willing to die for his dawg.

Treebie was watching them both, ready to make Two Gunz' death wish a reality if either one of them reached for anything besides a napkin.

They all took seats around two tables that had been pushed together. A bottle of champagne sat chillin' in a bucket of ice in the center of the table. Kiam thought that was strange because this was not a celebratory meeting.

The owner came out from the kitchen again and asked if anyone wanted to order dinner. "No, we're good," Kiam answered for his squad.

"We're good, too," said Dontae, speaking for Two Gunz and himself.

After the owner excused himself, the room grew quiet. The air between the two men that had ordered the deaths of each other's souljahs was heavy with distrust. Kiam sat quietly waiting for Dontae to reveal his hand.

196

"Where do I begin?" the young boss paused and rubbed his chin as he gathered his thoughts. When he had them clearly in his mind he continued. "Up until a few months ago I hadn't ever heard of you— "

"What about now? Do you know who the fuck I am?" Kiam interrupted him.

Dontae held his poise and chuckled. "Yeah Bleed, I know who you are now," he acknowledged. "And you should know who the fuck I am," he added with a smirk on his face.

"Like Biggie said—*you're nobody 'til somebody kills you*," Kiam one-upped him.

Beside him Lissha's pussy jumped, that was the type of boss shit that had her stuck on that nigga. Treebie's strap was already halfway out of her purse and JuJu couldn't wait to spill blood on the table cloth. He knew that if Dontae bit the bait Kiam was going to act the fuck up.

Two Gunz felt the vibe going in the wrong direction, he flexed his fingers and got ready to reach for his heat but Dontae remained cooler than a summer's breeze. Turning towards Kiam he asked, "We gonna talk or you wanna pull our dicks out and see whose is the biggest?"

"Big dicks don't pull triggers. Balls do. And since we both on that gorilla nut shit I'll be coming to see you real soon." Kiam began to rise from his seat.

Dontae thought about the losses they had already sustained. "Hold up," he put his hand up. "Before you bounce I want you to hear my offer."

Kiam wrinkled his brow giving Dontae the look of death; he was ready to say fuck it and see that nigga in the street but then a cooler head said hear this nigga out, he may give you the knife you need to cut his throat. Reluctantly he sat back down. "My time is important and very limited so I don't waste it. You sent word that you wanted to talk, so get to the point. I'm listening."

Dontae nodded respectfully, he had loss the pissing contest but he still had his dick and balls and in a minute he was gonna whip those muthafuckas out and show off his size.

Two Gunz relaxed his fingers and Kiam's people removed their hands off of their whistles. Looking Kiam squarely in the eye Dontae said, "We've both lost some men in this war but I'm willing to overlook my losses to bring peace between us. I don't fear you but I respect your ambition and the way you move."

Kiam accepted the props with a slight nod of his head and Dontae went on. "I know you're after The Boss of Bosses' status and I won't oppose you. Just don't fuck with what's mine. I don't give a damn about Wolfman and them because those muthafuckas ain't got no loyalty or principles. As soon as you started knocking nigga's head off they started forming fake ass alliances. When you turnt all the way up they started scrambling and turning against each other. Ain't no way I can ride with fake niggas against a real one."

Kiam ingested Dontae's claim as real spit. It didn't come out like dick riding, Dontae was just respecting how he rocked. "So what are you saying?" he asked him to clarify.

"I'm saying do what you do, playboy and I won't get in your way. If you wanna rule the world I salute you and I'll never come after you in anyway. Just leave what's mine alone. I won't help you get at Wolfman because he was the one that gave me my first pack. But as a show of good faith I'll deliver that weak ass nigga Money Bags Carter to you on a platter."

That was the type of offer Kiam couldn't refuse. "That's a bet. Bring me Money Bags Carter and I'll never move against you again," he agreed.

Dontae smiled, then nodded to his lieutenant. Two Guns reached inside his coat and pulled out a small cigar box and handed it to Dontae. Dontae placed the box on the table and slid it to Kiam. "Let there be peace between us," he announced.

Kiam didn't smoke but he decided to follow through with the ritual. He would pass the cigars around to his people and take one for himself, he just wasn't going to light up. He opened the box and stared at the contents inside then looked up at Dontae curiously.

Lissha, Treebie and JuJu strained to see what the box contained. Kiam picked it up and turned it upside down. A human ear, a tongue, and what looked to be a pair of eyeballs fell out on the table. Everyone looked at Dontae. Kiam looked back down at the small diamond money bag earring attached to the ear and knew exactly what had transpired.

198

JuJu tensed up and shot his eyes over at the twins signaling them to stay on alert. He didn't give a fuck if Dontae poured Money Bags Carter and his whole fuckin' crew on the table he didn't trust this nigga.

Dontae stood up and coolly announced, "Those belonged to Money Bags Carter. Like the Italians say, *he sleeps with the fish now*. From this day forward I won't allow anyone to see, hear or speak any evil against you." He leaned over and grabbed the champagne out of the bucket, popped the top and filled Kiam and his glasses. "To real niggas," he toasted.

Kiam looked in his eyes.to judge his allegiance. Dontae held a firm unwavering eye which to Kiam was the sign of an official nigga. He took the glass by the stem and tipped it towards Dontae. "And to a pact that I will not be the first to break," he vowed as they brought their glasses together.

Dontae nodded as he took the first sip. Kiam followed suit but kept a page marker in his mind. If Dontae even flinched towards betrayal he would make his mother regret taking a nut instead of swallowing it.

Chapter 30
Surprise

Faydrah swallowed a sip of water then sat the bottle down on her desk and twirled around in a circle in her swivel chair, stomping her feet excitedly. She was tickled pink as she looked at the ultra sound picture she had just gotten from her doctor. A routine check-up revealed that all her stress over not being able to fit her clothes was due to her being three months pregnant. With everything going on in her and Kiam's life she had totally ignored all the other signs.

She rubbed her hand across her belly and smiled even bigger as she thought about the fact of them being engaged, living together and now she was about to give Kiam his first child. "You got a good daddy," she said aloud continuing to rub her stomach with both hands.

Needing to hear his sexy voice, Faydrah reached over and grabbed the receiver and dialed Kiam's number. Just when she thought she was about to be sent to voicemail he answered. "Hey you."

"Hey, baby, where are you?" she asked in her pouty voice.

"I'm at JuJu's. Where are you?" he replied as he placed several bricks of that Schizophrenic on the table still in their caskets.

"I'm at work. Are you coming home tonight? I need to talk to you."

"Yeah, I'll be there when you get off. I realize I need to spend some time catering to my woman," he said, getting up from the couch and moving to the kitchen.

"I need you to handle your business real good. You been slipping, playa," Faydrah giggled as she twirled in her seat playing with the phone cord.

"Damn, a nigga been slippin'? Don't worry I got something for that ass tonight."

"Good 'cause I got something for you too."

"What you got for, Daddy?" His deep voice began to turn her on and a slight bit of disappointment surfaced as she realized she still had several hours before she could see him.

"I'll tell you when I see you. Let me finish up my work so I can get to my baby."

"A'ight, travel safe. Love you," he said.

"Love you more." Faydrah blew a kiss into the phone and hung up eager to finish her day and be out.

Kiam walked back into the living room and stood over JuJu and the twins as they divided the product and got it ready for delivery. In the last couple of weeks he had set the tone in the city, niggas was getting the fuck out of the way and the ones who refused were forced to surrender. Product was still jumping and keeping the cash flowing.

One thing Kiam learned when he was just a runner was as long as you keep them feinds clucking, your workers satisfied, and the competition on lock your pockets will stack while the next nigga starve. He knew for sure he was not going to be the hungry nigga.

"Y'all finish up and make the runs. I'll be off the radar tonight. I gotta take care of home. If something comes up that you can't handle hit my emergency line, other than that don't make me have to justify why I pay you so much," Kiam said, leaning over grabbing his gun and tucking it in his waist.

"You know we got this shit," JuJu said, standing up to give him some dap.

Isaac and Isaiah followed suit, they had mad love for Kiam. In a short period of time he had managed to change their whole lifestyle taking them from old school Chevy's with rims to Escalades and 600 Series Benz's with the top missing. They had moved out of their old apartment, turned it into a trap house and now they lamped in a condo out in the burbs. "Be careful boss," both of their voices rang at the same time.

Kiam chuckled, that twin shit always cracked him up. "A'ight y'all do the same." He walked to the door with the twins right on his heels making sure he got to his car safely.

"We gonna have to stop Kiam from traveling alone," Isaac said as he went to the window to make sure everything outside the door was still peaceful.

"You know how he do," JuJu responded.

"I don't give a fuck how he do. We ain't playing chase in the fucking school yard. We got niggas shook and you know how a scared, broke muthafucka can get," Isaiah pointed out.

202

JuJu nodded in agreement. "You right. Next meeting we need to set up some niggas to travel at least a few feet behind him and make sure he gets from point A to point B safely."

"That's all I'm requesting," Isaiah said, taking a seat and placing bricks in small duffle bags. His brother sat beside him doing the same.

"We all need to move differently," Isaiah said, looking back and forth between JuJu and Isaac. "We on a different level now, this is the stage where niggas try to dethrone the kings."

"Bruh, they will have to take the whole fuckin' castle 'cause I ain't trying to hear that shit," Isaac voiced.

"You already know," JuJu said. "Let's make these deliveries then call a small meeting with the lieutenants to start restructuring. Only a fool gets good advice then sits on it." JuJu reached out and bumped fist with his cousins.

Isaac and Isaiah nodded in unison. They had witnessed plenty of niggas rise and fall. Both of them swore that they would go down in a blaze of gunfire before they would surrender their crowns. Hooking up with Kiam was like catching lightning in a bottle and now that they had that shit in hand they planned to screw the cap on tight and protect that muthafucka with life or limb.

Faydrah drove through the city as if she was on a cloud. The light had left the sky and winter was all around her. Light snow had dusted the streets and people were moving quickly to their destination as the chill hit their faces. Normally Faydrah would feel a bit depressed because she hated the winter, but the smile that adorned her pretty face had been stuck there ever since she'd left the doctor's office that morning. She could not wait to share her good news with her boo.

When she pulled up in front of the house, she was a little concerned by the fact that weren't any lights on. Kiam's truck was parked in the driveway but it didn't appear that he was home. She picked up her cell phone and dialed inside. Kiam answered with a grunt.

"Hello?" Faydrah asked with suspicion in her voice.

"Where you at?"

"I'm outside but I didn't see any lights on."

"Bring your scary ass in the house. I told you I got something for that ass," Kiam joked as he peeked out the blinds at her.

"Whatever. Bye." She laughed and hung up. Faydrah grabbed all of her things and hopped out the car. As she turned her key in the door anxiety filled her body as she thought about how she should tell Kiam their good news.

When the door came open she was blown totally away by all that she saw. The living room was filled with over a dozen large black and white, scented candles that illuminated the room. The floor was sprinkled with black rose peddles, Gerald Levert and Keith Sweat were setting the mood with *Just One of Those Thangs*.

Baby, I still love you/I still love you baby, baby

Whenever we kiss and make up, girl/I miss you so bad/If I could tell you before, girl/You were the best thing I ever had/Sorry for all the wrong I've done

You were the only one/I need you to hold me, baby, baby/Like you used to, baby

Reminds me one of them thangs

In the den that sat off the living room Trapstar barked, trying to mess up the mood. Kiam had locked that little cock blocker behind the door this evening and Faydrah thought she didn't mind one bit.

She looked up and saw Kiam standing beside the couch wrapped in a thick black towel with a single red rose in his hand. Her eyes roamed from the top of his head down to the tip of his feet. All his chocolate was on full display and causing her mouth to water. When her eyes settled on his hand, his finger was motioning for her to come to him. She immediately sat her briefcase down, took off her coat, stepped out her shoes and walked over to where he stood.

When she got right up on him he ran the rose down her face stopping to rub it lightly against her lips "Can I have a kiss?" he asked in a deep whisper.

Lowering her eyes and licking her lips she responded. "You can have whatever you want." She took the rose into her hand.

Kiam placed his finger under her chin and placed a few tender kisses on her lips. Faydrah melted with every touch, her body was saying "fuck me" but her mind said "chill" and let him handle his business.

"You ready to let me treat you like a queen?" he asked, looking in her eyes.

"Yes," she said as he took her by the hand and led her to their bedroom.

Black and red rose peddles were laid out along the path and lighted candles sat on both sides of the staircase. When she got to the bedroom she saw he had decorated upstairs the same as downstairs with roses comforting her every step.

"Tonight it's all about you ma," he said as he walked her to the bathroom.

Kiam stood behind her, kissed and nibbled her neck as he reached around and began to unbutton her blouse. The silky material slid down her arms and chills filled her body as she felt the warmth of his breath tantalize her skin. "Umm," she moaned.

"Shhh. I'm just getting started ma," he whispered into the crook of her neck and shoulder.

Faydrah unbuttoned her pants and let them hit the floor. Kiam unbuttoned her bra then reached around and caressed her breast. His rock hard dick pressed between her cheeks causing an instant moistening between her thighs. She stepped out her panties then reached around and put her hand behind his head and slipped her tongue in his mouth. They stood naked and on fire as their hands and mouths explored all the sweet familiarities.

"You tryna get it started." Kiam said when she released him.

"I miss my baby."

"Come let me hold you for a little while." He dropped his towel and they stepped into the hot bubbling water.

Kiam took his time caressing and rubbing the sponge all over her body. He slowly washed every inch of her, massaging her muscles along the way. Faydrah put her head back and enjoyed the soothing caresses as Kiam made her whole body feel worthy of every touch.

When she was totally relaxed Kiam pulled her into his arms and rested her head back against his chest. They exchanged the "I love you's" and Faydrah stole a kiss.

"You know, no matter what, you will always have my heart and my soul," Faydrah said as his hands slid between her thighs.

"I know you're all mine and that's what intensifies my love," he said, biting into her neck and circling her clit with his finger, setting her pussy ablaze.

"Mmmm," she moaned as she felt his fingers push inside of her.

"Come for me baby," he whispered in her ear as her head rested on his shoulder.

"Baby, baby, baby," she cried out as he brought her to the edge of ecstasy.

"Give it to me." He pressed on her clit and circled faster.

"I'm giving it to you Kiam." She.gripped the edge of the tub and released. It came down in a heavy constant flow that made her dizzy with ecstasy. Faydrah laid her head to the side and tried to recover as he rubbed slowly up and down her pulsating lips.

Kiam reached over and gripped her breast in his hand and squeezed her nipples with the tips of his fingers.

"Baby, be gentle," Faydrah whispered.

"Why you always trying to make me be gentle?" His voice was thick with passion. "Lift up before I hold you down and make you do what I want you to do." he said stepping out the tub.

"You tryna put me outta commission," she said with a sexy grin.

Kiam lifted her up then pulled Faydrah to her feet. He grabbed a towel and carefully dried her off touching and caressing her body along the way. After tucking the towel around her chest, he grabbed another from the shelf and dried himself.

"I need to tell you something," she said, taking him by the hand and pulling him in front of her. "Sit down."

"What's up ma?" He looked up at her with low eyes as he took a seat on the edge of the Jacuzzi.

Faydrah placed her hands into his and took a deep breath. "Well," she paused.

"Well what?" He looked at her with a raised eyebrow.

"Somebody is going to be a daddy and it's not me," she sang with a smile.

Kiam's face went blank then his eyes moved down her body. He let go of her and placed his hands on her stomach. Faydrah placed hers on top of his. "We having a baby?" he asked.

206

Faydrah nodded her head.

"Thank you." he said as he felt a lump form in his throat.

"No, thank you. You are my everything Kiam." Her voice cracked and happy tears formed in her eyes.

Kiam leaned in, closed his eyes and kissed her belly. "I love you so much."

"I know."

Kiam wrapped her in his arms and rested his head against her stomach as he processed the idea that he was going to be a daddy. He stood up and took her face into his hands and kissed her deeply. When a light moan left her lips it was on.

Kiam lifted her up into his strong arms, carried her in the bedroom, and gently laid her.in the middle of the bed. He looked at her with utter appreciation and bowed at the seat of her thrown. He placed several kisses on her stomach then cupped his arms under her legs and pulled her sweetness to his lips. Faydrah pressed her head deep into the pillow as his tongue began to glide over her clit with the lightness of a feather. Placing her hands on his head she prepared herself for the passionate whirlwind that only he could wrap her in.

"Kiam," she whispered.

Kiam dared not answer and lose contact with her sweet pearl so he just lightly hummed and sucked as her legs began to tremble.

Faydrah twitched as Kiam ran his tongue between her lips then buried it inside of her.

"Oh, my god," she cried as she tried to wiggle away from his grip.

Kiam came up, placing himself over her and positioning his dick at her opening.

"I need to taste me on your lips," she moaned as she pulled him to her. She hungrily kissed him as he entered her slowly and each thick inch filled her to the core.

Faydrah got lost in the passion as she anticipated each stroke. Every time he pulled back she craved to have him back inside of her. With Kiam she never had to hold back she could give him every part of her. She closed her eyes and enjoyed her man as he pushed deep. The flicker of the candles lit the spaces between the darkness as Avant and KeKe Wyatt crowned *Nothing in This World* perfectly through their speakers.

I can picture us in the living room/by the mantel piece/and you're telling me you're loving me/with your hands on my thighs/while I'm staring in your brown eyes/and the expression on your face/is telling me you want more than a taste so tonight we're going all the way/we'll be loving 'til the break of day. There's nothing in this world I wouldn't do for you boy/I don't care what the others say now that I got you babe/No one can bring me joy like you girl/All the little things you do/It's all about you boo.

Kiam ran the tip of his tongue over her erect nipples as he answered her cries for more. He looked down into her gorgeous eyes and silently thanked God. It was unreal that after sitting in that cell for eight years he would end up back in her arms ready to spend the rest of his life with her and be able to create life in her precious womb.

"Eyez," he mumbled as she moved just right beneath him.

"Yes, baby," she cooed.

"Throw that pussy at me, baby," he moaned as he began to release deep inside her.

Faydrah spread her legs wider and moved in harmony with him. Kiam kissed and sucked her lips as she held him tight. Between her embrace was his whole world and he vowed to do everything he needed to do to keep her safe.

Faydrah was in heaven. She squeezed him tightly because he was the only thing real in her life and letting him go was not an option. They feel asleep in each other's arms happy and complete.

When Kiam woke up the next morning, he heard Faydrah on the phone telling her mother about the baby. He turned over on his side, spooned her into him, and placed his hand on her stomach and rubbed as if he was letting the baby know that daddy was right there. With her back to him and behind pressed comfortably against his groin, Faydrah continued her conversation. She giggled as she shared her excitement with her mom. A feeling of pride rushed over Kiam and invigorated him like an early morning shower. He laughed at himself as he lay there wondering if parenthood would turn him soft.

Never that he said as his eyes caught sight of his two bangers on the nightstand. He decided that he was gonna go even harder; he was gonna treat the streets like the foul hearted side bitch that it was. He would fuck 'em real good for another year or so then leave that bitch with nothing but a wet ass and a story to tell.

The only thing worthy of holding onto forever was lying in his arms.

Chapter 30
Facing the Bitter Truth

Lissha's love and respect for Kiam had multiplied tenfold since their heart to heart talk. Now she paid more attention to how he moved and the things he said. What stood out most, even more than his G, was his loyalty. A man that stood firm on his principles was sexy as hell. She wanted him more than she wanted to take her next breath but two huge obstacles stood in their way.

The first was Faydrah. Just the other day Kiam had told her that the bitch was pregnant, now her hold on him was stronger than the Jaws of Life. But not stronger than Lissha's desire to have him. She had decided to fall back for now because aggressiveness would have been seen by as disrespect to the code that he lived by. She would sit back and plot, and the turtle would eventually win the race.

In the meantime, she was about to face the second obstacle which was Big Zo. It both saddened and frightened her to think of what his reaction was going to be when she told him how she felt about Kiam. *Daddy can be so got damn selfish and overbearing.*

Lissha closed her eyes and leaned her head against the steering wheel as she waited outside the prison for visitation to begin. Her heart ached as she looked up at all the concrete and razor wire that was Big Zo's only reality.

She had been all in her feelings lately and hadn't answered his calls, but now she had some really good news to deliver to him along with her confession. She just hoped the good news would lessen the blow of what he would see as the ultimate betrayal. *I'm his baby girl, he'll understand. And it's not like I've already done it*, she tried to convince herself as she felt the push of tears in the corners of her eyes.

Big Zo spotted his LiLi as soon as he entered the visitation room. She was at the snack machines with her back to him. She must've felt his eyes on her back because she looked over her shoulder and their eyes met. She flashed him a smile and came walking towards him with her arms full of microwave sandwiches and a bottled juice.

"Hi, Daddy," she beamed as she stepped into his arms. As usual he smelled good and was as fit as a man half his age.

"Hey, baby." Big Zo hugged and kissed her then held her back at arm's length and looked her over.

She threw a tiny smile on her face. "Our table is over here," she said, leading the way.

Big Zo nodded at several men that were visiting with loved one's as he followed Lissha to their seats. He sat down across from her and Lissha placed the snacks on the table between them. "What do you want me to heat up first?" she asked, avoiding direct eye contact.

"I'm not hungry right now, maybe later. Where you been? I've been tryna reach you all week."

"Things have been hectic lately Daddy." She fumbled around with a bag of Lay's chips; she needed something to do with her hands to stop them from trembling.

"Your phone still works doesn't it?"

"Yes, I'm sorry," she apologized in a child's voice and casted her eyes to the floor.

Big Zo looked at her and his forehead creased. "Baby, is something wrong?" he asked. He had just talked to Treebie yesterday and she hadn't mentioned anything other than Wa'leek being in town causing discomfort. But she had assured him that he was running into brick walks.

"I'm good, Daddy. I'm probably just a little tired from the drive," Lissha lied as she waited for an opening to tell him the truth.

Big Zo nodded his head. "So what's been going on? Is Kiam holding things down?" He kept his voice low.

"Yeah, Daddy," she replied, brightening up some. "Kiam has the whole city shook and we're seeing more money than ever before."

Lissha went on to tell him about the mutilated body parts that Kiam delivered to their enemies and the pact that he had made with Dontae. She was careful not to speak above a whisper. Big Zo listened with a calculating mind. The more bloodshed and the more brutal the murders were that Kiam committed the more likely the Feds would come after him, making it a priority to get him off the streets. When their interest in him reached its zenith that's when he would contact them and offer them Kiam for a free get out of prison pass.

"Baby, it's almost time," Big Zo said.

212

Lissha knew exactly what he was referring to but her heart ached when she thought about it. "Daddy, I have some good news," she said, changing subjects and fidgeting with one of her rings.

Big Zo reached across the table and placed his hand on top of hers. "I need some good news, what is it?" he asked.

"Kiam found a lawyer that guarantees he can get your sentence reduced from life to thirty-five years, you'll be out in thirty and he only wants a quarter mil."

Big Zo did the math in his head and chuckled. He had only served a dime so far which meant he would still have twenty more years to do. "You call that good news?" he asked bitterly.

Lissha lowered her eyes again.

"I'm fifty-five years old. If I serve another twenty years in this muthafucka I'll be seventy-five when I get out. What the fuck am I gonna be able to do at that age?" he asked as if she had caused his situation.

"At least it's something, Daddy," she mumbled.

"What the fuck did you say?" he gritted, causing Lissha to shiver. She didn't dare repeat it. "Where the fuck is this all coming from? Stick to the got damn script." Big Zo squeezed her hands roughly.

Lissha stifled a cry.

He released her hands and looked her in the eye but she refused to meet his stare. Big Zo jumped to the only conclusion that would explain her wavering. "You fucked that nigga didn't you?" he accused on clenched teeth moving slightly forward.

Her heart hit her breast bone hard. "No," she answered truthfully but he didn't believe her.

"Yes you did, bitch!" Big Zo's hand was a blur. Whap! He slapped Lissha clean out of the chair onto the floor causing a few items from the table to scatter on her way down.

Heads turned at the sound of the commotion. The guard rushed over and asked Lissha if she was okay. "I'm fine. I slipped out of my seat," she said, getting to her feet. Lissha fumbled trying to pick up the sandwiches and settle back in her chair.

The guard looked from her to Big Zo who now had his arms folded across his chest. "You heard her, she slipped. Now push the fuck on and let me enjoy my muhfuckin' visit," he growled.

"Ok but I'm going to be watching you Carruthers," the guard warned then returned to his post.

Lissha's hands shook as she dabbed at tears with some napkins. She kept her eyes low and head down. The last thing she wanted to do was make him angrier than he already was.

Big Zo had zero compassion as he went the fuck off in a low but harsh tone about something she had just uttered. His face contorted into a threatening scowl and the heat that came off his words were hotter than a cheap pistol. "Bitch, don't you throw no other nigga in my face talking about how loyal he is. Fuck loyalty, that nigga is a pawn I'm the muhfuckin' king and don't you ever forget that."

"But he cares about you Daddy, doesn't that matter?"

"Do *you* care about me?"

"Yes. You know I love you and I always will but I don't want to do him like that."

Hearing those words come out of Lissha's mouth infuriated Big Zo. His nose flared in and out. Kiam was his only way out of prison. They had been planning this for years and now she wanted to back out. He leaned across the table and spat dead in her face. "I don't give a fuck how you feel. I own your ass, bitch. If you cross me you'll die with that nigga."

Lissha jumped back and wiped the glob of spit out of her face and looked at him with a hardened stare. "It's snitching, Daddy. And don't you remember what you told me about snitches? You said death to all of them muthafuckas. Do you remember what you had me do to some of those that testified against you?" Lissha said on tight lips.

"This isn't the same. Kiam's a pawn and pawns get sacrificed for the king."

"Telling is telling," she said, refusing to give him an out.

Big Zo laughed. "You should be the last person to condemn a muthafucka for telling," he said. "Or have you forgotten that you're the one that told me that your mother was creeping on me with Wolfman? Remember that?"

The recollection caused Lissha to drop her head in shame. Big Zo pounced on her while she was weak with regret. "You was just sixteen but you knew what you were doing. You knew it was wrong but you did it

214

anyway because you wanted me for yourself even though I was your mother's man and your stepfather. Is that loyalty Lissha?"

"I was young."

"But you knew the code didn't you? You knew that betraying your own mother's secrets was wrong. And after I put her ass out in the streets and cut her off you became my woman just like you planned all along."

Lissha sniffled as she lost the battle to hold back her tears. Big Zo could see he had successfully had the impact he needed to have on her so now it was time to lick her wounds.

Big Zo reached over the table and took her hand in his. "I'm not judging you baby, all I ask is that you don't judge me. Fuck everybody else as long as we remain loyal to each other. If you slept with Kiam I can forgive that—I love you just that much."

"I didn't sleep with him," she said.

Big Zo heard the honesty in her voice and that soothed his anger. He leaned across the table and kissed her. "I love you baby and that's why I'm willing to do this. I want to get out of here so that we can have a life together. Do you still want that?"

Lissha moved her head up and down.

"Who do you love?" he asked, stroking her hand.

"You Daddy," she replied.

"Well, look in my eyes and tell me what I need to hear."

Lissha lifted her head and looked into his eyes. "I love you Daddy and I will not betray you," she said.

When the visit was over, Big Zo hugged and kissed his baby girl goodbye. "You and me against the world," he whispered in her ear.

"Forever," she vowed.

But as Big Zo watched her turn and head towards the door he reminded himself *Trust No Bitch.*

As soon as he got back to his cell, Big Zo retrieved his cell phone from his hiding spot and dialed a number. As he waited for the party to answer he chastised himself for not choosing her over Lissha in the first place. The bitter truth was that he would do whatever it took to get out of prison.

Chapter 32
Snakes in the Game

Lissha drove the last ten miles of her trip in utter turmoil. Nothing could have prepared her for what happened on that visit. Only one other time had Big Zo put his hands on her and his vow to never do it again had just been broken. Adding insult to injury he had spat in her face as if she was the lowest form of life. Maybe she was, she thought.

Big Zo had given her everything she had ever wanted and all he demanded in return was loyalty. But he was asking her to do the very thing that he claimed to detest. Not only that, he wanted her to help him do it to the only nigga that had kept it one hundred with him— Kiam didn't deserve that. In a short period of time he had managed to capture her heart without even trying.

Lissha bit down on her bottom lip and tried to contain the tears. Her heart was in direct conflict with her duty causing her to seriously consider aborting the plans that Big Zo had designed to regain his freedom. If she turned her back on him he would probably die in prison. If she helped him set up Kiam, Kiam would suffer that awful fate. She just couldn't do it.

Lissha got off the expressway and drove straight to Kiam's house. She sat there staring at his truck and her conscious urged her to get out and tell him everything. Her heart became heavier by the second and her mouth felt like she was chewing cotton as she tried to formulate the words that she would say to him.

It occurred that it was too late to turn back now, the wheels had already been set in motion. If she went in there and told him the truth Kiam would consider her just as culpable as Big Zo. He would snap. He would probably blow her brains out and feed her to Treebie and Bayonna in a dish. And even if he spared her, the reality was she would never have him because he would forever hold it against her.

Kiam was a man that stood on more than his word. He stood on the actions behind them and because of that she knew exactly what she needed to do. As she drove off she gripped the steering wheel tightly and tears rolled down her face. The only choice she had was to stick to the script. Big Zo would forgive her momentary change of heart but had she lost his trust? she worried.

Lissha drove to her house parked and ran inside. Her first move was to call the girls and put them on point for tomorrow night. Big Zo wanted them to hit someone's spot that would assure that the death toll continued to rise.

After discussing it with her bitches in code talk, Lissha sat on her bed and tried to conjure up the evil from within to do the dirtiest and unthinkable acts that lay ahead of her. This was the life she had chosen and the dishonor she was about to commit was definitely about to have deadly consequences.

Faydrah had been cooped up in the house for the last two weeks and finally Kiam gave her the okay to hit the streets. She made her way to the mall and filled the trunk with all her favorites' shoes, pocketbooks and expensive perfumes. After driving through Legacy Village for something to eat, she headed to the nail spa around the corner from the diner.

"Hey, Ms. Faydrah," her nail technician said with a smile.

"Hey, Tiffany," Faydrah said, sipping her drink.

"You look so pretty, you all glowing and shit," Tiffany said, coming over and holding her arms open to give Faydrah a hug. A few of the regulars nodded and smiled.

"I feel pretty Tiff, but it's hard to believe at times," she responded with a smile.

"I can imagine, you use to be like I ain't having no kids," Tiffany turned her lips up mocking Faydrah. They both busted out laughing.

"I know right. Well Kiam changed all that," Faydrah said giggling and rubbing her little bump.

"Come sit down, what all you getting today," she asked, walking to the pedicure chairs.

"The works, girl I need it all. That man been keeping me locked up in the house."

"You know how they do, they can have the run of the earth but then tell us *stay yo ass in the house*," Tiffany said as she ran the water for the pedicure and set the massage chair.

Faydrah nodded her understanding, took off her coat and fur boots, and hopped up in the chair placing her feet in the hot bubbly water.

"Go ahead and relax mommy. I'll be right back." Tiffany said, going back to finish a manicure.

Faydrah threw her earphones in, turned on her Pandora, and closed her eyes.

Tiffany allowed Faydrah time to just chill then she did her feet giving her a thorough massage and French pedicure then onto her hands.

Faydrah collected her boots and headed to Tiffany's table and took a seat.

"So do you know what you're having yet?" Tiffany asked placing Faydrah's hands in the bowl.

"Not yet we'll find out next month."

"Is Kiam excited?" Tiffany asked, lifting her eyebrows up and down.

"He is more than excited, all he does is rub and talk to my stomach. Not to mention he gets to enjoy his favorite position," Faydrah said then laughed.

"Sheeiit. I know that's right. You know they don't play with that back action."

"His butt is spoiled."

"Well he deserves it. He is a good man and he had to do a lot of hand action over his eight year vacation so you better give him whatever he asks for," Tiffany said then slapped fives with Faydrah.

"Can't you tell I've been giving it to him?" Faydrah said, pointing to the little bump in her stomach.

They continued to laugh and talk as if they were the only two in the shop. Just as Tiffany was almost done she looked up and saw a woman walking into the salon with all high end labels and iced up. She walked over to the counter and requested, Cynthia, the woman with the table next to hers then strutted over and sat down with a confidence that read *bitch back the fuck up.*

Faydrah noticed the sudden distraction in Tiffany and looked over to where her gaze rested. When Faydrah looked over at the woman she gave her a small smile. The woman barley returned it as she stuck her hands in the bowl with poise and arrogance.

Tiffany twisted her lips to the side like *bitch please.* Then she gave Faydrah the *you see this bitch look* raising her eyebrows in the woman's direction.

Faydrah slightly shrugged her shoulders and held her hands out for Tiffany to finish. They started back into their conversation apparently not fazed by the woman's stank attitude.

"That rock is official," The woman said to Faydrah.

Faydrah turned in her direction. "Oh, thank you." Faydrah said, sliding it back onto her finger.

"He gave you a ring and you gave him a baby, huh?" The woman threw a smile on her face and continued to pry.

Faydrah looked at her hand then tried to be as diplomatic as possible. "Loyalty and good pussy earns rings. Pregnancy is just a result of both," she said, looking at the woman straight in the eyes trying to gage her angle.

"I hear that. I need to find me a nigga that folds to good pussy. You see I like jewelry," the woman bragged, holding her hand up.

"Well, keep looking. I hear one is born every second," Faydrah shot back, stood up and passed Tiffany a hundred dollars.

The woman nodded with a sinister smile on her face. "I wish you all the best."

"Thank you," Faydrah returned.

Tiffany came from around the table and walked Faydrah to the door. They swapped a few words about the strange interaction and Faydrah was out.

The smile dropped from the woman's face before the door could close. *Niggas swear they're a boss until they find out everything they love can be touched,* she said to herself as she unconsciously rubbed the Black Mamba tat around her wrist.

Chapter 33
Calculated Diversion

"**D**on't fucking play with me, run that money," the raspy voice boomed as the blood red eyes peered down at him.

"We ain't got shit here," he yelled from the other end of Treebie's rubber grip fo-five.

"Nigga, do you think I'm in the habit of putting a gun in the wrong nigga's face?" she smacked him across the mouth with her heat then put it between his eyes. "Your memory feeling jogged yet muthafucka?"

"Maybe we need to give him a reason to mourn," Bayonna said as she knocked one in the chamber and pointed it at his woman's head.

"Wait," Two Gunz yelled out from his kneeled position. He looked down at his little brother's dead body beside him; blood ran out of the hole behind his ear turning the thick white carpet red. They had killed him with no purpose other than to show their viciousness.

On the other side of Two Gunz, his baby mama was faced down with a pump shotgun to the back of her head. Two Gunz knew that neither of them would be shown any mercy so he refused to cooperate with the masked robbers' demands. "Get it how y'all live," he said, staring death in the face and refusing to tuck his tail.

Lissha usually stayed in the background and watched over everyone's shoulder. Not tonight, she stepped forward and blew the front of his head to the back. When his body twisted and fell to the side Treebie looked up with disgust. They had not gotten the information they needed and they had stayed a few minutes past too damn long.

She grabbed the girl by her ponytail and pulled her head back so that she was staring into those blood red eyes. "Bitch I don't have a problem killing a woman," she warned. I'm going to ask you one time where the money at and if you stutter I'ma let this trigger scream. Don't die over the next nigga's shit." She shoved her gun up under the terrified girl's nose. "Start bumping ya gums, bitch," she spat.

"It's in the basement," she cried as her whole body shook with fear.

Treebie pulled her up on her feet by her hair and led her towards the basement's stairs. Bayonna followed with her pump cocked and ready to cause more carnage.

Lissha ran Two Gunz' pockets then put an insurance shot straight through his heart. She stepped over his body and did his little brother just as dirty as she had done him, then she proceeded down the stairs to help her girls hit the safe.

When she got in the basement, Treebie was tying ol' girl up and Bayonna was filling the duffle bags. Lissha's eyes widened at all the stacks they had come up on. This looked to be the biggest lick they had ever come up on. "Yeah this nigga was sitting on Fort Knox," she mumbled to herself.

Treebie stood over the woman as Lissha and Bayonna drug the bags to the basement door.

"Kill that bitch and let's go!" Lissha yelled out.

"Nah, I think Wolfman would want us to spare the woman," Treebie pretended to whisper.

Behind her mask Lissha smiled, knowing that Treebie had just thrown salt in the game.

Treebie reached down and smacked the woman across the head with the gun drawing enough blood to make her signature known. She bent over and rubbed a crisp bill in the blood then stuffed it in the woman's mouth past the gag. "Blood Money, bitch," she boasted. "Tell a friend."

Chapter 34
Fatal Deception

Wa'leek hit the remote on the garage opener and pulled his car in next to Treebie's. Once the gate slid down in its place he turned off the engine and sat contemplating on what move he needed to make next. He had been in the city for well over a month and was no closer to Blood Money than he was when he first stepped foot back on enemy soil. It was plaguing him that he had scratched every inch of the city and still came up dry. One thing he knew he didn't have in his blood was defeat so he was not giving up on the hunt.

Frustrated at his lack of progress he stepped out the vehicle and headed inside the house. When he hit the lights it was apparent that Treebie was not home and from the looks of things she had been gone for some hours. There was no lingering smell of food nor the faintest hint of her perfume. No weed smoke was in the air and no scented candles burned. He walked over to the refrigerator and opened it wide. The only items that stared back at him was bottled water and a muthafuckin' bagel.

"How the fuck a nigga got a wife and ain't got shit to eat," he said, slamming the door and walking towards the living room.

Wa'leek stopped a few steps away from the couch as his thoughts returned to the difficulty he was having finding out the identities of Blood Money. He had chased down a dozen or more leads only to be left holding nothing but his dick in his hand.

He stood there reassuring himself that he had put the press down hard enough on muthafuckas. He indeed had, but obviously those Blood Money niggas moved with caution, and the fear they left behind had the streets afraid to utter their names. Shit was getting tight and if he kept asking around about them it was only a matter of time before the ones he was hunting would began to hunt him. He had to admit Treebie was right. It was time to get the fuck outta Ohio. He had his own shit pending in the Bricks and even though he had vowed to bring Riz some heads on a platter he wasn't trying to get his knocked off in the process.

Wa'leek took off his coat and threw it over the couch then headed to the basement. He hit the lights and walked straight to the bar. He could see a half lit blunt in the ashtray and three shot glasses on the bar. "Yo ass ain't cook but you got time to get high and drunk. Yeah I got something for that ass," he said aloud, shaking his head as he walked to the back of the bar to grab a bottle of Amsterdam.

He grabbed a glass and an ashtray and headed to the couch and took a seat. He poured himself a full glass then lit the blunt and began taking a few hits.

"Where you muthafuckas at?" he asked as he replayed the night that Blood Money almost took his life. He put the glass to his mouth and drank it half down. Taking a few more pulls of the blunt, he sat it in the ashtray and filled his glass back to the top and started thinking.

Where the fuck was Treebie at? She needed to bring her ass home and do what a wife was supposed to do for her husband. Wa'leek grabbed his phone and texted her to see where she was. When she didn't respond he texted her again and waited.

A couple of minutes passed without him receiving a reply so he called her number, ready to order her home. When he was sent straight to voice mail his mood shot from bad to worse. He threw his cell down next to him and kicked his feet up on the coffee table. When he leaned up to grab the blunt from the table something on the floor over by the lounge chair caught his eye. It was a black strap with something silver on it. Wa'leek squinted his eyes for a better look then took his feet down and went to retrieve it.

"What the fuck?" he said as he turned the object in his hands.

His hands became hot as he realized that the object was a voice distorter. The only other time he had seen one was the night those four Blood Money niggas ran up in the spot and robbed and murdered his homies. Why in the fuck did Treebie have a voice distorter? he asked himself.

I wanna find them chicks and murder them myself. Spanks words came back to him in clarity. *Chicks,* he had slipped up and said. Wa'leek knew that the tongue sometimes betrayed a guilty mind if a nigga wasn't careful.

"That muthafucka! He knew who they were all along!"

Now it all added up. Four masked robbers that killed indiscriminately and without mercy. Four friends who was as thick as thieves. *Treebie, that bitch Lissha, Donella and Bayonna. And Spank probably sets up the licks.* Wa'leek pieced it all together.

He balled up the voice distorter and stuck in his pocket. His eyes focused on a cabinet with a lock on it over by the bar. He looked around for

224

something to break the lock with but couldn't find anything. "Oh, you're coming off muthafucka," he said with determination. Then he stalked upstairs and retrieved a tire iron from inside the garage and hurried back down, chest heaving and thoughts burning.

Wa'leek beat the lock with the tire iron until it snapped open and clanged to the floor. He opened the cabinet doors and found a small cache of guns, black hoodies and pants and cases of those blood red contacts. The blood in his veins boiled like a pressure cooker.

The room seemed to spin as he thought about those red eyes staring at him as that bloody money was stuffed in his mouth. He recalled every detail of the robbery and murders in slow motion. Two of his homies laid face-down and executed. Others in the house tortured and killed with no regard. A hole blown through Riz's son Jamaal's hand. And the disrespect to him personally. They had stuffed a bloody bill in his mouth and taunted. *" This is Blood Money muthafuacka. "*

He had always wondered why he was spared too when it was urban legend that those niggas only left one to be the mouth piece of their terror. Now he had the answer and it was an insult of the worst kind. It wasn't dick up under that gear, it was pussy. His pussy.

"You fuckin' deceitful bitch," he yelled out as he took off for the steps.

Wa'leek grabbed his coat and moved to the garage, he would show Treebie what blood money really was when he got back. In the meantime he was going to show Spank that a country nigga could never outfox a nigga from up top. "That pussy ass muthafucka knew all along that I was sleeping with the enemy. Now he's about to find out why they call the Bricks *Dirty Jersey,*" he said as he backed out of the garage.

Wa'leek parked a few houses down from Spank's. The street appeared to be quiet and still which served him perfectly. He screwed the silencer on the end of his toolie, slipped it inside his coat pocket and went to serve justice. He didn't see Spank's ride in the driveway but that didn't deter him.

With a strong winter wind at his back and revenge in his pocket, Wa'leek walked up on the porch and knocked on the door. As he waited for someone to answer he turned sideways to watch the street and the door at the same time. If that nigga happened to pull up he was going to leave his cabbage well cooked.

"Who is it?" Jewel called out from behind the door.

"It's Wa'leek," he answered, stepping in front of the peep hole so that she could see him.

He heard her disengage the lock then she opened the door. "Hey Wah," she said, smiling at him like she was happy to see him again.

"How you ma?"

"I'm just fine. Spank isn't here but you can come in and wait for him. He just called, he should be here shortly." She stepped to the side to let him in.

"I don't know if I wanna come in," he said, looking down at the gun in her hand.

"Why not? I don't bite," she replied then her eyes followed his and she realized what he was staring at. "Oops. I don't need this for you but I gotta be careful you know how Spank is, he be doing the most." She sat the gun on the picture stand by the door and smiled at Wa'leek.

He stepped inside and followed her to the den. As they neared the room he could hear Wales song *Ambition* playing.

They gonna love me for my ambition/ ambition . . .

Wa'leek eased his hand in his pocket and quietly slipped his burner out. As they entered the den he raised his arm and shot Jewel in the back of the head. Pwwt! The silencer muffled the sound but did nothing to limit the damage. Jewel's pretty blond streaked tresses puffed out around her head like a halo. Blood and skull sprayed out of her forehead and she crashed to the floor on her face.

Wa'leek pumped two more shots in her then stepped over her body, took a seat on the couch and fired up a blunt that he found on the end table. As the smoke filled his lungs he waited for Spank to come home and walk into a death trap.

Spank came into the house with a bag full of money slung over his shoulder. He had just collected from some bricks he had fronted to somebody. He had to admit that the game was being sweet to him, he was getting paid from both sides and making off like a bandit.

"Jewel," he called out as he followed the sound of the music coming from the den. When he stepped in the room, he saw her stretched out on the floor in an unnatural twist. He froze in his spot then he bent over to see if she was dead.

"Blood Money nigga," the distorted voice said from behind him. Spank turned and looked up. The last thing he saw before he got sent to his Maker were a pair of blood red eyes.

Wa'leek stepped back examining his handiwork. The corners of his mouth formed into an evil smirk; he had two heads for Riz and three to go. He tucked his gun and eased out the house just as smoothly as he came in.

As Wa'leek drove back home with the bag of money on the seat next to him, he thought of all the ways he would torture Treebie before killing her. *'Til death do us part,* he said as he reached the house.

Treebie's other whip wasn't in the driveway so he knew that she wasn't home yet. It didn't matter, he was going to patiently wait on that ass to return then he would show her no mercy. Deception and deceit were unpardonable.

He hit the remote and pulled back into the garage. He waited for the garage door to come down then he grabbed the money off the seat and went inside the house. As he stepped through the door headed for the bedroom Treebie crept up behind him and put a gun to the back of his head. "You should've left well enough alone," she muttered.

Chapter 35
Deadly Silence

Kiam and Faydrah were snuggled up on the couch watching ESPN highlights before the big Sunday night football event. Trapstar was all underfoot so he took him in the den and locked him in their with some toys.

"Babe, why are you always locking my little doggie in a room?" asked Faydrah when Kiam returned.

"Because his little butt is a hater. Next time I'ma get you a pit bull," he said as he sat back down beside her.

"I don't want a pit."

"What do you want?" he asked putting his arm around her shoulders.

"You. Nothing but you and our baby," she replied, cuddling in his arms.

These were the type of days that a G could hold on to when the streets became cold and merciless. Every time he looked into Faydrah's beautiful face while rubbing her belly, it made him look forward to the day when he was able to retire from the game and put the heartless memories behind him.

Kiam knew that that day was a year or two away. It wasn't just about stacking more money for them to live lavish, it was also about his word to Big Zo. There was still some things that had to be done and on his life he would see them through. Loyalty never wavers, he said to himself then he returned his focus to his beautiful queen.

He leaned over and placed his head against her stomach. "What's up little baby," he cooed to his seed.

Faydrah looked down at him lovingly and stroked the back of his head. "Look at you," she said, "Nothing has changed from when we first fell in love. All that thug stuff goes right out the window when we're alone. And I can already see that this baby is going to have you wrapped around its finger."

"You already know," he agreed. "I'm going to spoil her just like I spoil her mother." Kiam sat back up and gave her some tongue.

Faydrah wrapped her arms around his neck and made the kiss last. When their mouths separated her face was flush, after all this time he still took her breath away. She reached out and wiped the corners of his mouth and Kiam stroked her wrist.

"By the way, it's not going to be a *she*. I'm going to give you a little man who will be as handsome and as strong as his daddy," she predicted.

"I'm one of a kind," he teased.

Faydrah grabbed a pillow off the end of the couch and playfully hit him across the head. "You're so dang arrogant," she said half-jokingly.

"My baby mama love it."

"You got that right sir," she laughed, thinking that sometimes he could be so silly.

Kiam saw the love in her eyes and he couldn't help but verbalize his appreciation. "Baby, I know I can be hard sometimes but I hope you know that my love and respect for you is forever. You are my peace in the middle of this shit storm. I thank you for always being here for me. That's real talk shorty," he said, leaning down and kissing her lips.

"You know I ain't going no where. You stuck with me for life." Faydrah held her hand up and shifted it from side to side.

"Yeah you still owe me for all that ice," Kiam said real smooth, stealing himself another kiss.

"No, you owe me. Your son is taking over my whole body." She giggled.

"That's because he's a boss. You better recognize," he said, rubbing her belly and smiling wide.

"Whatever, he is going to be a good boy." Faydrah got ready for their little "who's in charge" battle.

"I wanna be a good boy, Let me get some Sunday night wetness before the game," Kiam said, moving his hand from her stomach and sliding it between her legs from the back.

"You are so spoiled, you know that right?"

"Get up on my lap and spoil me some more," Kiam spoke deep.

Faydrah wasted no time getting into place and hooking a brother up. All that hot pregnant pussy had Kiam on cloud fifty-five. He sat back and let her do her thing; being the king had more benefits than money and power combined. In her he had a passionate and loyal queen. All of the money in the world couldn't replace that.

Kiam and Faydrah took a quick shower then prepared for the game. She popped a few bags of popcorn and poured them into a bowl with Cool Ranch Dorito's while Kiam let Trapstar out in the backyard to run around in the snow.

Kiam locked the back door and came back in the living room, sat in his recliner and pushed it back. "Come on ma," he yelled out.

"Don't be rushing me, while you all propped up," Faydrah sat the bowl in front of him then went back for his soda.

"Thank you, baby." Kiam hit her butt as she turned to sit down.

"Go ahead and get me hot and you're gonna miss your little game." She warned as she sat on the couch and kicked her feet up.

Kiam didn't even respond he wasn't trying to miss the Browns. Faydrah had that type of heat between her thighs that would make a man miss his mother's funeral if he got started.

He flipped back and forth between ESPN and Fox waiting for the kick-off. He grabbed the bowl of popcorn and began putting a serious hurting on it. Just as the teams took to the field Kiam heard his emergency phone ringing from the other room. He sat up in the chair and moved swiftly to his den.

"Hello."

"What's good?" Big Zo asked.

"Ain't nothin' Pops, just chillin' about to watch the game with my girl. Everything a'ight?" Big Zo sounded stressed.

"You heard from Lissha?"

"Nah, not today. Why? You need something?"

"I been calling her all day and no answer. I also hit Treebie and Bayonna and the same thing. All three of their phones are going to voice mail."

"A'ight, I'm on it."

"I'm worried, hit me as soon as you hear something."

"I will."

As soon as Kiam disconnected the call, Big Zo's worry came over him. In all the years of him knowing Big Zo he had never heard him sound so concerned. With all of the beef with Wolfman going on he could not discount anything.

Kiam hit Lissha's number back to back and each time he was sent straight to voice mail. When he tried to reach Treebie her phone sent him to voice mail too. "What the fuck is going on?" he wondered out loud.

"Is everything okay baby?" Faydrah called from the other room.

"Yeah," he called back to her but he wasn't so sure. He tried to reach Bayonna but she didn't answer either. Now he was really concerned.

Kiam immediately hit JuJu and after four rings he finally got an answer. "What's up boss?" JuJu slurred.

"Where you at?"

"At the crib. What's banging, you straight?" JuJu came to attention hearing the urgency in Kiam's voice.

"Is your woman with you?"

"Yeah she lying next to me. Why? What's up?" JuJu got out of the bed and walked into the bathroom closing the door behind him. Bayonna sat up, got out of the bed and walked close to the bathroom door to try and catch what was going on.

"You seen or heard from Lissha?" Kiam asked as he moved up the stairs and into his closet to get dressed.

"Not since yesterday afternoon. Why? What's up?"

"I don't know yet but get dressed and be on standby. Put the twins on pont we might have to go and turn the city blood red."

"Done." JuJu hung up and called the twins. When Isaac answered her relayed Kiam's message. "Get on point. I'll be over there in a minute."

Bayonna heard the door knob turn and ran back and hopped on the bed. JuJu didn't even look in her direction as he moved to the dresser and began throwing on his jeans and a shirt.

"Babe, what's the matter?" she asked, looking worried.

"Nothin'," JuJu said then moved to the closet grabbing his vest, gun, hoodie and boots.

"JuJu don't lie to me. I know the code. What happened?" Nervous energy filled her whole body.

"I need you to stay in the house. I got something to take care of. Don't open the door for nobody not even me." He looked at her with a firm eye.

"JuJu what the fuck is going on? If there's a problem you don't have to leave me at home I'ma ride or die," she reminded him.

232

"Just chill, ain't shit yet. But we at war. Just be on the alert and stop asking me the same question, when I don't answer it's for a reason." He strapped up then reached under the bed and detached his baby snug from the bed frame.

JuJu leaned in and kissed her lips and was out.

Bayonna grabbed her cell phone and called Lissha and Treebie and got no answer then she called Kiam and was sent to voice mail. "What the fuck is going on?" she said aloud then hopped up and threw on her clothes. Just as she was stepping into her boots her phone rang beside her.

Kiam moved around his room getting dressed and strapped and hitting Lissha's phone every few minutes. His mind began producing flashes of all the torture he had been putting on the streets and then the promise he made Pops to protect his daughter took over all those thoughts and for the first time regret crept into his veins.

Kiam rushed down the stairs taking two at a time. "I'll be right back," he looked Faydrah in the eyes.

"Where you going? I just ordered your pizza and wings," she said, walking towards him.

Faydrah was no fool. She could see the seriousness in Kiam's demeanor and a sinking feeling moved in her chest. "Babe, you okay?"

"Yeah, I'm good. Just chill until I get back. I just have to check on something."

Faydrah looked in his eyes and she felt tears forming in hers but she dared not let them fall. "You promise?"

"Yeah, ma. I promise." He reached out and took her in his arms. "Don't eat all of my food," he joked.

"Shut up. You better hurry back." She squeezed him tightly.

When Kiam heard a small whimper and felt her hand settle on his lower back, a lump formed in his throat. He hated that his lifestyle left her filled with worry every time he walked out the door but that was part of loving a man like him. He tried to reassure her that her nigga was built for whatever and that she didn't have to worry about him.

"You good ma, just let me handle this. I'll be right back." He squeezed a little harder and then let her go. "You know where the heat is at right?"

"Yes."

"Bring it downstairs and don't hesitate to use it," he said, locking eyes with hers.

Faydrah pulled back and held in all of her emotions, she knew the last thing he needed was for her to break. She understood that he needed a clear mind while he went to handle whatever it was that was so urgent or he might not make it back.

She forced a smile on her face and said, "Handle your business, baby." Trepidation seized her as she watched him walk towards the door.

Kiam knew that she was afraid for him. Like she knew him, he knew her just as well. He turned around and caught her wiping away a tear. "Eyez," he said, lowering his gaze to her belly then lifting it back up to capture her eyes with his. "I love you. Try not to worry."

"I can't help it baby," she admitted on low tone as she watched him leave out and close the door behind him.

As soon as she heard the locks click, she ran to the door and put her hands against it, "I love you too," she whispered. It felt as if she was giving him her last touch.

She took a deep breath as she felt herself becoming overwhelmed and on the verge of breaking down. *Pull it together Faydrah. You know he got it.*

It took a few minutes for her to get her breathing under control. But when she did, she put the chain on the door and moved back to the couch, grabbed a pillow and hugged it snugly within her arms.

As Kiam headed into the city, he tried to convince himself that Lissha was okay. He had noticed a change in her lately but he couldn't figure out what had caused it. He wondered if it was because he had told her about Faydrah being pregnant? If she was in her feelings over that it would explain her sending him to voice mail but why wouldn't she answer Big Zo's calls? And where was Treebie?

JuJu arrived at the twin's house in full kill mode. He stepped out of his truck taking big steps in the snow making a path to the porch. When he knocked on the door Isaiah opened it. He was dressed in all black and a hoodie pulled over his head.

234

JuJu's breathing was quick and intense causing thick smoke to escape his mouth with every breath.

"No word from Kiam yet?" Isaiah asked, moving to the side.

"Nah, I want you to head over to his house and hold post until we get back."

"A'ight. What about Bayonna?"

"She straight," JuJu said confidently.

Isaiah moved to the closet and grabbed his coat and tucked his guns and headed out the door. Isaac was seated on the couch taking a few shots of Jack to the head and loading his whistle. JuJu took a seat adjacent to his, took his cell phone out and laid it on the table. He stared at it for a minute then sat back and waited. He was hoping for the best but preparing for the worse.

Faydrah jumped when she heard the bell. Her first instinct was to go upstairs and get one of Kiam's guns. Then she remembered that she had ordered pizza. She moved to her purse and grabbed a fifty out of her wallet then walked to the door.

When she looked out the peep hole, and saw the boy with the *Dominoes* cap her nerves settled down. Her mouth watered at the memory of the last time she had their wings. With a smile of anticipation on her face she opened the door. Boom!

 The loud bang of the gunshot rung her ears and the delivery boy's brains splashed all over her face. His body lurched forward before crumpling down across her feet.

Faydrah screamed.

"Shut up, bitch!" barked the hooded figure, raising the gun up to her face.

Faydrah's eyes grew wide with fear as she stared at the weapon. She slowly stepped back but the intruder stepped with her. The cold air whipped in the door causing her shirt to blow. But the cold eyes at the other end of the gun was unaffected by the frosty wind.

"What do you want?" she asked in a frightened tone. "Please. You can have whatever you want. I didn't see anything" She continued to slowly back into the house.

"Bitch, I don't want shit you got except your life."

Faydrah looked at the eyes of her assassin and the heat drained from her body. She felt wetness trickle down her inner thigh settling in a puddle under her feet. A haunting laugh came in her direction then she heard bullets being pumped into the chamber. Trapstar was barking and scratching on the backdoor.

The attacker lowered the gun to Faydrah's stomach. "Please, I'm pregnant," she cried, covering her belly with both hands.

"Yeah I know." Pow! Pow!

"Noooooo!" she screamed as the first bullet tore through her left hand cracking her ring and entering high in her abdomen. The second bullet shattered her hip bone.

Faydrah fell back into the end table knocking the lamp over as her body crashed to the floor. Her heart beat fast as she tried to crawl away from the deliverer of death. She placed her hand on her stomach and began to shake when she saw all the blood that coated her palm. "My baby," she cried.

"Take that little bastard with you to the afterlife," the cold-hearted assassiness sneered. Then she stood over her and shot her in her beautiful face. "Die bitch," she spat and shot her again before turning and fleeing out the front door.

Faydrah lay whimpering on the floor. She tried to move but her legs no longer worked. When she tried to lift her head blood filled her eyes and stole her vision. She wanted to cry out but thick warm blood filled her mouth and choked off her cries. Then she heard someone whispering her name but the unfamiliar voice was in her head. She squeezed her eyes shut and the voice grew louder.

Death was calling.

Nooooo! Please! she cried inside. She wasn't ready to go. She wasn't ready to leave Kiam, they still had so much love to share, so many kisses to exchange and so many dreams to pursue. *And what about my baby? Please, all I ask is for a chance to hold him in my arms and see the pride on his daddy's face when he comes into this world.*

With the last strength remaining in her body, Faydrah willed her arms up and wrapped them around her belly. Sticky blood covered her shirt and wet her arms. Tears ran down her face into her blood filled mouth as a loud

236

sob came from deep in her soul. Death's call screamed her name drowning out her sobs. The louder it called the weaker she became.

As darkness began to envelope her, Faydrah slowly gave up the fight. She locked hands with the horrible fate that was hers and her unborn child's and surrendered to the cold and eerie silence of death. And with her final breath her thoughts left her and the baby and instead she prayed that Kiam would have the strength to send all their enemies souls to hell.

To Be Continued...
Trust No Bitch 3
Available Now!

BOOKS BY LDP'S CEO, CA$H

TRUST NO MAN

TRUST NO MAN 2

TRUST NO MAN 3

BONDED BY BLOOD

SHORTY GOT A THUG

A DIRTY SOUTH LOVE

THUGS CRY

THUGS CRY 2

TRUST NO BITCH

TRUST NO BITCH 2

TRUST NO BITCH 3

TIL MY CASKET DROPS

Coming Soon

TRUST NO BITCH (KIAM EYEZ' STORY)

THUGS CRY 3

BONDED BY BLOOD 2

RESTRANING ORDER

BOOKS BY NENE CAPRI

PUSSY TRAP I, II, III & IV

DREAM WEAVER

TAINTED

Coming Soon From Lock Down Publications

RESTRAINING ORDER

By **CA$H & COFFEE**

GANGSTA CITY **II**

By **Teddy Duke**

A DANGEROUS LOVE **VII**

By **J Peach**

BLOOD OF A BOSS **III**

By **Askari**

THE KING CARTEL **III**

By **Frank Gresham**

NEVER TRUST A RATCHET BITCH

SILVER PLATTER HOE **III**

By **Reds Johnson**

THESE NIGGAS AIN'T LOYAL **III**

By **Nikki Tee**

BROOKLYN ON LOCK **III**

By **Sonovia Alexander**

THE STREETS BLEED MURDER **II**

By **Jerry Jackson**

CONFESSIONS OF A DOPEMAN'S DAUGHTER **II**

By **Rasstrina**

WHAT ABOUT US **II**

NEVER LOVE AGAIN

By **Kim Kaye**

A GANGSTER'S REVENGE

Ca$h & NeNe Capri

By **Aryanna**

<u>Available Now</u>

LOVE KNOWS NO BOUNDARIES **I II & III**
By **Coffee**
SILVER PLATTER HOE **I & II**
HONEY DIPP **I & II**
CLOSED LEGS DON'T GET FED **I & II**
A BITCH NAMED KARMA
By **Reds Johnson**
A DANGEROUS LOVE **I, II, III, IV, V, VI**
By **J Peach**
CUM FOR ME
An **LDP Erotica Collaboration**
THE KING CARTEL **I & II**
By **Frank Gresham**
BLOOD OF A BOSS **I & II**
By **Askari**
THE DEVIL WEARS TIMBS
BURY ME A G **I II & III**
By **Tranay Adams**
THESE NIGGAS AIN'T LOYAL **I & II**
By **Nikki Tee**
THE STREETS BLEED MURDER
By **Jerry Jackson**
DIRTY LICKS

By **Peter Mack**

THE ULTIMATE BETRAYAL

By **Phoenix**

BROOKLYN ON LOCK

By **Sonovia Alexander**

SLEEPING IN HEAVEN, WAKING IN HELL **I, II & III**

By **Forever Redd**

THE DEVIL WEARS TIMBS **I, II & III**

By **Tranay Adams**

DON'T FU#K WITH MY HEART **I & II**

By **Linnea**

BOSS'N UP **I & II**

By **Royal Nicole**

LOYALTY IS BLIND

By **Kenneth Chisholm**

Trust No Bitch 2

www.ingramcontent.com/pod-product-compliance
Lightning Source LLC
Chambersburg PA
CBHW070104280626
47159CB00016B/1319